MAKER OF MANHOOD

"Mr. Carter, what is it?" Candy Pratt asked. "What do the signals from the *Vanderbilt* mean?"

The seventeen-year-old midshipman shifted his feet nervously on the deck of the *Delta Dancer*. With the murder of the first mate and the treacherous capture of Captain Rafe Taylor by the Union captain of the *Vanderbilt*, he'd become captain by default.

"They've demanded that we surrender the ship to them," he said. "If we don't, they are going to wait just outside the harbor and sink us the moment we leave port."

"What are you going to do, Mr. Carter?"

"I—I don't know. I wish the captain were here . . ."

"Well, I know," Candy said suddenly. "We are going to fight, the first thing tomorrow."

And in Candy Pratt there grew the knowledge of what she must do. Midshipman Jesse Carter was barely out of adolescence, unsure of his manhood. Despite her passionate love for Rafe Taylor, to save his ship and his men, she must give Jesse Carter his manhood tonight . . .

The Making of America Series

THE
RAIDERS

Lee Davis Willoughby

A DELL/JAMES A. BRYANS BOOK

Published by
Dell Publishing Co., Inc.
1 Dag Hammarskjold Plaza
New York, New York 10017

Dell TM 681510, Dell Publishing Co., Inc.

ISBN: 0-440-07249-2

Printed in the United States of America

First printing—September 1984

Chapter One

Had a sea gull ventured twenty miles off Cape Charles, Virginia, on the afternoon of November 19th, 1861, it might have looked down upon the sparkling blue water of the Atlantic to see two ships a mile or so apart. From the vantage point of the sea gull's great height and because of its superior speed, the ships may have appeared to be stationary. However, the long, white feathers which were the ships' wakes would easily belie that illusion, for the ships were sailing at top speed. In fact, one ship was in pursuit of the other.

The ship being pursued was the Confederate raider, *Delta Dancer*. It was racing through the water under a cloud of canvas and with its engine ahead all full. She was making nearly seventeen knots, and Captain Rafe Taylor, who was standing on the stern just beneath the fluttering Stars and Bars, felt that if they went any faster, the ship would lift right out of the water. He studied the Union blockade enforcer that was chasing the *Delta Dancer*. Even in the past few minutes he had noticed that he was opening up the distance. There was no way that ship was going to catch him. The captain of the Union ship must have realized it as well, for Rafe saw the flash of a firing cannon and realized the bow chaser of the Yankee ship had just fired at him The ball fell far short, and he knew that the Yankee captain had loosed the shot in frustration. Rafe laughed the rich, hearty laugh of a man who realizes that he has won. Once again he had concluded a successful voyage. Three Union commerce ships captured and one man-of-war defeated in battle. Now he was running through the very teeth of the Union blockade to put in to Chesapeake Bay. He had an important message for the Confederate government in Richmond.

"More speed, Mr. Herrick, more speed!" Captain Charles Raymond shouted. "He's getting away!"

"Cap'n, we've got the safety valve tied down now," Mr. Herrick answered. "We can't go any faster. The *Delta Dancer* is faster than we are!"

"Damn!" Captain Raymond said. He raised his binoculars to his eyes and saw a man standing on the stern of the Confederate raider. He couldn't be sure, but it looked almost as if the man were laughing at him.

"Damn!" Captain Raymond said again. He pounded his fist into his hand angrily, then ran his hand across the top of his head as if to brush the hair from his eyes, though, in fact, there was not a hair on his head. He was only forty years old, but he was completely bald. It was a condition he made no effort to hide. In fact, he used it as his trademark, and he took pride in the fact that his men, in secret, called him Old Cannon Ball. He was short and muscular, and not that unlike a cannon ball in appearance or disposition. He was a powerful man who had had made more than one adversary regret ever having crossed him.

"Gun crew to the bow chaser!" he called.

"Cap'n, she's well out of range of the bow chaser," Mr. Herrick reminded him.

"I know it, Mr. Herrick," Captain Raymond said. "You might say I'm just sending our friend Mr. Taylor a calling card."

Captain Raymond put the glasses back up to his eyes and watched the flight of the cannon ball. It fell far short, as he knew it would, but it was his way of hurling a curse at Rafe Taylor.

Taylor was an insolent young pup. If he had

known two years ago how things were going to turn out, he would have broken Taylor, when Taylor sailed as his first lieutenant.

"Richmon'! We're comin' into Richmon', the capital of the Confederacy!" the conductor called proudly as he walked through the lurching train car.

One of the passengers in the car who responded to the conductor's call was Captain Rafe Taylor. He was a tall, blue-eyed, sandy-haired man, whose face had the deep tan of one who had stood countless watches on deck in the tropical sun. He was twenty-seven years old, but weather and the stress of command made him look older than his years.

After Rafe had eluded Captain Raymond, as well as other blockade ships of the Union Navy, he put into Norfolk, right under the noses of the patrolling Union ships. He left the *Delta Dancer* under command of his first lieutenant, Mr. Mc-Corkle, then boarded the midnight train at Norfolk. He changed trains in Petersburg at four a.m. and reached Richmond at just past sunrise. One year ago, this same trip would have been made in less than three hours. Then the trains traveled at nearly forty miles per hour. That was no longer the case, as a new law designed to protect the railroads from undue wear limited all trains to ten miles per hour. Rafe looked through the window of the car as the train crossed the James River on its approach to Richmond. The city was spread out on the opposite bank of the river.

The capital of the Confederacy was normally a city of some thirty thousand souls, though its numbers were now greatly swelled by its position as capital of the South and by the advent of war. It was, like Rome, built upon seven hills, a fact which was not lost upon the politicians of the city.

The principal part of the city, however, was built upon one hill, and on that hill was located Capitol Square with the capitol building, which was designed by Thomas Jefferson, guarded by a mounted statue of George Washington.

Rafe had been in Richmond many times before, and he knew that there was really only one business thoroughfare, a north-and-south street known appropriately enough as Main Street. Along this street were located all the hotels, banks, newspaper offices and principal stores.

The city was covered by a low-lying layer of smoke, not only from the smokestacks of the mill but also from the chimneys of houses all over the city. That was because the morning was gray and cool.

It was November 20th, 1861, and Rafe was hurrying to the Confederate government in Richmond to deliver some distressing news. Mr. James Mason and Mr. John Slidell, two dignitaries who were to represent the Confederate government in the Court of St. James and in Paris, had been seized from a British mail packet by a Union warship. Rafe, whose swift ship, *Delta Dancer*, had delivered the two commissioners from Charleston to Nassau, heard the news at Nassau, and he'd returned immediately so he could inform President Davis and his cabinet.

As soon as the train stopped, Rafe hurried to find a hack and, providing a generous tip, ordered the black driver to drive him swiftly to Capitol Square. Once there, however, any further attempt at swiftness was impossible, due to the red tape of the bureaucracy which was already in place in the new government.

"I don't care what kind of news you have; you don't get in to see the President without an appointment," the despotic little clerk informed him.

"Don't you understand what I'm telling you?" Rafe asked in a voice which could barely contain his irritation. "Mason and Slidell have been seized by the Yankees."

"I can make you an appointment on Friday next," the clerk said, looking at his ledger book as if he hadn't even heard Rafe's words.

A rather short, stout man with white, wavy hair and chin whiskers was walking through the Great

Lobby. He saw Rafe at the clerk's desk and came over to him.

"You're Captain Taylor, aren't you, sir?" the man asked, extending his hand in greeting.

"Secretary Mallory," Rafe said, relieved to see the Secretary of Navy. "Yes, sir, I'm Rafe Taylor."

"I thought as much. I met you earlier this summer when you were commissioned, I believe. What are you doing in Richmond, sir? Is you ship disabled?"

"The *Delta Dancer* is in fighting shape, Mr. Secretary. She's in Norfolk now, taking on supplies. Mr. Secretary, I'm very glad to see you. I've come bearing distressing news."

"Oh? What news?"

"Our ambassadors, Mason and Slidell."

Mallory chuckled and held up his hand to interrupt him.

"They aren't ambassadors yet," he said. "They can't be until we are recognized as a country. For the moment they are only commissioners, with no more authority than the commissioners of any business establishment."

"No, sir," Rafe said. "For the moment they are prisoners."

"What? Prisoners, you say?"

"They were taken from the British mail packet," Rafe said. He hit his fist into his palm. "I feel responsible, sir. If I had taken them all the way to England myself, this wouldn't have happened.''

"No, it isn't your fault at all," Mallory said. "Don't you see, we wanted them to travel by foreign ship, because the moment they were on board the vessel of another nation, they were, in fact, accorded commissioner status. Does President Davis know of this?''

"I don't believe so, sir," Rafe said. "I came as fast as I could, after I received the news. I arrived in Norfolk at eleven last night and took the next train. I fear all my haste was in vain, however, as this gentleman—" Rafe pointed to the clerk and let the word *gentleman* slide out with a note of sarcasm—"allows that I will be unable to call upon the President until Friday next.''

Secretary Mallory stroked his whiskers for a moment.

"Captain, I have an appointment with the President at one o'clock this afternoon. Suppose you meet me in my office at a quarter till? I'll take you to the President.''

"Thank you, Mr. Secretary," Rafe said. He rubbed his own chin and felt the stubble of a two day's growth of beard. "I, uh, feel like I should get cleaned up first. What hotel would you recommend?''

"They are all crowded with visitors to the capital,

I'm afraid. But I've always been partial to the Hotel Crillion.''

"The Crillion it will be, then," Rafe said. "And I'll see you at a quarter till one—with my thanks, sir."

"No, Captain. The thanks of our nation should go to you and men like you. If we are to succeed, it will be on your efforts, not ours."

The first year of the War Between the States had brought several victories to the South, reinforcing the Southern view that the Hessians of the North, as the Union troops were often called, were no match for Southern gentlemen. Already there was unrest in the northern press and most Southerners were convinced that the war would soon be over. All over Richmond, hotels and fine restaurants were crowded with men in colorful, braided uniforms representing such units as Bailey's Battlers, Morgan's Marauders, Wilson's Warriors, and perhaps a dozen others, none of which had ever seen combat. In fact, many of these units didn't even exist other than as elite social clubs to provide elegant uniforms for their gentlemanly members.

Rafe found that the Hotel Crillion, like all the other hotels in Richmond, was exceptionally crowded. Uniformed men and well-dressed women were so numerous in the lobby that a normal conversation was quite out of the question. The only way one could be heard was to yell just a little louder than his neighbor, and that, of course, only intensified the bedlam.

Captains and majors and colonels who had never commanded a man nor ever heard a shot fired in anger waved drinks and cigars as they discussed tactics and strategy. The women, who were also caught up in the excitement, were just as noisy as the men. Occasionally the high-pitched shrill of a woman's laugh could be heard above all else.

"You are in luck, sir," the hotel clerk said. "A room was just vacated."

"Good," Rafe said, signing the register. "I trust you have facilities for a bath?"

"You will be on the third floor, sir. There is a public bath at the end of the hall with a stove for heating your water."

Rafe took the key and his grip up to his room. He had not worn his naval uniform on the train, though he did bring it with him. He thought it would be proper to wear it now, since he would be with the Secretary of the Navy when he met President Jefferson Davis.

When he reached his room, he took the uniform out of the grip and hung it up to allow the wrinkles to fall out.

Down at the end of the hall of this same floor, in the public bath, Candice Pratt had just finished her bath. She stood up in the tub and reached for a towel.

Candy was a beautiful young woman of twenty-two, with a luxuriant head of tawny hair. Her brown eyes were almost gold, and even here, in the privacy of her bath, they revealed a lust for life which could scarcely be contained. She had a fine, slender form with high-rising breasts and long, tapered legs. She was humming a little song as she stretched for the towel, but she interrupted the song when she found the towel just out of reach. She had to step out of the tub, and so her nudity was fully exposed when the door was suddenly, and unexpectedly, thrown open.

Candy looked around in surprise, then gasped, for she saw a tall, blue-eyed, sandy-haired man standing before her. He was carrying a towel draped across one arm, and he looked as surprised to see Candy as she was to see him. His look of surprise, however, soon turned to interest, as he stood there and took in her beauty with unabashed admiration.

"Well, good morning, ma'am" he said as easily as if he had passed her on the street.

"What?" Candy asked. She was so shocked by his sudden appearance that for a long moment she made no attempt to cover herself. Only when she saw his appreciative stare change into a broad grin did she come to her senses. Quickly she grabbed the towel—and managed to restore some modesty, if not dignity, to the scene. "Who are you, sir? And why are you here?"

"I am Captain Rafe Taylor," the man said. He held up his towel. "And I am here to take a bath."

"Well, as you can see, this bathroom is occupied," Candy said.

"Yes, so I see." The intruder's smile widened.

"You call yourself a captain, sir," Candy said angrily. "That presupposes you are a gentleman. I've never known a gentleman to barge into a lady's bath!"

"I'm sorry," Rafe said easily. "I've never known a lady to take a bath in a public place without first locking the door."

"I . . . I thought I did lock the door," Candy said.

Rafe touched his eyebrow in a lazy salute.

"Finish your bath in peace, madam. I shall stand sentry duty outside your door."

Rafe withdrew and closed the door behind him. Candy dried herself, then dressed quickly. She was terribly embarrassed by the incident, and she blushed mightily as she dressed. She realized that a man had just seen her nude. It was the first time in her life that such a thing had happened.

It was a mortifying experience, yes, but, despite the embarrassment and shame, Candy was vaguely aware of another sensation which she didn't fully understand. She had experienced a degree of forbidden pleasure. She couldn't explain it, but neither could she deny it. She had noticed what a handsome man Captain Rafe Taylor was, and she had been pleased at his obvious appreciation of her own charms.

After Candy dressed, she opened the door, hoping to find him gone. Instead, he was still standing in the hall, as if faithfully discharging a duty to protect her from any further unwanted entries.

"I see you are still here," she said, trying to make her voice sound flat and unemotional.

"Yes, and lucky for you, I am," Rafe said. "There was yet another who would have intruded on your bath, had I not turned him away."

"I thank you, Captain," Candy said, still keeping the tone of her voice flat. She noticed that, for him calling himself a captain, he was not in a uniform. Instead, he wore a rather ordinary-looking brown suit. "Captain of what?" she asked.

"I beg your pardon?"

"You introduced yourself as Captain Taylor," Candy said. "But there are so many captains and majors and colonels, all with glorious uniforms, that one can't keep up with them. You are wearing no uniform at all. Of what magnificent regiment are you an officer?"

Rafe laughed.

"I'm glad to see that someone else has noticed

this strange phenomenon of officers by the legion. When last I was in Richmond, I bought a pair of boots from a mere lad. This morning, I saw this same lad playing billiards, only he was dressed in the uniform of a major. But about my own case. The truth is, madam, I serve in no regiment at all.''

"You are at least honest about that," Candy said. "Though I wonder why you would bother to call yourself a captain, if you don't avail yourself of the opportunity to wear a uniform?''

"Yes," Rafe said with a smile. "Why indeed?'' He could have told her that he was master of the *Delta Dancer.* Many people had already read of the exploits of his raider, and perhaps she had as well. But Rafe thought that would appear to be bragging, so he held his council. "Perhaps the fact that I am not taking advantage of my title will convince you that I am not to be classed with the ballroom warriors with which Richmond is so rife,'' Rafe suggested.

"And thus classified, you feel emboldened to take advantage of a lady in her bath?'' Candy charged.

"No, madam," Rafe replied seriously. "I beg of you, do not think my ill-timed intrusion was planned. It was a mistake for which I most heartily apologize.''

Candy looked at him for a moment. She had

failed to lock the door, and that was her fault. The look on his face when he first entered her bath was one of total shock. He couldn't have faked that. And, after all, if she would admit it to herself, she would realize that her anger was directed more at herself than at him. That was because she felt guilty over the forbidden pleasure the incident had evoked. She returned his smile.

"You are forgiven, sir," she said. "Only next time, do be a good man and knock before you come in, won't you?"

"Yes," Rafe said with a sly smile. "I promise. Next time, I will knock before I come into your bath."

Candy, who was dressed now, started down the stairs to meet her father. She thought about Rafe's promise. Somehow it seemed to carry more than the sum total of its words.

Rafe had been a lieutenant in the U.S. Navy when the war broke out, having graduated from the U.S. Naval Academy at Annapolis. He had served his country proudly, but he was a Virginian by birth, and when Virginia seceded from the Union, he felt compelled to resign his commission and go with his conscience. He took no pleasure in the action; in fact, it pained him to have to treat as an enemy flag that banner which he had so faithfully defended.

As the war was not a social event for him, he had not bought a new uniform. Instead, he modified his U.S. Navy uniform by replacing the gold buttons of the U.S. with the silver buttons of the Confederacy. The U.S. Navy lieutenant's stripe was removed from his uniform, and the three stars of a lieutenant commander in the Confederate Navy were added. He wore a silver belt buckle crested with the gold letters CSN. Though he had gone to no pains to have a special, elaborate uniform made, the result of his alterations was a uniform which was very impressive in its elegant simplicity.

As Rafe once again entered the Great Lobby of the capital building, he saw two men standing near the foot of the stairs which led up to Secretary Mallory's office. One of the men was wearing a double-breasted, dark green uniform with a scarlet blaze between the rows of buttons. His rank was that of colonel. It was a very colorful uniform, but of what Rafe had no idea. He chuckled to himself as he climbed the stairs to the second floor.

"He is the Commanding Officer of the Richmond Lancers," Mallory said with a chuckle, answering Rafe's question a moment later.

"The Richmond Lancers? Who are they? I've never heard of them."

"Oh, they are a most elite group," Mallory said. "They have disdained the use of firearms and drill once per week with lances. They have taken an oath to provide a shield around the city and repel the Yankee invaders with nothing but a lance and Southern courage.''

"I'm sure everyone feels safer," Rafe said, laughing.

"Yes, you can well imagine how effective they would be against mine balls and grape. But, of course, we will never find out, for even if the enemy were on the James River Bridge, I doubt that these fellows could be found. However, I am told that they are most skilled on the dance floor at the many balls being given in Richmond.''

"God help us, Mr. Secretary, if this war goes any furthur and we have to depend on fools like that," Rafe said.

"Yes, well, fortunately, those who fought at Bull Run and in Wilson Creek weren't fools. We can trust that there are enough men like them, and like you, Captain, to carry our cause. Ah, there is the President's office.''

The door to the office opened and a man stood there, looking out. He was a slim man, just a little over medium height, with high cheekbones and thin lips. He wore chin whiskers and he smiled at Mallory.

"Steven, right on time, I see," he said. "And this is our Captain Taylor?''

"Yes, Mr. President," Mallory said. "Mr. President, Captain Taylor is much too modest to speak of his exploits, but, as Secretary of the Navy, I take great pride in telling you a little about him. He is master of the ship *Delta Dancer*. The *Delta Dancer* is a steam-powered, screw-driven, sloop-rigged ship, which, under sail and steam, can make eighteen knots.''

President Davis whistled. ''That's very fast, isn't it?''

''Fastest thing on the ocean, Mr. President,'' Rafe said. ''On that matter I will speak, as it is a tribute to the ship and the men who sail her, and not her master.''

''But her master is responsible for her glorious record,'' Mallory went on. ''The *Delta Dancer* has captured no fewer than twelve merchant ships, and has defeated in battle three ships of the line of the U.S. Navy.''

President Davis shook Rafe's hand. ''Sir, it is indeed a privilege to meet you. Please, come in, won't you?'' he added, inviting them into his inner office.

The President's office was unprepossessing, furnished with a desk and a few chairs and little more. Jefferson Davis was a practical, uncompromising man. He was intelligent and proud, and his conversation was often embellished with the words of a scholar.

''And now, Captain, tell me what you know of

the apprehension of Messrs. Mason and Slidell,''
the President invited.

"The information I have, Mr. President, is
skimpy, but, I believe, accurate. On November
8th, while still in the Bahama Channel, the *San
Jacinto*, a Union warship under the command of
Captain Charles Wilkes, stopped the British mail
packet, *Trent*, and removed Mason and Slidell
from her under force of arms.''

"Were there any wounded?'' Davis asked.

"No, sir. The Trent was unarmed and she struck
colors immediately when Captain Wilkes issued a
demand that they heave to.''

To Rafe's surprise, President Davis laughed aloud
and hit his fist into his hand.

"Rejoice, gentlemen, for our two commissioners have accomplished far more than I ever dared
to dream,'' he said. "We have won a major victory as a result of Captain Wilkes' *faux pas*.''

"How so, Mr. President?'' Mallory asked. "Our
two representatives are now in prison, and we
have no voice in any foreign court.''

"Don't you see, Steven?'' the President replied.
"By taking Slidell and Mason from a British vessel,
the United States has committed an act of war. We
may expect Great Britian not only to recognize our
independence but also to help us in our battle,
much as France helped in the first War of Independence.''

"Do you really think the British will go that far, Mr. President?" Rafe asked.

"I think there is every chance that they will," President Davis said. "At the very least, they will humiliate the Federal government by forcing them to release our commissioners with apologies. Even that will be a valuable prize, for it will recognize us as a belligerent party, and that is the first step in national recognition." He chuckled again. "All in all, I would say this has been a wonderful year for the South and a disastrous year for the North. We have soundly defeated them in every engagement both on land and at sea. And now we have won a decisive political coup with the Slidell and Mason affair. I predict, gentlemen, that Dr. Pratt's mission to Washington will be a success."

"Dr. Pratt's mission?"

"Yes, Dr. Arnold Pratt," President Davis said. "You have heard of him, I'm certain. I am to meet with him." Davis looked at his watch. "In fact, he and his daughter may be in the outer chamber even as we speak. I am sending him to Washington to make one final effort in effecting a peace."

"Do you really think there is a chance for that, Mr. President?" Mallory asked. "After all, if Washington doesn't recognize us as a government, there is no reason to believe they will receive an emissary of our government, is there?"

"Dr. Pratt will not be going as an official emissary of our government," President Davis said. "He is going to appear to declare, after much soul searching, his loyalty to the Union. He was a schoolmate of Governor Salmon Chase, who, as you know, is not only the Secretary of the Treasury but was an active seeker of the presidential nomination for the Republican Party. Governor Chase is certain to have a great deal of influence in the Federal government, and once Dr. Pratt has reestablished his friendship, he will then begin to plead our case."

"Isn't that a little dangerous for Dr. Pratt?" Mallory asked. "If it is ever discovered that Dr. Pratt is using his friendship to influence the policy of high government officials, he could be tried as a spy."

"Yes, that possibility certainly exists, and as has already been demonstrated, the officials in Washington are not adverse to using the hangman's rope. But can we ask less of our statesmen than we do of our soldiers and sailors?" Davis replied. "Do they not risk their lives every day? You, Captain, have often risked your life at sea, have you not?"

"Yes, of course, but I am used to such risks."

"And so should we all be, under the circumstances. Besides, it is a risk worth taking, if it is taken for peace."

"Do you think there is any chance of success?"

"We can pray that there is a chance," Davis answered. "After all, gentlemen, we are actually brothers with the gentlemen from the North. All of us have served the United States flag in one capacity or the other, and we can't help but sorrow at the suffering we have already caused each other. Wouldn't peace be better for us all?"

"Yes, of course it would," Mallory answered. "Dr. Pratt's friendship with Secretary Chase not withstanding, I can only hope that Dr. Pratt will find himself dealing with reasonable men."

"Surely, sir, there are some reasonable men remaining in Washington," President Davis said. "Perhaps you would like to meet the good doctor and his daughter? His daughter is going with him. Governor Chase has a daughter who is the same age as Dr. Pratt's daughter, and it is hoped that a friendship between the two young ladies would strengthen Dr. Pratt's position."

"I have not met Dr. Pratt's daughter, though I have heard that she is a young lady of great beauty," Mallory said.

"Exceptional beauty," President Davis said. "Captain, you are unmarried, I believe?"

"Yes, sir."

"Then I've no doubt that you will appreciate Miss Pratt. She is called Candy, and, I assure you, a more beautiful young lady has never graced the fair Southland.''

"What man would not be pleased and honored by such a prospect?" Rafe replied.

President Davis opened the door and spoke to someone in the outer office. A moment later, a tall, dignified-looking man with white hair and a white spade beard came into the room. With him was his daughter. When she and Rafe saw each other, there was a mutual, though quiet gasp. Standing there before him was the same beautiful girl whose bath he had interrupted earlier in the day.

"Ah, Miss Pratt," President Davis said. "I have the honor of presenting Captain Rafe Taylor, master of the Confederate raider, *Delta Dancer*."

Quickly, and without displaying the least sign that he had ever seen her before, Rafe took her hand in his, made a courtly bow, and put her fingers to his lips.

"Mr. President, I have never known your words to be inadequate before," he said. "But in describing Miss Pratt's beauty, you have fallen woefully short."

Chapter Two

(**From** *Harper's Weekly*, January 4, 1862)
1862
Harper's Weekly wishes its friends a Happy New Year. It has every reason to do so, for it believes firmly in the prospects and promises of the coming time. Nor can it be unmindful of the prosperity which has followed it during the eventful year that now closes, a prosperity which it may fairly say is not altogether undeserved. With a weekly issue of 120,000 copies, an illustrated journal like this is necessarily a power in the land. Today, at least, while it compliments all others, it may be forgiven for not forgetting itself: especially if

it means, in good faith, not to forget itself in the coming year, but to serve its friends as faithfully as in the past.

A Happy New Year! It can hardly fail to be that. The tempest upon our Southern horizon is already wasting itself away, and it will leave the land fatter and fairer in all good purposes and principles. The cloud that rolls up for the moment from the East, beyond the sea, is a cloud that is transparent, and a peaceful sky shines through it. We have come in the last year to our national consciousness. We have proved to ourselves that the sons are worthy of the sires. The proof has cost money and blood, and will yet cost more. But that retrospect makes even the dark year of war welcome, and the consequences will make each future year of our lives a Happy New Year.

"Father, listen to this," Candy laughed, reading from "Humors Of The Day," in the *Harper's Weekly*. "The story is told of a certain New Zealand chief, that a young missionary landed at his island to succeed a sacred teacher deceased some time before. At an interview with the chief, the young minister asked, 'Did you know my departed brother?' 'Oh yes! Me deacon in his church.' 'Ah, then, you knew him well: and was he not a good and tender-hearted man?' 'Yes,' replied the deacon with much gusto, 'he very good and very tender. Me eat a piece of him!' "

Candy laughed heartily at the joke when she finished reading it.

"Candy, I hope you do not allow others to know you appreciate jokes of such a callous nature," Dr. Pratt said. "It is unladylike. Help me with this confounded tie, would you? At times like this, I wish I could dress in military uniform, the better to be free of such nonsense."

"Let the others strut and fret about in their uniforms," Candy said, as she adjusted the tie at her father's neck. "There are so many of them that they have quite lost their appeal. Those men who will garner the most attention at the President's reception will not be in uniform."

Dr. Pratt chuckled. "As if anyone is going to waste time looking at the men when there will be such unattached beauties there as you, Kate Chase and Susan Cameron. Especially as you insist upon wearing a dress with such a scandalously low neckline."

"Kate said that Mrs. Lincoln wears such dresses," Candy replied. "It is proper to wear dresses in accordance with the style set by the hostess."

"Yes, well, Mrs. Lincoln is not young and attractive. You are."

Candy laughed—a light, lilting laugh. "I know

what has you worried. You fear my head will be turned by some young, handsome Union officer."

"The thought had crossed my mind," Dr. Pratt admitted. "Despite the fact that we have, by grace of Sam Chase's influence, been admitted to Washington society, we must not forget that we are Virginians, engaged in a war with the Federal government."

"I won't forget," Candy said. She finished tying her father's tie, then stepped back and looked at it. "There, you look quite the gentleman now," she said.

A gold watch chain stretched across Dr. Pratt's vest, and he reached into his vest pocket to pull the watch out.

"We are too punctual," he said. "We've left ourselves fifteen minutes. Very well, we shall merely await the Chase carriage in the parlor of this boarding house."

"We most certainly will not!" Candy said. "Father, I would simply die of embarrassment. I would just die!"

"You would be embarrassed to wait in the parlor?" Dr. Pratt asked, puzzled by his daughter's strange reaction. "Why would such a thing prove embarrassing?"

"Father, really," Candy said. "One never shows such anxiousness. It simply isn't done. We will wait here until Governor Chase sends his driver for us.''

Dr. Pratt sighed and sat down. "Very well," he said. "Hand me the *Harper's Weekly*. I shall need something to while away the time.''

Candy handed the paper to her father.

"Hello, what's this?" Dr. Pratt asked, looking at the cover of the magazine. There was a woodcut on the cover which showed a brig being destroyed by cannon fire from a long, low, sloop-rigged ship flying the Confederate flag. The masts and smoke-stack of the Confederate ship were slanted back at a rakish angle, and even though it was just a drawing, one could almost see the great speed of the ship.

"Did you see the cover of this magazine?" Dr. Pratt asked. "This ship is the *Delta Dancer*. Isn't that the ship of the young naval officer we met in President Davis' office?''

"I don't recall meeting anyone," Candy lied. Even as she spoke the words, she felt her face burning and an uncomfortable heat suffusing her body. She had seen the drawing earlier in the afternoon when she purchased the magazine at the newsstand. Sight of the ship had brought to her immediate memories of meeting Rafe Taylor, not in the office of the President of the Confederate States of America but in the bathroom of the Hotel Crillion.

"Of course you do," Dr. Pratt said. "He was a tall, handsome man, I'm sure you'll recall."

"I suppose so," Candy said. "He just slipped my mind."

"He's not likely to slip the minds of the U.S. Navy," Dr. Pratt said. "He's already captured or destroyed over thirty enemy vessels."

The caption of the picture read: "The pirate *Delta Dancer* firing at the brig *Joseph Parks* of Boston, sketched by one of the crew of the *Delta Dancer*."

"Hmm," Dr. Pratt said. "One of Captain Taylor's men is quite an accomplished artist."

There was a knock at the door then, and Dr. Pratt rose to answer it. A liveried gentleman was standing in the hallway, just outside the door. He bowed politely.

"Dr. Pratt, the governor's compliments, sir, and he begs you and Miss Pratt join him."

"We'd be delighted," Dr. Pratt said, then looked at Candy questioningly. "It is quite acceptable to go now, isn't it?"

"Really, father," Candy said under her breath.

Candy stood in line with her father, Secretary Salmon Chase and his daughter Kate, as they waited to greet President Lincoln. The President was standing just inside the door of the room, greeting everyone as they arrived. A small chamber orchestra played music from the far side of the room, but there was no dancing, nor could there have been on the thick, rose-colored carpet on the floor.

The first person she encountered was the President's military aide, Colonel Lamon. Colonel Lamon was at least five inches shorter than the President, but, then, so was everyone else in the room. Even from outside the door, Candy could see the President's face clearly because he was so tall. She heard her father give their names to Colonel Lamon, and Colonel Lamon whispered the names to the President. She curtsied to the President as she stood in front of him.

"Miss Pratt, you are the third beautiful young maiden to pass before me in as many minutes," the President said, smiling broadly. Candy was struck with the expression in his eyes. "There was Miss Cameron, Miss Chase, and now you." Lincoln turned to General McDowell who was standing close by. "General, I have just hit upon a brilliant idea. Suupose we fielded a division made up of single young ladies, all as lovely as these three. Why, then the enemy would throw down their guns willingly, for who could wage war against such beauty?"

Those within earshot of the President laughed, though the laughter of some was controlled and embarrassed, for many still had difficulty in accepting the "backwoods Mr. Lincoln" as the President.

Even Kate Chase had called Lincoln "the baboon who occupies the White House," and there were many among the more sophisticated who felt a need to apologize for President Lincoln.

Though Candy and her father had been in Washington for several weeks now, this New Year's reception was the first time she had ever seen the President. She had seen dozens and dozens of pictures of him, both photographs and woodcuts, so she knew what he looked like. Or at least she thought she knew. She had, from the pictures, always deemed him to be ugly, and his own self-deprecating remarks often spoke of his homeliness. And yet . . . there was something about him now, whether in the texture of his skin or the depth of his eyes, which tended to soften his looks. There was a great gentleness about him which didn't come across in pictures. There was something else, too, she noticed. As the evening wore on, Candy could hear repeated bursts of laughter from those nearest the President, yet, for all his joking, there was something sad about him. She couldn't quite make it out. It was as though he knew a great and tragic secret of which he could not unburden himself, and so he had to bear its sadness alone. Candy moved though the room meeting officers, ladies and high-ranking government officials, but no matter where she was in the room, she was constantly aware of Lincoln's presence. She felt almost as if his eyes followed her, though, of course, they did not.

Suddenly there was a loud pop, like the report of a pistol, and a woman screamed.

My God! Candy thought. Someone has shot the President! She felt a sudden chill go over her body; then, inexplicably, there was a burst of laughter. She saw that the President was leading the laughter, and he held up a white glove, the side of which was obviously ripped out.

"Don't be alarmed, folks," the President quipped. "I reckon, when they surveyed this big mitt of mine for gloves, they came up about an acre short. The popping sound you heard was the seam bursting."

"Mr. President, I hope the person who stitched your glove is not the same person who is stitching Professor Lowe's balloon," someone said, and again there was laughter.

"As I've no intention of ever going aloft in the Professor's infernal machine, I'll not waste time worrying about such a thing," Lincoln said.

The reception resumed its normal course after that, and a few moments later Candy found herself standing with her father in front of Secretary of State Seward. They were talking about what was being called "the *Trent* affair." The *Trent* was the name of the British mail packet from which the two Confederate envoys, Slidell and Mason, had been forcibly—and, by international law, illegally—removed. England had threatened war if the United States did not "make right their actions."

"I am faced with this dilemma," Seward was explaining to those who were gathered around him. "If I decide this case in favor of my own government, I must disavow its most cherished principles and reverse and forever abandon its essential policy."

"How so, Mr. Secretary?" he was asked. "Have we no right to remove war material from ships at sea, even though those ships be neutral?"

"I remind you, gentlemen, that we went to war against England in 1812 for the same cause which now comes between us. Could we, in 1862, debate one side of a question, upon which principle we sacrificed so many valiant lives in defending the opposite side in 1812? No, gentlemen, our national pride is wounded, to be sure, but our honor is entirely unstained."

"So what is to be the outcome? Are Slidell and Mason to be allowed to go to France and England, there to work their treason against us?"

"Yes," Seward said. "I have informed Her Majesty's government that I will release Slidell and Mason at their pleasure."

"Sir, how can you submit to the British at such a time? Don't you realize that submission will only be interpreted by the South as a sign of weakness?"

"Look, suppose we refused to release Slidell and Mason. Suppose we responded to the English baiting now. What would it accomplish? We might, and we probably would, do infinite injury to British commerce. We might even overrun Canada, and thus add that wild and worthless region to our dominion. But would Canada compensate for the dissolution of our Union? There is no question that the navy of Great Britain is at present so superior to ours that our blockade of the Southern ports would be speedily broken, and thus the great object for whose accomplishment we have taken up arms would be placed beyond our reach. The war between the insurrectionary and the loyal States would be prolonged indefinitely, and our ultimate success would be rendered extremely doubtful.

"We have no choice but to comply with the demands of the English, and as those demands are simply to recognize the right of the seas, a right we have already fought a war for, then I say we shall do it."

"I, for one, agree," General McDowell said. "One war at a time is quite enough for me, thank you."

Rafe Taylor sat on a piling at the East End Pier in Baltimore, holding an open sketchbook on his lap. Dr. Pratt had commented that someone on board the *Delta Dancer* was an artist. That someone was Rafe, for now there was taking shape on his pad a beautiful drawing of the United States warship, *Vanderbilt*.

The ship was long and lean with clean, beautiful lines. It had side-mounted paddlewheels amidship, with two rakish smokestacks. There was a fore-and-aft mast carrying sail and six cannon mounted on each side, plus a pivot gun at the bow and another at the stern.

Rafe, posing as a newspaper artist, had interviewed one of her officers, new to the Navy, though experienced as a merchant seaman.

"Isn't she a beauty, though?" the officer asked. "She cost nearly one million dollars, and she was built by Mr. Jeremiah Simonson especially for Commodore Vanderbilt. Mr. Vanderbilt then gave her to the government as a free gift. She is 340 feet long, 49 feet of beam, draws 33 feet, and displaces 5,268 tons. She is propelled by two engines of 2500 horsepower and is the fastest ship afloat. I guarantee you, the *Vanderbilt* will best the *Alabama* or the *Delta Dancer*."

"She is a beautiful ship all right," Rafe agreed. He finished the drawing, then closed the cover.

"Commander Raymond is aboard, sir. He is the ship's master. Would you care to meet him?"

"Uh, Commander Raymond?"

"Aye, sir. Charles Raymond."

"Thank you, no," Rafe said. "I would like to,

but I must hurry to make the deadline for my paper.''

Rafe waved to the helpful officer, then walked quickly to quit the dock area. He had once been first lieutenant to Charles Raymond. It wouldn't do to see him now, for Raymond would recognize him immediately and have him placed under arrest.

Unlike Captain Semmes of the *Alabama*, Rafe's likeness had not appeared in Northern newspapers. His ship, the *Delta Dancer*, was well-known by name, if not by appearance, because it had appeared many times in Northern papers. Rafe had drawn pictures of engagements and mailed them to the Northern press, and they had often responded by publishing the pictures. It had created a great deal of notoriety for Rafe and his ship. Lieutenant Thomas McCorkle had questioned Rafe the first time Rafe sent out a press release; then Rafe showed him what he was doing. His drawing of the *Delta Dancer* was just different enough from its actual appearance to confuse everyone. Captains of seagoing vessels actually kept drawings of the *Delta Dancer* at hand when they were at sea, only to be surprised when Rafe attacked them, because there was enough difference between the drawing and the actual ship to totally mislead them.

On the other hand, Rafe had an authentic drawing of nearly every warship the United States Navy had commissioned as pirate chasers.

The *Vanderbilt* was a very beautiful ship, and no doubt she was fast. But a few well-placed shot in her exposed side paddles would render her completely helpless. The *Delta Dancer* was propelled by screw, and as it was underwater, it was practically invulnerable to cannon fire. In any battle between the *Delta Dancer* and the *Vanderbilt*, Rafe knew that the *Delta Dancer* would emerge the victor, despite the *Vanderbilt's* superior speed.

Three blocks away from the docks, the cold winter air began to chill Rafe through to the bone, so he turned in to a saloon which he knew to be frequented by seamen, but by only a few officers. He knew nearly every officer-of-the-line in the Regular Navy, though there were a few merchant marine officers who had been pressed into regular naval service and whom he didn't know. It wouldn't do to frequent an establishment where he might encounter some of the officers he had served with. The Grog Bucket, however, would have no such officers. Most of the sailors he had known in the Regular Navy had come with him when he offered his services to the South, even those who were northern-born. Long-time sailors nearly forgot where they were born. They owed their allegiance to their ship and to their officers, and Rafe had been an officer who engendered such loyalty.

The room was filled with smoke, not only from the pipes and cigars of its patrons but also from a fireplace which was drawing badly. Despite that, it was warm and inviting, and Rafe, seeing an empty table quite near the fireplace, took a seat, grateful to be in out of the cold.

There was a loud burst of laughter from a table near him, and Rafe looked over to see half a dozen men and as many painted women drinking and enjoying each other's company. They were all seamen, but they appeared to be merchant seamen, and at least two of them spoke with English accents.

"I thought ye said this place would be free of officers," one of the men said in a whisper which carried louder than he'd intended.

"Aye, that I said 'n' that I meant," one of his companions answered.

"Then what'd be that gentleman what jus' took his seat there, iffen he ain't an officer?" The man indicated Rafe, and Rafe felt a moment of apprehension. Had he been recognized?

"Do you know the gentleman?"

"I never set eyes on him before this minute," the first speaker said. "But I knows officers when I sees them."

Rafe smiled. He wished he had that man on his crew. An instinct like his was one of the most valuable talents a man could bring to a ship which served as a raider.

The second man turned in his chair and looked directly at Rafe.

"Is my friend right, mister? Be you a ship's officer?"

"I congratulate your friend on his keen observation," Rafe answered. "I have served in such a capacity, though now I am but a humble newspaper artist." Rafe held up his tablet.

"See, Pete, he ain't nothin' more'n a artist now," the sailor said.

Rafe's explanation seemed to satisfy the men, and they returned to their own conversation, leaving him alone.

Rafe drank a hot rum and looked through his sketchbook. He looked at the *Vanderbilt*, which ship he had just drawn, and at the *Oneida*, *Galena*, *Tuscarora* and *Crusader*, all of which had been assigned the duty of searching for the *Delta Dancer*.

As if unbidden, Rafe turned the page beyond the drawing of the ships, and there he saw sketches he had made of Candy Pratt. One sketch was of her head and face only. In it, he managed to catch the exact expression, not only in her face but also in her eyes, that he had seen the last time he saw her. There was a light in her eyes—of curiosity? interest? desire? Rafe didn't know exactly what it was, but he had drawn it, and as he studied it, he could almost read it as if she were standing in front of him. Of course, his drawing was done in pencil,

and therefore did nothing to convey the blush of
her cheeks or the gold of her hair and eyes.

There was another drawing he'd made of her on
another page, one that he looked at only when he
was sure he was alone. Rafe looked around the
room and saw that, though not alone, he was, at
least, being ignored. He turned the page to look at
the other drawing he had made of Candy. In this
drawing she was standing beside a bathtub, holding a towel to her body. The towel managed to
discreetly cover that most intimate spot at the junc-
ture of her legs, though the long curve of her
naked thigh was completely visible. Only one breast
was completely covered; the other was exposed by
a fold in the towel, so that the nipple, thus seen,
was as vividly portrayed as a spring rosebud. In
this drawing, as in the other, there was the same
compelling expression in her face.

Rafe stared at the drawing for a long moment,
then felt a quick, flaring heat throughout his body.
His stomach tingled, and there was an uncomfortable pressure in the front of his trousers. Rafe took
a deep breath and closed the tablet. He took another drink, and as he turned the glass up to his
lips, he saw a young girl working the tables. She
was not heavily painted and garish-looking like the
other women in the place. Instead, she was lithe of
form and moved with an easy grace. She had long,
light brown hair, not quite as tawny as Candy's

blonde tresses, but nearly so. Her eyes weren't brown with gold like Candy's; they were blue, but they were clear and innocent-looking and in that, like Candy's eyes.

Once the girl glanced up to catch Rafe looking at her. She smiled and blushed and returned to her task of clearing away the empty tables.

Rafe signaled to the bartender.

"Aye, sir, 'n' what could I be doin' for you?" the bartender asked.

"That girl," Rafe said, pointing to the girl who was working the tables. "She isn't a whore like the others?"

"No, sir. That girl is my daughter."

"I see," Rafe said, prepared to drop the subject.

"You've an interest in her, then?" the bartender asked, keeping the subject alive.

"And if I do?" Rafe replied.

"With the right price and gentlemanly behavior, I might be willin' to allow you a visit with her."

"You've a room here?"

"Aye, right at the head of the stairs," the bartender said. "Do you have five dollars in coin?"

Rafe stacked the coins on the table.

"Go on to the room," the bartender said, raking the coins into a pocket on his apron. "I'll send the girl right up."

Rafe started for the stairs, then stopped at the foot and looked over toward the girl. The bartender was talking to her. She looked over toward him and smiled, ever so shyly, and nodded her head. Rafe went on up to the room.

The room was dark, even though there was a window, and Rafe was surprised to see that it had grown dark since he'd come into the saloon. He walked over to the window and looked through it, down into the alley below. He could see a couple of street bums who had wrapped themselves in blankets to keep warm. They were lying against the back of the building across the alley, and they had stacked up some empty crates to act as a windbreak. Rafe turned away from the window and lit a lantern which was on a table beside the bed.

The door behind him opened and the girl he had seen downstairs came in. She smiled self-consciously at Rafe.

Rafe had brought his bottle up with him, and he pulled the cork with his teeth. The light from the lantern was caught by the rum and it glowed a brilliant amber, as if it had captured a bit of the lantern's fire. There was an empty glass on the table; the girl pointed to it.

"Would you be offerin' a girl a little drink now?" she asked. Her voice was low and husky, and for all her innocent look, there was no shyness to it.

Rafe looked at her as he poured the drink. She

was pretty enough, he hoped, to act as a surrogate Candy Pratt. Maybe she could at least dull some of the aching want he felt.

The girl took the glass, then quickly, neatly, tossed the drink down. She smiled again and wiped the back of her hand across her mouth.

"I know what you want," she said. She undid the buttons of her dress, then pulled it off, over her head. She wore nothing beneath her dress, and Rafe was surprised to be treated to the sight of her naked body so quickly.

The girl folded her dress carefully and placed it on the table, then walked easily and unashamedly to the bed. Her body was subtly lighted by the lantern, and the area at the junction of her legs was darkened by the shadows and by a tangle of dark hair which formed an inverted triangle. She turned down the covers of the bed.

Quickly, Rafe took off his clothes and lay down on the bed beside her. His need was very evident, and the young girl took a gasping breath through pursed lips.

"Oh, dear, you are ready, aren't you?"

She rolled against him, kissing his open mouth with her own, and Rafe felt her tongue dart and probe against his lips. He positioned himself so that he was over her.

The young girl received him with a short, joyful

gasp. She wrapped her legs around him and met his lunges by pushing against him.

Rafe could feel all the hunger of his soul collecting then, bunching up in a small spot just between his shoulder blades. He closed his eyes and mentally changed this girl to Candy Pratt. With thoughts of Candy in his mind, the pleasure began spreading out, whirling around and around to take up all parts of his body, drawing heat and sensation from every point, until, finally, in a burst of agony which turned to ecstasy, he felt himself exploding into this young girl who writhed beneath him. Even as he sprayed his seed into her, he could feel her pulsating in the throes of her own pleasure, joining him in the rapture of the moment.

Much later, when the lantern had been turned very low and there was only the dullest glimmer of light still in the room, Rafe, thinking the girl beside him was asleep, got out of bed. He padded across the cold floor of the room and looked through the window again. Now the inside of the window was covered with cold moisture, and he wiped a circle with his hand, then peered through. It had begun to snow, and the two blanket-wrapped bums were tucked up under boxes, oblivious to the weather.

Rafe heard the springs of the bed creak, and he turned around to see the young girl sitting up. She had drawn her knees up under her chin and her arms were wrapped around her legs. She was still totally nude and the effect she presented was erotic, though, oddly, chaste, as none of her more intimate charms could be seen.

"Does she know how much you love her?" she asked.

"What?" Rafe asked quietly.

"The woman you were thinking about," the young girl said.

"What makes you think I was thinking of anyone else?" Rafe asked, surprised by the young girl's comment.

"I don't paint my face, and dissipation has not yet taken its toll of me," the girl said easily. "But I am not the innocent I appear to be. I have been with many men. When a woman has been with as many men as I have, she learns to know what is in his mind as they make love. There was another woman in your mind, wasn't there?"

"No," Rafe said. He smiled. "I mean, yes. But it is foolish. I have only seen her twice and we have hardly spoken."

"And yet you feel a great need for her," the girl said. It wasn't a question; it was a statement.

"Yes," Rafe admitted.

"Did I help ease some of that need?"

"Yes," Rafe answered, smiling. He came back to the bed and sat down beside her. He put his hand on her neck and squeezed it gently. "You helped a great deal."

"I'm glad," she said. She looked toward the window. "It is snowing."

"Yes."

"Have you a place to go tonight?"

The *Delta Dancer* was anchored in a secret cove over on the outer banks. He would not be able to find a ferry to take him across tonight.

"I was going to find a hotel room," he said truthfully.

"No," the girl said. She raised her arm and put her hand on his shoulder. That action exposed one of her breasts, small, but perfectly shaped, tipped by a nipple which looked like a glowing ember. "Stay here with me."

Rafe felt the need returning.

"All right." he smiled, slipping under the cover, then pulling her down to him. "That sounds good to me."

Chapter Three

Washington was a gay, exciting town, aswirl with handsome, uniformed men and lovely young ladies. There was an endless round of parties, receptions and shows, all of which managed to keep Candy entertained.

Notwithstanding the gaiety of the city, the war was still going on. It was a war which, in its beginning, had been seen as little more than a riot that could quickly be put down. However, battles out West soon changed that way of thinking. In the cold winter snows of Missouri the armies met time and time again, with each skirmish building upon the other until gradually, inexorably, the number of dead and dying kept growing.

At first, Dr. Pratt was able to find some favorable response in the halls of Congress, as well as in the administration itself, to his proposal that a peace conference be convened. But as the number of dead kept growing, even those people who had been receptive to him hardened their position. Now it was known that, whether its existence was recognized or not, the Confederacy was no mere uprising of a few rebellious spirits. It was a nation with an army, brilliantly led and well-armed.

The Navy of the South was practically non-existent, though the Northern press was full of stories of the voyages of the *Alabama* and the *Delta Dancer*. On February 12th, 1862, *Harper's Weekly* carried an editorial which summed up the frustrations of the North with regard to Captain Rafe Taylor and the *Delta Dancer*.

THE DELTA DANCER

Certainly, if Captain Rafe Taylor were on our side, we should give him dinners and invite him to receive his fellow-citizens at the City Hall. The Delta Dancer *rivals the* Alabama. *She dances in and out under the very noses of our guns. They smell her and snort, but she skips away. She will arrive blithely in Liverpool or Southampton, and a week afterward, while she is comfortably lying there,*

*the news we send of her burning or her cap-
ture will set all Europe laughing. It is a joke;
we may as well own up to it, and laugh too.
Certainly, crying won't help it.*

*The truth is, our Navy has been utterly
inadequate to its task. The career of the* Delta
Dancer *cannot help but be mortifying to us,
not because its movements are so important
in themselves, but because Captain Taylor
shows a skillful audacity which inspires admiration and begets confidence.*

A week or so later, Rafe was sitting on a coil of
rope on the quarterdeck, reading the paper. The
ship was under way at sea, moving by sail alone,
in order to preserve coal. Rafe chuckled and put
the paper aside. It had come aboard the *Delta
Dancer* yesterday, when Rafe stopped a ship which
was one week out of New York and making for
Spain. The ship had been of Spanish registry, and
after a perfunctory inspection, Rafe had let it go.
The captain had been gracious enough to give Rafe
the newspaper, thus allowing Rafe to catch up on
the news and, incidentally, read an article about
himself.

"Cap'n?" Lieutenant McCorkle said, coming to
the quarterdeck.

"Yes, Mac?"

"Lookout reports smoke on the horizon."

"Where away?"

"Dead a'starboard, sir," McCorkle said.

Rafe got to his feet lightly, then, instead of yelling up to the lookout, climbed the mast himself. When he reached the top tee, he held onto the mast and reached for the sailor's glass.

"Where is she?" he asked.

"There, sir, a bit o' smoke is just creepin' up," the sailor said, pointing in the direction he had indicated.

"Aye," Rafe said. "I see her."

"Merchantman, sir?"

"My bet is she's a warship," Rafe said. "After us, more than likely. No commercial ship is going to be wasting steam when they've a good trade wind. But a warship tryin' to catch us would tie down the safety valves."

"We gonna show tail, Cap'n? Or are we gonna fight 'er?"

Rafe looked at the man in the lookout and smiled. He knew that such a question on any other ship would be tantamount to insubordination. On board the *Delta Dancer*, however, every man-jack shared in the prizes the ship captured, and thus everyone had more than a casual interest in what went on.

"I'd like to do neither," Rafe said. He looked at the sun, already low in the west. "If we run, we'll get so far off the trade routes that we could let a big, fat prize slip right through our hands. On the other hand, if we fight, we might get so badly hurt as to not be able to repair in time for a prize ship."

"Glory, Cap'n, we got to do one or t'other," the lookout said.

"Maybe not," Rafe said. He pointed to the sun. "If we can stay out of her way until the sun sets, we might be able to double back, avoid her entirely, and be sitting here when a nice, fat ship comes along."

Rafe slid down the rope to the deck where he was met by Lieutenant McCorkle.

"I've alerted the men, sir," McCorkle said. "The sharpshooters have drawn rifles, and the other men have sharpened axe and cutlass to repel boarders."

"Good," Rafe said. "Mac, tell the engineer to make steam."

"Aye, sir. I'll have him use the good smokeless coal."

"No," Rafe said. Rafe walked over to the rail and put his hands on it as he looked toward the horizon where the ship had been spotted. Now that he knew where to look, he could see the tiny wisp of smoke which had given the ship's position away. "No, use the dirty coal."

"Beggin' your pardon, sir, but that stuff'll show so much smoke they could spot us from Nassau."

"Good," Rafe said mysteriously. "That's just

what I want. Tell the engineer to wet a blanket and throw it in the fire.''

"Sir?''

"I want this fella, whoever he is, to know exactly where we are,'' Rafe paused, then looked at McCorkle and smiled. "Till sundown,'' he added.

McCorkle laughed out loud.

"I get it, sir. We're suckerin' him in.''

"Yes,'' Rafe said. "At least, I hope we are.''

"Cap'n, the sails are visible,'' the midshipman on watch said. The midshipman was a young man named Carter. He had been in his first year at the Naval Academy when war broke out. Rafe knew that Carter had given up as much as anyone in order to fight for the South. It would have been very difficult for him to have the brigade of midshipman while he was still in school. The traditions, the esprit, the ideals of the academy were very strong.

"Can you tell anything about her?'' Rafe asked, reaching for the midshipman's glass.

"She's barkentine-rigged, Cap'n,'' Carter said. "Square-rigged on the foremast, fore'n'aft-rigged on the main and mizzen mast. She's a sidewheeler. Cap'n, it's the *Vanderbilt*!''

"Well, well, it's our old friend Charles Raymond,'' Rafe said, opening the glass and looking toward the approaching vessel. "I guess now we'll find out just how fast the *Vanderbilt* really is.''

"Cap'n, engineer reports steam, sir," McCorkle said.

"Very well, Mr. McCorkle. Take up a heading of east by sou'east."

"Aye, aye, sir."

Rafe looked through the glass again. He had taken a course directly away from the *Vanderbilt's* line of travel, thus preventing Captain Raymond from being able to cut the angle on him.

He closed the glass and handed it to the midshipman.

"I'll be in my cabin," he said. "Call me if there is any change."

"Aye, sir," Carter replied.

Rafe went to his cabin and sat at his desk. He began to write in the log, noting the time and location of the sighting of the pursuing ship. There was a chance he would have to fight Captain Raymond. He knew that Raymond was a ferocious adversary; he had fought with him on slave patrols before the war. He wasn't overly concerned about that, though. His was a well-trained crew, each man with a vital interest in the outcome of the battle. The crew of Captain Raymond's ship, Rafe knew, would more than likely be composed of eighty percent conscripts. No matter how good Raymond was, most of his guns would be marred by unskilled hands. Raymond and his officers and the few experienced men he might have would have their hands full just trying to prevent a panic. If it came down to a battle, Rafe would have the advantage in the quality of men who were serving with him.

The ships were something else. The *Delta Dancer* was a trim, fast, excellent ship as a commerce raider. It had no armor, however, whereas the *Vanderbilt,* like most other Union warships, had, at the very minimum, sheet cables protecting their sides and engines.

"Cap'n, I thought you might appreciate a bit of soup," the cook said through the door to Rafe's cabin. "Iffen there's to be a fight, I won't know when you can eat again."

"Thanks, Eb," Rafe said, opening the door. Eb brought in a tray which held a bowl of hot beef soup, a piece of bread and a flask of wine.

"See that the men are fed, too," Rafe said.

"Aye, Cap'n," Eb replied, withdrawing without further comment.

Rafe ate his soup, and as he ate, he opened his sketchbook to look at the drawing of Candy.

Suddenly the beat of the engine stopped. Rafe was on his feet and to the door of his cabin instantly.

"Mr. McCorkle!"

"Aye, sir, I'm checking on it," McCorkle answered.

There was a sudden burst of steam, then a scream

from the position of the boiler. Rafe ran toward the boilers and saw a cloud of steam escaping. He saw two men dragging a third away.

"What happened?"

"The slide bearing froze on the engine, Cap'n," one of the sailors said. "Then the pressure built up 'n' a fitting let go. It could've been worse; the boiler could've burst. Iffen that had happened, we'd all be goners."

"Who was hurt?"

"Frenchy, sir."

"Bad?"

"He'll be dead afore mornin'—and the better off for it," the sailor said.

Rafe looked over at the ship's surgeon who was administering to the scalded man.

"How are we on laudanum?"

"We've got quite a bit, Cap'n."

"Give him as much as it takes to ease his pain."

"Aye, sir," the surgeon answered.

"Cap'n, the *Vanderbilt* is gainin' on us," McCorkle said of the pursuing ship.

"All right," Rafe said. "We have no choice; without an engine we'd be so badly outmaneuvered that we couldn't begin to fight her. We have to get away from her."

"Cap'n, even with steam, the *Vanderbilt's* likely as fast as we are."

"We've no choice, Mr. McCorkle. Crowd on all the sail you can. Hang out the crew's laundry if need be. We've got to give her the slip."

"Aye, sir."

"Cap'n, her bow gun just fired, sir!" the lookout called down.

Immediately after the lookout's call, there was a sound, like an unattached freight car rolling down the track. On the heels of that sound was a low, distant thump, like thunder. A shell burst in the water about one hundred yards in front of the ship.

"They're using an eleven-inch gun for a bow chaser," Rafe said. "They have the range on us."

"The bastards must have seen the steam and think we burst our boiler," McCorkle said.

Rafe saw a flash of light and realized the gun had fired a second time. A second later, the rushing of the shell and the thump of its firing. The second shell fell one hundred yards short.

"Damn, they have us bracketed," Rafe said grimly. "Come hard to port."

"Helmsman, hard to port!" McCorkle shouted.

The ship answered the helmsman's command just as the third projectile was launched by the distant ship. The abrupt course change caused the shell to punch harmlessly through an upper sail, then splash in the water.

"They've switched to solid shot," Rafe said. "They think they have us ranged. Good. This way they won't be able to adjust their shooting as they would if they were firing explosive shell.''

"We can dodge their long-range shooting, Cap'n," McCorkle said. "But every time we make a zig like that, we lose time. They'll be catchin' up with us soon."

Rafe looked at the sun. Only a sliver of it remained above the horizon.

"Maybe not," Rafe said. "If we can just stay out of her way until dark."

Candy had quite enjoyed the evening concert presented by the Orchestral Union of Washington. The concert had opened with an overture, *Lenora, Number Three*, by Beethoven, and had closed with the overture to *Merry Wives of Windsor* by Nicolai. Candy had attended the concert with her father, as the two young ladies with whom she had made such friends were no longer available. Kate Chase had married young Captain Sprague of the Union Army, and Susan Cameron's father had resigned his cabinet position and had been posted as an ambassador to Russia. Candy missed the companionship of her two friends. It wasn't that she didn't enjoy attending concerts, dinners and receptions with her father. In fact, in the social whirl of wartime Washington, her position as official hostess for her father was important. Still, she would have enjoyed the opportunity to have more contact with women of her own age.

"Oh," Candy said as they reached the lobby of the theater. "My gloves."

"Your gloves?" Dr. Pratt said.

"I had them right here," she said. "They were in the pocket of my wrap; I know they were. Now they're gone."

"Perhaps they're back at the seat," Dr. Pratt said. "I'll go for them."

"Thank you," Candy said.

Candy stood in the lobby and smiled and exchanged pleasantries with the others as they crowded out. She moved over to the side of the lobby to be out of the way, when a small, mustachioed man approached her.

"Miss Pratt?"

"Yes," Candy said.

"I have a message from General Beauregard to your father."

"What?"

"Here," the man said, shoving an envelope into her hands.

"Wait; what is this?" Candy asked, but the small man moved quickly and within a moment had disappeared into the crowd.

Candy looked at the envelope the man had given her. Why would General Beauregard send a letter to her father? She was consumed with curiosity, so

she removed the envelope and opened the letter.
The writing made no sense.

Imshallxmcrmosvsthieverifvreabvelittlexm
fallsvrjonmsurndayatmmtwopmserignalvmr
edrmravndwihivterjoketsfrojklmtxurmners
hxvijljlfqergomndsisaoikedyuonrtfaoilaus
fuyretphedciwtyqamtamtllpuyoimntsaegreme
duprownaiutomniuce

"Here are your gloves," Dr. Pratt said, returning a moment later. The crowd had very nearly
gone by the time he returned. "They were lying
neatly on the arm of the chair. Someone must have
found them and put them there, realizing we would
return."

"I suppose so," Candy said, almost absently.

"What have you there?" Dr. Pratt asked, pointing to the envelope.

"I don't know," Candy said. "A strange little
man just handed this envelope to me and said I
must give it to you."

"To me?"

"Father, he said it was from General Beauregard."

"No," Dr. Pratt said. "It can't be. President
Davis agreed that our mission here was too important to take a chance on it being compromised by
the exchange of any messages."

"Let's throw it away at once," Candy suggested.

"We can't do that."

"Why not? Father, if your mission is too important for you to be contacted, then it is certainly too important for you to take a chance on being caught with such a message in your possession."

"It may contain critical information which would be damaging to the South," Dr. Pratt said. He put the message in his coat pocket. "I can't just let it fall into government hands."

"But what good will it do for you to keep it?" Candy asked. "It is in some cipher which I can't understand."

"Nor I," Dr. Pratt said. "But I don't want to dispose of it here. When we get home, I will burn it."

"Father, let's go home right away," Candy said.

"We can't, dear; we are to attend a reception at Secretary Stanton's home."

"I don't like him," Candy said.

Dr. Pratt chuckled. "Well, after all, he, like everyone else in Washington, is our enemy. You're not supposed to like him."

"I liked Secretary Cameron."

"You liked his daughter Susan," Dr. Pratt reminded her. "And you have barely been civil to Mr. Stanton, ever since he replaced Cameron. It is no wonder that he seems cold to you. You have given him little opportunity to warm up to us. And need I remind you, young lady, that our job is to influence as many as we can, and that certainly would include the Secretary of War.''

Candy and her father had been walking as they were talking, and now they were on the street in front of the theater. It was a warm, balmy night, with a breeze which carried with it a threat of rain. The breeze blew Candy's dress out to one side, and Dr. Pratt had to hold onto his hat to keep it from blowing away. He saw a cab and waved at it, and the driver clucked at his horse, then swung around to pick up the fare.

The cab was enclosed so that, though the wind made the carriage shake, it at least didn't threaten to take Dr. Pratt's hat away. They gave the driver the address, then settled back into the seat.

"Father, do you sometimes feel guilty?" Candy asked.

Dr. Pratt sighed. "To the degree that I am enjoying the comforts of Washington, while in Richmond our fellow countrymen are beginning to experience the shortages of war, yes," Dr. Pratt said. "But, as to carrying on a deceit against the government here, no, I don't feel guilty at all. After all, what am I trying to do here? I am trying to influence certain people into bringing about a peaceful settlement to this war. In that, I feel that I am saving the lives of thousands of men, from the North and the South. Now, if I were involved in some overt act of espionage, yes, I might feel guilty.

"Hold it up there, driver!" someone shouted in a gruff voice. "Stop that cab."

"What is it?" Candy asked. "What's going on?"

"I don't know," Dr. Pratt answered in a voice which showed as much confusion as Candy's.

Candy stuck her head out the window and saw a mounted patrol of soldiers blocking the road. One of the soldiers, a captain, got down from his horse and walked over to the cab. He opened the door.

"Miss Pratt. I would like to ask you and your father to get out of the coach, please."

"You—you know who we are?"

"Yes, ma'am," the officer said. "We surely do know who you are."

"Then, if you know us, Captain, why are you stopping us?" Dr. Pratt asked. "You have clearly made a mistake here. We are on our way to a reception being given by the Secretary of War."

"Yes, sir," the captain answered. "I know, for that is how I was told I could find you."

"I don't understand," Candy said. "Find us for what? What do you want?"

"Miss Pratt, Dr. Pratt, it is my duty to inform the two of you that you are under arrest."

"Under arrest? Arrest for what?" Candy asked.

"Espionage, ma'am. You were given a note this evenin' by a Rebel spy, were you not?"

"No!" Candy said. "I don't know what you are talking about."

"Your pa does, don't you, sir?" the captain asked. "What did the note say?"

"I don't know," Dr. Pratt said quietly. "It is in cipher and I can't read it."

"Never mind; we have people who can read it," the captain said. He held out his hand. "Would you give it to me, please?"

Dr. Pratt sighed resignedly, then reached into his coat pocket for the letter. It was ironic, he thought. He was a Confederate agent, but he wasn't the one they were looking for. He didn't even know what this letter was about.

The *Delta Dancer* was running full and by under heavy sail. At sundown Rafe had struck the regular sails and hoisted his "special" sails—special, because they weren't the ordinary white sails with which most ships were equipped. Rafe had an extra set of sails dyed black for sailing at night. Many were the times he had been able to approach enemy merchant ships in the middle of the night because his sails were black and, from any distance at all, virtually invisible. Always before it had been a weapon of attack. Now he was forced to use this same system of stealth to retreat.

The thought of retreat galled him, but he really had no choice. Without steam he would be helpless in a battle which required meneuvering, and as the *Vanderbilt* had eleven-inch guns to his 64-pounder smooth bores, he would have to be able to maneuver if he was to stand a chance in any battle with them.

"Can you see anything?" Rafe asked, staring out into the dark.

"Aye, Cap'n, she's still out there," the lookout called down. "I saw sparks from her stack a while back."

"Damn," Rafe said, pounding his fist into his hand. "Raymond must have guessed which way I would go and cut the angle. At this rate he'll be alongside by sunup."

"Maybe we can double back," McCorkle suggested.

"How many hours till sunup?"

"I make it about four hours, sir."

"No good," Rafe said. "Without power we'll have to beat against the winds and the current. By sunup we won't even be hull-down yet, let alone sail-down. If we're anywhere on the horizon, he can catch us under power."

"I wish we were as fast as that bastard who's chasin' us," McCorkle said. "If we had steam, we could make it."

"Yeah," Rafe said. "And if frogs had wings,

they wouldn't bump their ass every time they jump after a grasshopper."

"I'll get the gun crews ready, Cap'n. I guess we'll be fightin' come sunup."

"Grasshoppers have wings," Rafe mused.

"Sir?"

"Grasshoppers," Rafe said. "They have wings and the *Vanderbilt* has steam."

"Yes, sir," McCorkle said, not quite understanding what Rafe's strange remark meant.

"Don't you see?" Rafe asked.

"No, sir," McCorkle admitted.

"If the mountain won't come to Mohammed, Mohammed will go to the mountain," Rafe said. "We can't run away from Captain Raymond, but the captain can run away from us."

"Aye, he could if he wanted to. But why would he want to be runnin' from us now? He'd get the better of us in any fight," McCorkle said.

"Rig a lugsail on the dinghy," Rafe ordered.

"Aye, aye, Cap'n," McCorkle said, still not understanding what Rafe had in mind.

Rafe went to his cabin and got the hurricane lantern. It was especially designed to burn in the fiercest storm, being vented to allow air for the flame, but shielded to keep out the water. He lit the lantern, then brought it out on deck, in direct violation of his own imposed security.

"On deck, douse that light, you crazy son-of-abitch!'' the lookout shouted. Then, when he saw that Rafe was the one with the light, he coughed and recanted. "I'm sorry, Cap'n, I didn't know it was you. I was just trying to maintain light discipline."

"And you've done a good job of it, too, Pig Meat," Rafe said. "But bear with me, laddie. There's a reason for my madness."

"Aye, sir," the big sailor known as Pig Meat answered. If it had been anyone else, he would have been certain that the man had gone mad. But he, like everyone else on board the *Delta Dancer*, had absolute faith in the captain.

"Mac, assemble the crew," Rafe ordered.

"Aye, Cap'n," McCorkle said, watching in amazement as Rafe hung the lantern from the sternpost, then opened the shutters to the brightest glow. "Uh, Cap'n, that light'll be visible for ten miles or so."

"Yes, Mac, that's what I'm counting on. Have you rigged the lugsail on the dinghy?"

"Aye, sir."

"Good, good. Now, assemble the crew."

Less than five minutes later the entire crew of the *Delta Dancer* was assembled on deck. As those who had been on the gun deck came up and saw the lighted lantern, they gasped. A few made comments on the stupidity of showing a light when they were trying to sneak away in the dark. When they saw that their captain was not only aware of the light but was indeed the cause of it, they fell silent in curiosity. Not doubt, just curiosity. What was going on? They stood by in twos and threes, some leaning against the railing, some against the mizzen, a few around the swivel gun.

"Men, I have a plan. If it works, why, I imagine you will all be calling me a clever fellow," Rafe said. "If it doesn't work, well, we'll be none the worse for it than we are now, for unless something happens, we'll be in a one-sided battle tomorrow, sure as a gun is iron. And, without our engine, I don't have to tell you which side will be favored."

"What's your plan, Cap'n?" one of the men called.

Rafe chuckled. "Well, it has to do with this lantern. Or did you all think I had gone completely daft and was using this to look for Andy's glass eye?"

Andy was the bo'sun. He had a glass eye which had been made for him in China out of jade. Andy referred to it as his poke, and he was always borrowing money on it. He had lost it a couple of days earlier, and there was a twenty-dollar reward for anyone who could find it. There was a smattering of polite and nervous laughter at Rafe's attempt to make a joke of the situation. It wasn't much of a joke, but it did help relieve the tension of the moment, and that was its purpose.

"The truth is," Rafe went on, "I hope to use this lantern to lure our Yankee friends into a wild goose chase. I'm going to put this lantern in the dinghy, set the lugsail and send her flying before the wind. If the Yankees fall for my trick, they'll be chasing the dinghy all the way to Africa, while we. . . ."

"Beat back against the wind," McCorkle said, now understanding clearly.

"Yes," Rafe said. He sighed. "At least, that's what I hope. Well, men, what do you say?"

"What do we say?" one of the men shouted back. "I say three cheers for the Cap'n!"

The sailor's shout was immediately answered by three rousing cheers.

"All right, Mac, set the bait," Rafe said. "And we shall see what we shall see."

McCorkle started to put the lantern in the dinghy, when Midshipman Carter spoke up.

"Not there," he said. "At the top of the mast."

"What?" McCorkle asked, surprised that a midshipman would correct him.

"Well, uh, sir," Carter said, clearing his throat nervously. "If the lantern is supposed to be on the sternpost, then it would be about that high from the water."

"The lad's right, Mr. McCorkle," one of the

other sailors said, and McCorkle, laughing, moved the lantern to the top of the mast as per Carter's suggestion.

There was no shortage of help as the dinghy was put over the side. The sails were set and the dinghy started its quiet journey, while the *Delta Dancer* came about and took up a sharp tack about one hundred and ten degrees away from the original line of progress. Within half an hour the lantern was a tiny, bobbing light far in the distance.

"Now," Rafe said, "all we have to do is wait until morning. By then we'll know if I'm a fool or a genius."

"Cap'n Raymond, sir! She's showin' a light!" the lookout suddenly shouted.

Raymond raised his binoculars and saw, as the lookout reported, that the *Delta Dancer* was, indeed, showing a light. He let out an explosion of sound which may have been a laugh, though, as such an expression was rare with him, it was really difficult for anyone to know.

"By thunder, Mr. Herrick, we have him now!" he said. "Reduce speed one-third."

"Reduce speed, sir?"

"Aye," Raymond said. "I don't want to run over him in the dark. We'll just stay on him all night long; then, at dawn, we'll open fire."

"Cap'n, without steam he won't be able to maneuver," Mr. Herrick said.

"A decided advantage to us, don't you think?" Raymond replied.

"Yes, sir, of course it is," Mr. Herrick said. "But Rafe will know that as well. Surely you will give him the opportunity to surrender?"

"Mr. Herrick, I know that you and Mr. Taylor were friends in Annapolis," Captain Raymond said. "I have spent my entire naval career aware of the protection you and the other Academy graduates extend to each other. In the peacetime navy, you conspire together to prevent other more deserving men from reaching higher rank. Do not think I am unaware of the plotting you and your friend Mr. Taylor did against me when you both served with me on the *Vermont*."

"Captain Raymond, you err, sir. Rafe and I were friends, yes, but we engaged in no plots. Such a thing would be mutinous."

"And you think Rafe Taylor incapable of mutiny?"

"Rafe Taylor is an honorable man, sir."

"An honorable man, you say? And yet he has violated his oath of allegiance to the United States to serve in the Confederate Navy."

"Yes, sir, but I still consider him my friend."

"He can be a friend no longer, sir. Mr. Taylor is an enemy to the United States, and, by thunder, you are sworn, by oath, to make him your enemy as well. I am going to sink Mr. Taylor, and the pirate ship *Delta Dancer*, at first dawn. Do you understand me, mister?''

"Aye, Cap'n," Herrick replied.

"Very good. Now, Mr. Herrick, I am going to hold you personally responsible for seeing to it that the bunch of landlubbers and shore rabble Secretary Welles has given me for a crew are turned out and at their guns by first light.''

"Aye, sir," Mr. Herrick replied.

"I am going to turn in now, Mr. Herrick. See to it that we do not lose contact with the *Delta Dancer*.''

"Aye, sir, we'll stay in close contact," Herrick said. He looked at the light again, then lowered the glass with a confused expression on his face, then raised it and looked again.

"Cap'n Raymond?''

"What is it, Mr. Herrick?''

"That light. Don't you think there is something peculiar about it?''

"It's a standard stern lamp," Raymond answered.

"Yes, sir, it is," Herrick said. "But why would Rafe be showing a stern lamp? He knows we are here, and he knows that we know he lost his engine.''

"Maybe Rafe Taylor is just making a dumb mistake," Raymond suggested.

"No, sir, I don't think so," Herrick replied. "Besides, there's something else. The course is very erratic. He's wandered two points since we first spotted him."

"Maybe the boiler explosion damaged the rudder as well," Raymond suggested.

"I don't know, Cap'n. There's something funny about that light."

"Follow it, Mr. Herrick." Raymond ordered; then he turned to leave the deck for his quarters.

"Aye, sir," Herrick replied.

"I'm going to turn in now, Mr. Herrick. See to it that we don't lose contact with the *Delta Dancer.*"

For the next few hours the crew of the *Delta Dancer* paced nervously back and forth on the deck, searching the horizon for any sign of the pursuing ship. Finally, there was a streak of pearl gray in the east, then pink, then the golden blaze of full day as the sun came full-disk from the water.

Though there was actually only one official lookout, there were, perhaps, half a dozen men in the braces, and as many telescopes. Those on deck looked up at their elevated partners anxiously, as the lookouts, real and self-appointed, searched the horizon all the way around.

"Cap'n," the lookout shouted down from his uppermost perch.

"Aye?"

"No ships in sight, sir!" he shouted happily.

The crew of the *Delta Dancer* responded with a rousing cheer.

Captain Raymond was dreaming. In his dream he was being introduced to President Lincoln by Secretary of the Navy Welles. Secretary Welles was describing Raymond's great naval victory over the *Delta Dancer*, and, in appreciation, the President was, personally, promoting Raymond to the rank of Flag Officer. Artists for *Harper's Weekly* and *Leslie's Illustrated* fought for the right to do his likeness for their journals, and everywhere he went, men wanted to shake his hand.

He was awakened by a knock at his cabin door, and for a moment he lay there, irritated by the intrusion.

"What is it?" he called.

"Cap'n, it's me, sir," Herrick said. "I think you'd better come on deck, sir."

"On deck? Yes, on deck. Have we closed with the *Delta Dancer*?"

"No, sir," Herrick said.

"No? What do you mean, no?"

"Perhaps you'd better come see for yourself, sir," Herrick suggested.

Angrily, Captain Raymond hurried to the deck. He saw some of the crew gathered near the port railing, and he pushed his way through them, then looked at what they had been looking at. He saw a skiff from the *Delta Dancer*; it was rigged with a lugsail and showing a lamp from the top of the mast. A sailor from the *Vanderbilt* had furled the sail, and now the boat was bobbing, dead in the water.

"I fear this is what we followed all night, sir," Herrick said. "We lost them."

Raymond squinted his eyes and looked at the boat for a moment. He rubbed the top of his bald head; then he smiled.

"No, Mr. Herrick, we didn't lose them. We sunk them."

"What? Sir, you can't be serious!"

"I'm quite serious," Raymond said. "We must have hit her with one of our shells, and she sunk during the night. She put her skiff over, but before she could evacuate her crew, she went down with all hands. That is precisely the report we will make. There will be prize money for all the men."

"Hurrah!" the men shouted, and word spread through the ship's company like wildfire that they had sunk the *Delta Dancer*.

"But, Cap'n, you can't really believe that," Herrick protested a few moments later when the two officers were away from any chance of being overheard by the celebrating crew.

"Of course I don't believe it," Raymond said.

"Do you think me a fool?" Raymond rubbed the top of his head again and looked down at the skiff. "But if Taylor thinks I believe it, he may grow incautious. He got me this time, but he can't escape me forever. I'm going to get him, Mr. Herrick. You can count on that. I'm going to get Rafe Taylor."

Chapter Four

The police officer who had been appointed to escort Candy took her into the courtroom and sat her behind a table. The table was very near the judge's bench and separated from the gallery by a railing. The gallery was already full of spectators, but there were still people coming in, even though they were relegated to standing along the walls.

"Where is my father?" Candy asked the police officer who had taken a seat just behind the railing on the first row. "You said he would be here."

It had been a little over a week since Candy and her father were arrested while leaving the theater. They had been taken to jail and separated, and Candy had not been allowed to communicate with him since that time.

It had been a long, frightening week in jail. Candy was kept in a cell all alone, and she had seen no one except her guards—and them only when they fed her. She had not been charged with any crime, nor had she spoken with a lawyer. When they told her this morning she was going to trial for espionage, it was the first information she had been given. When they told her that her father was also being tried, and that they would be tried together, she felt a sense of joy over the opportunity to see him again, even though it was tinged with fear over the outcome of their ordeal.

Candy turned to look through the courtroom at those who had come for the sensational trial. She saw many of the same people here she had seen at the many receptions and parties she and her father had attended over the last few months. Some of the same young women were there, dressed in butterfly-bright dresses and stylish hats, just as if this, too, were a party.

Candy turned away from them, embarrassed to look at them and embarrassed to be looked at by them. Candy, who had an expert eye for fashion and who normally wore simple but very stylish clothes, was now wearing a very plain, unadorned dress of gray, one provided by the jail. Her hair was combed back in a severe bun because she had been unable to take care of it while she was in jail.

There was an increased murmur of voices from

the gallery and Candy looked up to see why. She saw her father being brought in through the side door, and she gasped and stood up. He looked so tired and haggard, not at all like the strong man she knew.

"Father!"

"You'll have to sit down, miss," her police escort said.

"Father, are you all right?" Candy ran toward her father, but before she could get to him, tow court bailiffs grabbed her and held her back.

Somewhere deep inside him, an ember of Dr. Pratt's old self remained, and that ember sparked into life when he saw the guards grab his daughter.

"Let her go, you fools!" Dr. Pratt commanded, and the bailiffs and police officers, accustomed to obeying their superiors, reacted to Dr. Pratt's authoritative voice. Candy was free to go to his arms.

"Father, how happy I am to see you. Are you all right?" she asked, weeping in relief. Her time in solitude had caused her to think all sorts of things. She imagined he had been beaten and tortured or, perhaps, already taken to the gallows and hanged.

"I'm fine, darlin', just fine," her father said, putting his arms around his daughter and holding her close to comfort her. He brushed his hand over her hair. "Now, let's go sit at the table and not give these damn Yankees any more of a show than necessary,'' he suggested. It was as if seeing his daughter had caused him to be reborn. The tired and haggard man who had come to the door of the courtroom was left outside in the hallway, and the man who came inside was the strong father Candy had always known.

Her father was a well-known surgeon and a man who had influenced the shapers of his society, so Candy had always been proud of him. But she was never prouder of him than she was at this moment.

''All right,'' Candy said, and she turned and saw the bailiffs and police officers still standing back in obedience to her father's command. Her eyes were wet with tears, but the tears were not of fear or sorrow. They were of defiance and pride.

Candy and her father took their seat behind the table, where another man joined them. He whispered to Candy.

''I am Theotis Van Doren,'' he said. ''I am counselor for you and your father.''

''Where have you been?'' Candy hissed angrily. ''If you are my counselor, shouldn't you have come to talk to me? Shouldn't you listen to my side?''

''Sshh, dear, it's all right,'' Candy's father said, patting her hand softly. ''Trust me, darlin'. It's all right.''

Two men came to the other table then, one in

military uniform and the other in mufti. They were the prosecutors. But prosecutors of what? Candy wondered. With what crime were they being charged? If it was just the letter, she was certain there would be no problem. The letter had obviously been delivered to her by mistake. Besides, it was in code and she had no idea what it even said.

"All rise!"

There was a scrape of chairs and a rustle of clothing as everyone in the courtroom stood in response to the court clerk's command. The murmuring grew quiet. A horse-drawn trolley passed by outside, and the clopping of the horse's hooves and the clanging of the trolley bell seemed unduly loud.

There was a moment's pause; then the court clerk cleared his throat.

"His Honor Judge Emmet L. Dawes, Judge of the Federal Court of the District of Columbia, presiding," the clerk called.

A tall, very heavyset man with white hair and large mutton-chop sideburns entered the courtroom. He was wearing a black robe and carrying a small gavel. When he reached the bench, he withdrew a handkerchief from his sleeve and blew his nose loudly. He struck the gavel once, then sat down. The courtroom sat with him.

"Mr. Clerk, call the case," the judge said. His voice was merely conversational, but it was deep and resonant, and Candy could hear him as clearly as if she had been standing right in front of the bench.

"The United States of America versus Dr. Arnold Pratt and his daughter Candice," the clerk said. "The charge is treason."

"Treason?" Candy gasped. "My God, Father, are we to be charged with treason?"

Again her father patted her hand reassuringly. "It will be all right," he said quietly.

"Are both counsels present?"

"Counsel for the defense is present, Your Honor."

"The prosecution is present, Your Honor."

"Mr. Prosecutor, make your case."

The prosecutor in civilian clothes stood. "Your Honor, I call Mr. Thomas Weakes to the stand."

A small man stood and walked up to the witness stand to be sworn in.

"That's the man!" Candy said. "That's the man who gave me the letter."

"Yes," her father said. "I know."

"Would you identify yourself, please?" the prosecutor asked the witness after he was seated.

"My name is Thomas Weakes, and I am an agent for the Pinkerton Detective Agency."

"What?" Candy asked in a confused whisper.

"Mr. Weakes, have you ever seen either of the defendants?"

"Yes," Weakes said.

"Would you tell the court where you saw them?"

"At the Concert Union Hall," he said.

"And what was the occasion of your meeting?" the prosecutor asked.

"One of our agents intercepted a coded message which was being delivered by a courier for General Beauregard of the Confederate forces. With the intercepted message in hand, I posed as that courier and delivered the message to Miss Pratt."

"Would you identify Miss Pratt for the court, please?"

Weakes looked over toward the defense table and stared directly at Candy. His eyes reminded Candy of the eyes of a rat jealously guarding a piece of pirated cheese.

"The woman at the defense table is Miss Candice Pratt."

"I see. And how did you happen to choose Miss Pratt?"

"We didn't just happen to choose her. She and her father have been under investigation for some time."

"Why?"

"Secretary Stanton suggested that we examine the loyalty of Dr. Pratt and his daughter. Dr. Pratt is well-known in Washington circles as being an advocate for the Southern cause."

"Hang the damn Rebel-sympathizer to the nearest telegraph pole!" someone suddenly shouted.

That shout brought other demonstrations from the gallery and caused Judge Dawes to rap his gavel sharply several times to restore order.

"Your Honor, I object," the defense counsel, Mr. Van Doren, said quickly. "Such a statement is very inflammatory."

"Mr. Sinclair, you can justify this investigation, I suppose?"

"Yes, Your Honor, we are prepared to present several witnesses who will testify to the fact that Dr. Pratt has openly lobbied for a policy of appeasement," the prosecutor said. "But, in accordance with an agreement we have already entered into with counsel for the defense, it will not be necessary for us to do that."

"Is that true, Mr. Van Doren?" the judge asked.

"Yes, Your Honor. We have an agreement with the prosecution," Van Doren said.

"Then why did you object?"

"Our agreement did not call for prosecution inciting the gallery."

"Then, I ask you, Mr. Sinclair, if you have an agreement already, why introduce material of an inflammatory nature?"

"For now it is important to establish why Mr. Weakes singled out Dr. Pratt and his daughter as recipients of the message. It gives the articles of our agreement validity.''

"What agreement are they talking about?" Candy asked quietly. "I've made no agreement."

"Shh, it's all right," Dr. Pratt answered.

"I will allow the information regarding Dr. Pratt's lobbying to stand. Objection overruled," the judge said. Again he pulled out his handkerchief and blew his nose loudly. "Mr. Sinclair, you may proceed."

"Did Miss Pratt accept the note?" Sinclair asked. Sinclair was a tall, thin, bony man with chin whiskers only, and as he asked the last question, he turned toward Candy and stroked his chin whiskers.

"Yes," Weakes said.

"Did you tell her where the note came from? Did she clearly understand that it was a treasonous message from a Rebel general?"

"Yes, sir. I told her that it was a message for her father from General Beauregard. She couldn't misunderstand."

"And she accepted it without question?"

"Yes, sir."

"And what do you make of that?"

"Objection, Your Honor. That's calling for a conclusion," Van Doren spoke up.

"Mr. Van Doren," the judge said patiently, "do you or do you not have an agreement with the prosecution?"

"We do, Your Honor."

"Then, why object? I deem this testimony as important to establishing the truth and not subject to objection. No more objections. Conclusion, Mr. Weakes."

"Well, sir, when she took that note without question after I told her who it was from, why, I knew that the note was intended for her father all along," Weakes said.

"Your Honor, Colonel Barnett, who is representing Secretary Stanton and the War Department, will continue the questioning, with your indulgence," Sinclair said.

"Very well," His Honor replied, blowing his nose sonorously yet another time.

Colonel Barnett stood, but he didn't approach the witness. Instead, he asked his question from the table.

"Mr. Weakes, it is not unusual for people of our city to receive letters from southerners, is it? I mean, after all, there are many of us who have members of our own family in the South. This tragic war has set brother against brother and father against son, so the mere fact that she agreed to accept a message from General Beauregard is not, of itself, a treasonous act, is it?"

"No, sir," Weakes replied. He looked at Candy again, and this time he screwed his face into an expression of hate. "It was what was in the message that counts."

"What was in the message?" Candy asked aloud, unable to sit by silently any longer. "I don't even know what was in the message!"

"Quiet!" Judge Dawes shouted, banging his gavel down sharply. "Young woman, while you are in my court, you will observe all the rules of courtroom behavior. You are not to speak without permission, do you understand me?"

"Your Honor—" Candy started again.

"Do you understand me?" Judge Dawes repeated, again bringing his gavel down sharply. "Because if you don't understand me, I can have you gagged."

"I understand, Your Honor," Candy said quietly, defeated by the system.

"The girl is telling the truth," Weakes said. "Neither she nor her father could have any idea what was in the message."

Candy looked up in surprise. Could it be that this man who had tricked them was now going to come to their defense?

"Why is that?" Colonel Barnett asked. "You are convinced that her father was to be the recipient of the note, are you not?"

"Yes, of course."

"Then why do you say that they didn't know the contents of the message?"

"They couldn't know, because we arrested the

two of them before they could get back to their key.''

"Their what?"

"Their decoding key," Weakes said. He pulled a piece of stiff paper from inside his jacket pocket. The paper had several holes punched in it.

"You see," he said. "Every rebel spy in Washington has one of these keys. The messages are all written so that it looks like nothin' more'n a bunch of letters. But when you put this key down over the message, why, the holes show you just the letters you should read. When we put this key down over the message, it read—" Weakes cleared his throat, then read in a flat, expressionless voice— "I shall cross the river above Little Falls on Sunday at two p.m. Signal red and white rockets from Turner's Hill. For God's sake, don't fail us. Fire the city at all points agreed on at once."

There was another sudden outbreak of excited voices.

"Did you hear that? They were plannin' on burnin' down the city," someone said angrily.

"Hang 'em," Another shouted. "Hang both of 'em."

Judge Dawes pounded his gavel repeatedly until he was finally able to restore order.

"If there is one more such outbreak," he said sternly, "I shall have this courtroom completely cleared."

The voices quieted.

"Now," Judge Dawes said. He blew his nose. "I can understand public indignation over such treasonous acts, but we will not abandon the laws of the Republic in order to save the Republic. Pray, continue with your case, Colonel Barnett."

"Your Honor, if it please the court, my colleague and I are now going to invoke the articles of agreement with the defense, to which we previously referred," the military prosecutor said. He sat down, and Mr. Sinclair stood up again.

"Very well," Judge Dawes said.

"Dr. Pratt, would you take the stand, please," Mr. Sinclair asked.

"Father, what is this?" Candy asked. "What's going on?"

Dr. Pratt kissed Candy on the cheek, then stood up and walked slowly to the witness stand, where he was sworn.

"Dr. Pratt, what have you to say in regard to the information which has thus far been presented to the court?"

"Sir, I believe we have an agreement?" Dr. Pratt challenged.

"Oh, yes," Mr. Sinclair said. He turned to the judge. "Your Honor, the prosecution withdraws its case against Candice Pratt and asks that the court dismiss her."

"Very well," Judge Dawes said. "Miss Pratt,

all charges against you are dropped and you are
dismissed. You may stand down from the defense
table."

"What?" Candy asked, standing up quickly.
"What is this? What's going on here?"

"Miss Pratt, the charge of treason has been
dropped. Do you wish to be charged for contempt
of court?"

"I want to know what's going on here?" Candy
asked again.

"Your father made a deal," Van Doren said,
reaching up for her to try and calm her.

"A deal? What kind of a deal?"

"We made an arrangement with the prosecution,"
Van Doren said. "Your father agreed to plead
guilty to everything if they would drop all charges
against you."

"But why?" Candy asked. "Why would he
plead guilty when he's not guilty?"

"Darlin', please," Dr. Pratt called from the
witness stand, and there was such anguish in his
voice that it arrested her attention at once. She
looked at him and held her hand out toward him,
though when she took a step, she was quickly
restrained, not only by Van Doren but also by one
of the court bailiffs.

"Father, I—" she started, but he interrupted
her.

"Please," he said. "I have given this a lot of

thought. It it best. Believe me, darlin', what I am doing is for the best.''

"Bailiff, escort Miss Pratt to a seat in the gallery," the judge said. "If there is no seat in the front row, make one for her."

"Yes, Your Honor," the bailiff said. One of the men in the front row got up voluntarily, and Candy sat down, somewhat dazed by the sudden and unexpected turn of events.

"And now," Judge Dawes said. "May we continue?"

"You have a statement you wish to make, Dr. Pratt?" the prosecutor asked.

"Yes," Dr. Pratt said. "I hereby plead guilty to the charge of treason, and I accept full responsibility for all treasonous actions I have committed while in Washington."

"I have nothing further, Your Honor," the prosecutor said.

Judge Dawes blew his nose again, then turned to the jury.

"Since the defendant has entered a plea of guilty there is nothing for the jury to decide. The jury is dismissed. Court is adjourned, and I shall return within the hour to pass sentence."

Candy was allowed to go to the holding room to be with her father while they waited on Judge Dawes' decision. There was a table in the room,

surrounded by chairs, as this was the room where
lawyers sometimes met with their clients. Van
Doren was in the room with them, as were two
armed soldiers. Candy and her father embraced for
a long, agonizing moment; then they walked over
to look through the barred window. The bright
flowers outside the window belied the somber mood
inside.

"Why?" Candy asked. "Father, why did you
do it? Why did you plead guilty? You had nothing
to do with that letter and you know it."

"Darlin', what's the difference whether or not
the guilt comes in through the back door?" Dr.
Pratt asked. "The truth is, I am a registered repre-
sentative of the Confederate government, and as
such, I am guilty of treasonous action by not
making my position clear. If they investigate any
further, even these bumbling fools would discover
that, and if they do, I'm afraid some of the innocent will suffer along with me."

"What innocent? Who are you talking about?"

"Secretary Chase, for one. Sam and I have been
friends for a long, long time, my dear. I did what I
did because of what I felt to be a responsibility to
honor. If I attempt to fight this any further, I might
very well compromise Bill Chase, and he is innocent of all save a friendship which transcends
politics. I will not do that to him. When I learned

that I could plead guilty and end the investigation now, plus guarantee your freedom, I accepted."

"But what is to become of you?" Candy asked.

"I will have to go to prison, of course," Dr. Pratt said. "But Mr. Van Doren has assured me that as soon as peace is established, I will be released. Look at it this way, my dear: I am nothing more than a prisoner of war, and I dare say my own conditions of confinement are likely to be much better than that of our soldiers who are taken prisoner on the battlefield. Now, be brave, my dear. This must be done."

"I'll—I'll try," Candy said.

The door to the room opened and a messenger stuck his head in.

"The Judge is returning."

Chapter Five

Rafe Taylor wrapped his muffler around his neck and pulled his hat down low over his eyes as he walked along the Long Wharf in Boston harbor. It was the last week of February and, though warm for this time of year, still quite cold to one who had so recently been in the tropics of the Caribbean.

The dock boards were slickened with the previous night's rain as well as by the spray tossed up by the cold, rolling sea. A small bit of bread, wet and sodden, lay along the edge of the dank boards. A rat, its beady eyes alert for danger, darted out to the prize, grabbed it, and bounded back to the comparative safety of one of the numerous warehouses.

Behind Rafe, and tied to the mooring slips of the Long Wharf, were more than a dozen ocean-going vessels—some with elegant wheel boxes to each side; some, like the *Delta Dancer*, sleek and screw-propelled; some that were solely dependent upon sail power. All had great masts which stabbed into the sky, with rigging hanging from their yards, their rope and webbing whistling in the wind. One merchant vessel nearby was being unloaded, and it rocked gently as barrel after barrel of its cargo was being rolled down the gangplank by a group of muscular stevedores, black and white.

Rafe's ship had arrived during the night. They had lain out of the harbor entrance until the harbor pilot and a tugboat arrived at six this morning to make the arrangements for it to be towed in and docked. Now Rafe was going to the engine works to see to the repair of his engine.

The steam engine of the *Delta Dancer* was of a very special design, and an effective repair could only be made at the B.T. Thompson Engine Works in Boston. Without the steam engine, the *Delta Dancer* was totally ineffective as a commerce raider and was actually in danger of being sunk if caught in its damaged condition.

It was for that reason that Rafe decided to take a chance and put into Boston. It really wasn't quite as risky as it seemed. Boston was far enough north that there was practically no chance that anyone on the docks would recognize the ship or any of Rafe's crew. Also, Rafe carried papers of registry with the English Board of Trade which identified his ship as an English Armed Merchantman, and he had blank bills of lading which he could fill out to show the recent discharge of cargo at any port of his choosing. Another thing which would help was the fact that Captain Raymond claimed the *Delta Dancer* was sunk, and it had been reported in all the papers. That bit of misinformation would enable Rafe to carry off his deception. If everyone believed the *Delta Dancer* to be sunk, no one would try to connect this English Armed Merchantman with the Rebel pirate ship, as the *Delta Dancer* was called.

A few skillful cosmetic changes to the *Delta Dancer* made it appear as if she were a cargo sloop, armed only as protection against the Confederate raiders. With her name boards changed to read *Niagara*, Rafe felt relatively safe in putting in to port in Boston. The *Boston Evening Transcript* carried the news in the "Shipping Intelligence" column of the paper.

Arrived, sloop Niagara, *departed from Liverpool, 29th ultimate, arrived up at 8:00 this morning.*

The Niagara *carries a report which may substantiate Captain Raymond's claim that he sunk the Rebel pirate ship* Delta Dancer. *The*

Niagara reports arriving too late to help the infamous pirate ship as it was in its last stages of distress. It is said the Delta Dancer *went down with all hands.*

Niagara is without cargo, having discharged its load in Bermuda. It is in Boston to effect repairs to its steam engine, having suffered a breakdown just after quitting Nassau.

Rafe had never been to the B.T. Thompson Engine Works, and so he felt relatively easy in going in to arrange for the repair. The shop faced the waterfront, with just a small office in front of the building, and a large, noisy machine shop in the rear.

The windows were so dirty that one could scarcely see through them, but it wasn't the shop's reputation for cleanliness which had attracted Rafe; it was engineering skill.

Rafe stepped through the door. The inside was as disorderly as the outside suggested. There was a counter piled high with papers and drawings. A clock on the wall was an hour ahead, and a calendar was a week behind. Gears, valves and other engine components lay about, here as a paperweight, then as a doorstop.

There was a desk on one side of the little room, and a middle-aged man sat there reading a copy of the *Boston Evening Transcript*. He wore glasses which were almost as dirty as the front window, and Rafe couldn't help but wonder how he could see anything through them. The reader looked up as Rafe approached his desk.

"Yes, young man, what can I do for you?" he asked.

Rafe extended his hand. "Are you Mr. Thompson?"

"Yes," the man said.

"I'm Stephen Glover, Master of the steam sloop *Niagara*," he said. "We had an engine breakdown at sea."

"What's wrong?"

"It's the slide valve," Rafe said. "The sleeve broke and the valve jammed."

"It's one of my engines?"

"Yes," Rafe said.

Thompson rubbed his chin and studied Rafe for a moment. "What ship did you say? The *Niagara*?"

"Aye."

"What kind of ship is the *Niagara*?"

"She's an armed merchantman. A screw-powered sloop."

"Armed, you say? Why would you arm a merchantman?"

"Perhaps you haven't heard of the Confederate raiders," Rafe suggested. "The *Sumner*, the *Alabama*."

"Aye, and don't forget the *Delta Dancer*,"

Thompson said. "I heard she was sunk, but I don't believe it."

"Yes, well, with such predators at sea, my owners thought speed wasn't enough. So they armed my ship and sent us to sea."

"I don't recall fitting the *Niagara* with any of my engines."

"The engine was taken from the *Belle of the West*," Rafe said. He wasn't lying; the *Delta Dancer* had taken its engine from the *Belle of the West*.

"*Belle of the West*, yes," Thompson said. "I remember her. She belonged to a shipper in Virginia as I recall. I was afraid she would be doing blockade running by now. She was certainly fast enough. How did you come by the engine?"

"The *Belle of the West* was dismasted in a storm and scuttled in Liverpool. My owner bought her for the engine."

"I see. Well, fair enough. Tell me, lad, when the bearing froze, were any of your men injured?"

"Aye," Rafe said quietly. "We had one killed by scalding."

Thompson closed his eyes for a moment, then sighed. "Then I'll be repairin' your engine for no cost," he said.

"No, sir, you don't have to do that. I've the money to pay for repairs," Rafe said.

Thompson held up his hand. "If one of my engines is the cause of death of a God-fearin' seaman, then the least I can do is repair the engine without askin' for money."

"I appreciate that, Mr. Thompson; really, I do," Rafe said, surprised by the man's act of kindness. If some of the firebrands in the South could meet more Yankees like B.T. Thompson, perhaps this war would have never come about. "But I really couldn't do that. I have to pay you. It's the owners, you understand."

"Aye," Thompson said. "Well, then, lad, suppose I charge you a fair amount, and you make that payment not to me, but to the Sanitary Commission. You know they are providin' all the medicine and bandages and doctorin' tools for the battlefield hospitals in this war."

"Yes," Rafe said. He knew that the Sanitary Commission was treating all wounded equally, be they North or South. He could give the money to them with a clear conscience.

"I've been readin' about the *Monitor*," Thompson said. "Do you know of her?"

"I don't think so," Rafe admitted.

"She's an ironclad, designed by a fella named John Ericson."

"You don't mean the *Virginia*?" Rafe asked.

"The *Virginia*?"

Rafe felt himself flush. He had nearly given himself away with that statement. Everyone except the Confederate Navy called the *Virginia* the

Merrimac, the name it was known by when it was a ship of the line for the Union Navy.

"I mean the *Merrimac*," Rafe said. "It's the Confederate ironclad we've heard about, but haven't yet seen. I think the Confederates renamed her."

"They had no more right to rename her than they had to her in the first place," Thompson said. "She's the *Merrimac*."

"Right," Rafe said.

"Well, the *Monitor* is our answer to her. She's an ironclad, too, the likes of which the world has never seen before. And as I say, I've been reading about her, and it comes to mind I've got some sheet iron of the same kind which was used to plate the *Monitor*," Thompson said. "I'd be happy to plate your vessel for you. It would turn away any ball those Rebel pirates might throw at you."

Rafe thought about armor plating. It would, indeed, give his ship an advantage over the wooden-sided pursuit ships which were after him. But its very weight would also slow him down, and he was convinced that his ship's speed was worth as much toward protecting them as any armor plate would be. Besides that, he needed the speed to be able to chase down the commerce ships which were his targets.

"I don't know," Rafe said. "Like I said, the *Niagara* is of British registry. I'm afraid the ship's owners are more interested in how fast I can move the cargo from port to port than in any protective armor.''

"Aye, 'n' how fast their pockets can be lined, too," Thompson said. "I've no doubt the British bastards are truly enjoyin' this war. They're standin' aside, watchin' with delight, ready, like a vulture, to move in the moment there's bones to be picked clean. The really sad thing is, every man-jack that's killed in this war is American, be he North or South. We're God-fearin' Christian folk, and we should end this war.''

"I agree with you," Rafe answered. He did agree with Thompson, but in truth, he would have told him so, no matter what, because he didn't want to take any chances of getting into a political argument.

"Tell me, lad, if you'd not be wantin' your hull plated, what say I build an armor box around the engine? I can protect her boiler and the works with no great sacrifice in weight.''

"Yes," Rafe agreed. "I think I would like that.''

"Here, read the paper while I draw up the plans for your approval. There was fightin' at a place called Fort Donelson, out in Kentucky someplace. It was a pretty big battle, with lots of bloodshed.''

"Who won?" Rafe asked.

"I suppose you can say we won," Thompson said matter-of-factly. "We drove the Secesh away and took the fort. But there was an awful lot of killin'."

It had been· a while since Rafe received any news and he accepted the paper eagerly. He read of the great battle in Kentucky. The Union commander was a man named Grant. U.S. Grant. Grant had demanded "Unconditional Surrender," and the newspaper made much of his initials, U.S., and indicated that it stood for Unconditional Surrender. There was another story, though, which struck Rafe with its honesty. The article wasn't written in the normal, glossed-over terms of glorious victory. It was written by a man who had been there and was sickened by what he saw.

"Dead bodies, stark and stiff, lie in every conceivable position, distorted in the death agony, or stretched out with faces staring upward, washed by the pitiless rain. Here and there are limbs torn away by shot and shell or cast aside in the hasty field offices of the surgeon. Dead horses lie scattered over the ground. The air is heavy and tainted with odors of decomposition. The traces of the late mortal struggle are abundant, the ground ploughed and torn, and the forest trees broken and rent to shreds by the plunging missiles. It will take years to efface the marks of this combat.

Both armies are terribly handled and cut up. The lapse of time does nothing to lessen or modify the sad reality of the late battle which cost America, North and South, the lives of so many fine men.

Rafe folded the paper over and put it aside for a moment. The article was so sobering as to be almost a shock. Rafe had engaged in battle at sea, and he had seen the effect of shot and shell, not only against the vital parts of a ship but against the human body as well. A ball which happened to hit a man in the chest left very little which could be recognized as having ever been a human being. And yet, if ten or fifteen of his men were to be killed or wounded, or indeed if his ship were to go down with all hands, it would be nothing in contrast to the losses in the land battle just described.

Thousands of dead and maimed on the Federal side and, Rafe knew, at least that many on the Confederate side. How could brother slaughter brother? Rafe remembered a quote he once heard. The quote seemed particularly appropriate now. He said it aloud.

"What fools these mortals be!"

"What's that?" Thompson asked, coming back to show him the drawing of the armor plate he had just completed.

"Nothing," Rafe said sheepishly, embarrassed

at being overheard. "I was just mumbling, that's all." Rafe looked back at the newspaper.

Rebel Spy, Sentenced to Hang

The first two words of the article jumped out at Rafe as if they were printed in red ink. The first two words were: Candice Pratt.

Rafe read the article quickly, feeling a sinking sensation in the pit of his stomach. Was Candy about to be hanged?

Candice Pratt, daughter of condemned spy, Dr. Pratt, wrote a letter of appeal to President Lincoln today, begging that her father's sentence be commuted. She reminded President Lincoln that her father had entered a plea of guilty in an agreement with the prosecutor and, as such, should be spared.

The prosecutor admits that he and Dr. Pratt did have an agreement, but it was only that the charge of treason against Miss Pratt be dropped. Miss Pratt, who is as guilty as her father, would do well to thank the Federal Government for her own life, for there are many who would be pleased to see the young lady climb the scaffold steps alongside her treasonous father.

The hanging is set for two weeks hence.

Rafe looked at the dateline of the paper. It was today's paper, February 24th. That meant that he still had time to do something, providing the sentence hadn't been prematurely carried out. He knew that sometimes such sentences were executed early.

"What do you think of the idea?" Thompson asked.

"What?"

"Armor plate around the engine and boiler. Here, this is my drawing."

"I, uh, would have to get the approval of my owners," Rafe said. In fact, he would like to have armor in those critical areas, but now he had no time. He had to get to Washington before it was too late to do anything about Dr. Pratt. Of course, Rafe really had no idea what he could do, but he was certainly willing to try something. "Listen, how long will it take to replace the slide valve?"

"Oh, the better part of a week, I'd say."

"What? No sooner?"

"Listen, lad, you should know what a delicate instrument the steam engine is. A mistake on a valve tolerance could cause the boiler to burst. You wouldn't want that now, would you?"

"No," Rafe said. "I suppose not." He ran his hand through his hair in frustration. If he couldn't have the engine repaired in less than a week, then he may as well have the armor plate installed.

"Go ahead with the armor plate," he said. "As long as it doesn't take any longer to install."

"I can put it on at the same time; there won't be a bit of trouble," Thompson said, smiling broadly over the opportunity given him to tinker with armor plate. In his own mind he was convinced that he could be as brilliant an engineer as Ericson, the Swedish immigrant who designed and built the *Monitor*. Maybe this would give him a chance to prove himself.

Rafe left directions as to how to find his ship, then hurried back to the *Delta Dancer*. When he arrived, he saw his first mate, McCorkle, talking with one of the sailors, and he signaled to him to meet him at the stern rail.

"Are we gonna get the job done?" McCorkle asked as he leaned on the taffrail.

"Yes," Rafe said. "Thompson is going to do it for us. Oh, and I've ordered armor plate put around the engine and boiler."

"Aye, now that's a good idea, sir," McCorkle said.

"Mac, I'm going to leave everything in your charge," Rafe said. "I'm going away."

"Beg pardon, sir?" McCorkle asked, shocked by the statement. "Going away? Going away where?"

"To Washington," Rafe said. "You remember the girl I told you about—Candy Pratt?"

"Remember? You showed me a drawing of her. How could I ever forget?"

Rafe had shown McCorkle a drawing, though not the nude drawing he had done.

"You can understand, then, why I must go to Washington," Rafe said. "She's in danger. Or at least her father is, and for this girl, it may well amount to the same thing."

"What sort of danger is her father in?"

"They are going to hang him in a couple of days," Rafe said. "If they haven't already done so," he added under his breath.

"Hang him?"

"For treason," Rafe said. "You see, he and his daughter have been in Washington for some time now, but they are, in fact, working for the Confederate government."

"Whew," McCorkle said. "I see what you mean about them being in danger. But if they have already been caught, what can you hope to do?"

"I have no idea," Rafe said. "Maybe when I get there, if I get there in time, I'll come up with something. I only know that I have to go, Mac. I can't stay here when I know what's going to happen."

"All right," McCorkle said. "You want me to wait here for you?"

"No, I think it would be better if you left as

soon as you could. No sense in pushing our luck to the limit.''

"What about you?''

"I'll meet you in Whiteakers' Cove in the Chesapeake in two weeks,'' Rafe said.

"What date?''

"This is the 24th. Let us say ten days from now. That would be March 6th. That will surely give you enough time to finish the repairs and sail down there, and me enough time to accomplish whatever I can there.''

"What if you aren't there?''

"If I'm not there, leave without me. The command of the *Delta Dancer* is yours,'' Rafe said.

McCorkle smiled. "Be there,'' he said. "I'm not ambitious.''

Rafe boarded the New York mail train, which left from the Boston and Providence Railroad Depot at 8:30 that evening. The train wasn't scheduled to arrive in New York before midnight, at which place he would have to change trains for Philadelphia, then change trains again for Washington. It would be a long and tiring trip, but it was the fastest route available to him, and it would put him in Washington by evening of the next day.

The first part of the trip, from Boston to New York, passed easily enough. He was able to sit up in his seat without getting too tired. There was a wait of an hour and a half in New York before he could proceed to Philadelphia, so that by the time he boarded the Philadelphia comfort train, he was exhausted.

The phrase "comfort train" meant only that the seats, which had been little more than wooden benches on the mail train, were thinly padded. Rafe managed to find a seat by the window and, using his flat, sailor's hat as a pillow, leaned his head against the window and slept.

A vendor was hawking patent medicine at the railroad station in Philadelphia. The medicine, Helmbold's Extract of Buchu, was a guaranteed cure-all. The vendor, a tall, hawk-nosed man in a black coat and high hat, was set up one corner of the depot waiting room, and the passengers who were between trains found his spiel more entertaining than a long wait, so they gathered around to listen, while he droned on, punctuating his speech by stabbing a long, bony finger into the air.

"I guarantee my Extract of Buchu to cure all diseases arising from habits of dissipation, excesses and imprudences in life, and impurities of the blood."

Rafe smiled at all the miracle cures attributed to the medicine, then went into the depot dining room for a breakfast of ham and eggs.

There were several soldiers in the depot, and

here and there, throughout the waiting room, were tables with coffee and writing material for the use of the soldiers who were in transit. It gave Rafe a funny feeling to be "behind the lines," so to speak, for, in fact, these very men were his enemies. He saw one young soldier, barely seventeen, hobbling along on crutches. One of his trouser legs was empty and tucked up. The soldier was carrying a bag and dropped it. Rafe hurried over to pick it up.

"Thank you, sir," the soldier said. "I left my other leg at a place called Cape Girardeau, in Missouri. It's takin' a little gettin' used to."

"Yes," Rafe said. "I can see that it would."

"You a sailor?" the young soldier asked.

"Yes," Rafe answered. His clothes were seafaring clothes, though without the silver or brass accouterments which would identify him as Navy. Still, he was a little surprised the young man had noticed. The young man laughed.

"You're wonderin' how I knew?"

"A little," Rafe admitted.

"I can spot a sailor from a mile away. It ain't just their clothes, you unnerstan'; it's the way they walk 'n' stand, like as if they always have a rollin' deck under their feet. I know, 'cause I almost was one."

"Almost?" Rafe asked.

The young man smiled sheepishly. "I shipped out on a whaler oncet," he said. "I was sick from the day we left till the day we come back, 'n' I took an oath to the Almighty that if He'd ever get me back home, I'd never go to sea again. Where you headed?"

"Washington," Rafe answered.

"Too bad. I'm bound up Boston way. Iffen you was goin' there, why we could ride together 'n' swap yarns."

"Yes," Rafe said. "It's too bad."

The conductor called the Washington train then, and Rafe waved at the young, crippled soldier, then hurried on to the last leg of his trip.

Rafe settled down into his seat and looked through the window of the car as the train backed out from the loading shed. He looked for the young soldier, but there were dozens of wounded men, many with only one leg or one arm, so the soldier he had spoken with was difficult to find. He was glad; he didn't really want to see him again. He wished he hadn't seen him in the first place. When he spoke, he became a real person. Rafe was a combatant. He had engaged in mortal combats with Union ships of war, and they had exchanged shot and shell on many occasions. He had seen ships burn and sink as a result of his cannon fire. It was one thing to take a detached point of view and consider other ships merely enemy vessels which must be destroyed before they destroyed him, but it was quite another when he stopped to think that those ships were manned by sailors, some as young and innocent as the boy with the missing leg.

Rafe closed his eyes and tried to squeeze the thought out of his mind. Such a thought wasn't healthy for the captain of a commerce raider.

Chapter Six

Candy shifted positions on the sofa, but it didn't make the waiting any easier. She had spent ten hours here today, and as many the day before, and the day before that. She was in the anteroom of the White House, hoping for an opportunity to speak with the President.

Candy had hit upon this idea as a last resort for saving her father. Letters had done no good; pleadings with Secretary Stanton had been fruitless, and the lawyer had informed them that their legal appeal had been denied. There was nothing left now except for Candy to make a personal appeal to the President. Despite what she had heard about Lincoln when she was still in Richmond, her own personal knowledge of him convinced her that he was a kind man. She knew he would be sympathetic to her plea if she could just reach him, but that was not so easy to do.

Candy knew that Secretary Chase would be able to arrange an audience with the President, but her father had been most explicit in demanding that she not go to him for fear Secretary Chase would be compromised by their friendship. That left only one way open to her. She would have to go down to the White House and take her chances with something known as "Public Audience." Every day, a few lucky members of the public would be allowed in to talk with the President.

Most were self-seeking charlatans, demanding a high-ranking commission in the Army or an appointment or some other type of favor. They were an unpleasant lot to be around, and Candy could understand why so few were actually admitted. But she wasn't like them. Her case was genuine, and she felt unfairly put-upon at having to wait day after fruitless day to see the one man who could spare her father.

An Army sergeant who had been controlling the crowd of people all day looked up at the clock on the wall and cleared his throat.

"Gentlemen," he called; then looking pointedly at Candy, he added, "and lady."

There was a smattering of laughter, and Candy felt her cheeks flush.

"It is six and one half of the evening. There will be no more Presidential audiences granted today. Those of you who wish to do so may return tomorrow. Thank you."

"What do you mean no more audiences?" someone grumbled. "I been here for over three hours. I'm an important man; I've got better things to do than cool my heels for three hours and then not get to see the President."

Three hours, Candy thought. She had been here for ten hours a day for eight days now. Eighty hours she had waited for the President, and she realized that she was no closer now than she had ever been. The people around the President didn't understand the sense of urgency to her mission. Or, and Candy really didn't want to admit this to herself, they did understand, and it was precisely because they did understand that she was being denied access to the President.

It was obvious that Secretary Stanton wanted her father's sentence carried out and he would do all in his power to see that it was. Secretary Stanton held a lot of power, and Candy knew that she was fighting an uphill, and possibly a losing, battle. But she knew that she had to try. No matter how hopeless the situation seemed, she had to try! Her father was going to be hanged unless she could do something to prevent it.

Candy moved over to the desk and signed the register book which would get her this far tomorrow; then she went outside.

The sun hadn't actually set, but a heavy cloud bank had built up in the west and the sun was behind the bank so that the evening was growing dark early. A breeze whipped a piece of paper across Pennsylvania Avenue and plastered it to a fence. The same breeze blew Candy's skirt against her legs and thighs, outlining her body and disclosing the fact that she wore no bustles or stays in her dress. She held her hat to her head and walked quickly along the street, hurrying to get back to her room before the rains came.

A horse-drawn trolley car clacked by on the street, and for a moment she contemplated spending a penny for a ride, but the trolley car was full of soldiers and some of them were singing quite boisterously. She really didn't feel like sparring with any drunken soldiers, so she let the trolley pass on by.

It was about a five-minute walk to her room, and in that five minutes it grew dark enough that the lamps of the houses and shops began to project golden squares of light through the windows and onto the street in front of her.

It started raining as she walked the last few

blocks, and when she was almost home, the rain was hard enough to drench her thoroughly, even though she was in it but a short time. As a result, she was soaking wet when she finally reached the boarding house where she lived.

Normally, Candy went in through the front door of the boarding house. The rain was so severe, however, that she took the shortest way in, which was through the kitchen door.

In the kitchen were a couple of black women, hired as cooks by the boarding house, who were washing dishes from the supper meal. Candy had missed supper again, though it had to be paid for in her boarding rent. The black women looked around when they heard the door open, and when they saw Candy dripping wet, they smiled.

"Lord, chile, don' you know 'nuff to get in outta the rain?" one of them asked, and the other laughed at her joke.

"I guess not," Candy agreed sheepishly.

"Has you et?" one of the cooks asked. "Supper's all gone, but I could maybe scrape up some peas 'n' pone fo' you."

"No," Candy said. "Thank you, I'm not hungry."

She was hungry, but she didn't relish the idea of eating cold peas and cornbread. Instead, she just went up the back stairs to her room.

The hallway was nearly dark, but despite the

lack of light she could see a man standing in the shadows, just outside her door. She stopped and looked toward him.

"Candy?" the man spoke.

"Yes?" Candy was curious about who it was and who knew her well enough to address her by her first name. She took a few more steps toward him, then stopped and gasped. It was Captain Rafe Taylor, the man she had met in Richmond.

Candy felt first a sense of curiosity. What was he doing here? Then she felt a little twinge of anger from the sudden memory of the time he had taken advantage of her. That was followed by a reluctant memory of the pleasure she experienced each time she recalled that moment. Of all the sensations, curiosity was now the strongest, and she gave in to it.

"What are you doing here?" she asked.

"I came to get you and your father out of here," Rafe said.

"You're too late," Candy said. She was all the way up to him now. "My father is in jail."

"Waiting to be hanged—I know," Rafe said.

Candy sneezed, and that was when Rafe noticed that she was soaking wet.

"You'd better get inside and get out of those wet clothes," Rafe said.

"You're right," Candy said, sneezing again. She unlocked the door to her room and Rafe, without being asked, went in with her. Rafe turned up the gas and the lamps flared on.

There was a dressing screen in the room and Candy stepped behind it, then began slipping out of her dress.

"What do you mean, *you know*?" she asked. "You came here to get my father and me, and yet you know he is in jail?"

"Yes," Rafe said. He sat down in a chair and glanced toward the dressing screen. He could see Candy's head and bare shoulders above the screen; then, with a gasp, he realized that the mirror was positioned in such a way that he could see her reflection. He leaned back and enjoyed the sight without the slightest bit of guilt. In a moment Candy was completey nude, with her skin shining pink and damp from the rain. Rafe's breath became labored.

"I don't understand," Candy was saying. She didn't realize Rafe could see her, and she changed clothes slowly. "If you say you know my father is in jail, why did you come?"

"I told you," Rafe said. "To get you and your father out of here. We're going to get him out of jail."

"How?"

"Leave that to me."

"Won't that be dangerous?"

"Yes," Rafe said. "I'm touched that you are concerned for me."

"Not for you, for my father."

Rafe laughed. "As it stands now, your father is going to be hanged. Can you think of anything more dangerous?"

"No," Candy said, and despite herself, she laughed. "I guess not. Listen to me. My father is about to be hanged and I am making a joke about it."

"Your father isn't going to hang. We're going to stop it. The red one," Rafe said. In the mirror he saw that Candy was reaching for a dress. There was a red dress right next to the yellow one she was reaching for, and that was what Rafe was talking about.

"I beg your pardon?"

"Wear the red dress," Rafe said. "I'm taking you out to dinner tonight."

Candy looked up and saw Rafe's eyes in the mirror. She knew then that he could see her, and had been able to see her while she was dressing.

"Did you enjoy the show?" she asked. There was more teasing in her voice than anger.

"Yes, very much," Rafe admitted. "I'm glad to see that you aren't too upset."

"Why should I be upset?" Candy asked. "It's not as if you haven't seen me before."

Rafe laughed at the easy way Candy accepted

the situation. "I've made a reservation for us at the Columbia House."

"Don't you think you should have asked me first?" Candy said, but Rafe was pleased to see that she put the yellow dress back and selected the red one.

"It isn't entirely for pleasure," Rafe said. "We're to meet someone there. We're going to have to make a few arrangements, if we are to get your father free."

"Rafe, I wish you wouldn't offer me hope unless there is a really good chance we can do this," Candy said. Rafe was pleased to see how easily she used his name.

"I'm not offering you hope, Candy. I'm making you a promise. We are going to get your father out of jail."

They ate well in the Columbia House. Candy finished the last of her chocolate mousse, then patted her mouth with her napkin and looked across the table at Rafe. It had been a long time since she had eaten that well or enjoyed a meal as much. For the last several weeks, during her father's incarceration, she had been so busy trying to arrange for a commutation of his sentence that her meals, when she had eaten, were eaten on the run. They had been enough to sustain life, but little more.

She had not only forgotten how satisfying good food could be; she had also forgotten how delightful a meal could be in pleasurable company. And, she discovered, Rafe Taylor's company was most pleasurable.

Rafe was as handsome as any man she had ever met. That was no surprise to her; she had noticed his good looks from the moment of their first unconventional meeting in the bathroom in Richmond. What was surprising to her, however, was his easy sense of humor, his gentleness and concern, and the deep, exciting tremor of his voice. He excited her when he looked at her, and he excited her when he talked to her, and she knew that, if he wanted, he would be able to have his way with her.

"Would you like another?" he asked.

"Pardon?"

"The chocolate mousse," Rafe said easily. "Shall I order another?"

"No," Candy said, blushing that he had noticed her appetite. "I must have eaten like an urchin. It's just that I've been eating so irregularly lately, I had forgotten how good a meal could be."

"I know what you mean," Rafe said. "Oh, here is our contact."

Candy looked around toward the door of the dining room. There was a rather heavyset man there, dressed in the uniform of a colonel. "I don't see anyone but an Army colonel."

"That's our man," Rafe said. "He is in command of the military police detachment."

"He is willing to help us?" Candy asked. She gasped. "Is he a Southern sympathizer?"

"Not exactly."

"Then I don't understand. Why will he help us?"

"It's a business arrangement," Rafe said. He was unable to go any further because the colonel saw them and came to their table. Rafe offered him a chair.

"Miss Pratt, I believe we met at the Cameron reception," the colonel said. "I am Colonel Aldrich."

"Yes," Candy said. She didn't recall meeting him exactly, but she felt she had seen him before. It may have just been the eyes. His eyes were very deep with little red lights way at the bottom. They were disagreeable eyes and she had seen them on many men who, when they met her, seemed barely able to control the lust they felt. It was odd; she knew that Rafe wanted her, and yet she had never seen quite the same look in his eyes.

"Is everything set?" Rafe asked.

"Have you the package?" Colonel Aldrich replied.

Rafe reached inside his jacket pocket and pulled out an envelope. It was fat, and when Colonel

Aldrich looked inside, Candy saw that it was full of Federal greenbacks.

"Five thousand dollars," Rafe said. "Would you care to count it?"

"Not here," Colonel Aldrich said. "I'll count it after I leave. If it is all there, the deal will go through. If not, no deal."

Candy gasped. "Rafe, what is this? What's going on?"

Rafe put his hand across the table and took hers. "Don't worry about it," he said.

Colonel Aldrich chuckled. "Don't you think your daddy's worth five thousand dollars, Miss Pratt?"

"But surely you don't expect to be paid for saving a man's life?"

"Why not?" Colonel Aldrich hissed. "He's a condemned criminal, isn't he? It isn't like it was just anyone."

"Rafe, I—" Candy started, but Rafe shushed her and addressed himself to Colonel Aldrich once more.

"What are the arrangements?"

"At three a.m., Dr. Pratt will suffer an attack of severe stomach cramps. He will be removed from the prison and taken to the hospital by two guards. The guards are in league with me. When they reach the corner of Virginia Avenue, they will stop the ambulance and let Dr. Pratt go. They will later claim they were accosted by armed men and had no choice. You must be there to take Dr. Pratt from them.''

"All right, I'll be there,'' Rafe said.

"No,'' Candy said. Rafe looked at her. *"We'll* be there,'' she corrected.

Colonel Aldrich put the money in his coat pocket and patted the outside of the pocket gingerly. "One hundred dollars each for the two guards, and the rest for me. If this war continues long enough for other such opportunities to present themselves, I shall be a wealthy man,'' he said.

Candy watched him leave, then turned to Rafe.

"He is helping us free my father, so I suppose I should be grateful,'' she said. "But I can't find it in my heart to feel anything but contempt for such a creature.''

Rafe laughed. "Brigands know no politics,'' he said. "There is a man who would sell out his entire country if he thought there was profit enough in the venture.''

The rain which had come earlier in the evening was gone now, but it had cooled the air so that when they stepped into the street after dinner, Candy shivered.

"Are you cold?'' Rafe asked. He took off his jacket. "Here, wear this.'' There was a cab near the entrance of the restaurant, and Rafe helped

Candy into it, then climbed in beside her and gave
the driver the address of Candy's rooming house.

"Won't you need your jacket?" Candy asked.

"No," Rafe said. "I spend a lot of time on deck
at night. I'm used to the night air."

"What's it like on board a ship?"

"Freedom," Rafe said.

"Freedom? I should think just the opposite.
After all, you are cooped up in such a small
space."

"No, you don't think of the ship as being your
limitations," Rafe said. "It's sort of hard to explain,
but you become one with the ship. Then you have
the entire ocean as a boundary. And when you are
far at sea, away from sight of any land, you begin
to get an idea of how puny man's bickerings are.
The sea is so wide, and the sky so deep. And the
stars, Candy. You have never seen stars like the
stars on a clear night at sea."

"I should like to go to sea someday," Candy
mused.

Rafe chuckled.

"Why are you laughing?"

"I hope you're serious," he said.

"Why?"

"You will be going to sea soon enough. You
and your father. That's part of the plan."

"Oh," Candy said. "Oh, how wonderful."

Candy clapped her hands together once, almost

childlike in her innocence, and when she did, Rafe
put his arm around her and kissed her.

At first Candy didn't even think to resist. It
seemed so right, and the sensations at her lips and
the stirrings in her body were so pleasurable that
she lost herself in the kiss. Then she realized that
she was riding in the back of a cab, and not only
the driver but all of Washington could see what
was going on, and she pulled away.

"No," she murmured. "Not here, not now."
Then, though she couldn't believe she heard herself speak the words, she added, "Wait until we
reach my room."

Candy clung tightly to Rafe's arm for the rest of
the ride to her boarding house. The lobby of the
boarding house was quiet and empty, and they
walked through unseen, then up the stairs to the
hallway which led to Candy's room. There, in the
dark of the hallway, and with her heart pounding
fiercely at the sweet unknown which waited for
her, she fumbled with the key until she felt his
strong, confident hands take the key from her and
unlock the door.

Once they were inside, they were into each
other's arm in an instant, mouth to mouth, body to
body, with his hands moving impatiently through
her hair, and her tongue, as if by its own volition,
exploring his mouth.

Candy wasn't quite sure how her relationship

with Rafe had reached this point, but it was here, and she felt her insides growing white with the heat of building passion.

Suddenly, and unexpectedly—or, was it unexpected—strong arms lifted her up and carried her over to her bed.

"I want to love you, Candy," Rafe's husky voice whispered. "I want to love you more than I have ever wanted anything in my life."

Rafe smothered Candy's face with kisses, all the while busying his hands with the fastenings and catches of her dress. Hesitantly, and with her inexperience showing, Candy began to clutch at Rafe's clothing, and within a moment they were both naked, with the silken caress of air across bare skin.

Candy had kept her eyes closed most of the time, as much in innocent embarrassment as from sweet fear. She opened them and looked into Rafe's face to see reflected there an expression of wonder and want. She didn't realize that her own face mirrored Rafe's expression.

She had felt Rafe's eyes on her nude body before, and she had warmed to the sensation. Now, for the first time, she felt the touch of him, and the gentle warmth exploded into white-hot flame as his fingers scorched her skin with the heat of passion.

His fingers touched her neck, then moved gently

down the neck, across her bare shoulders, and onto the slope of her breasts. They stopped over one nipple and he kneaded it exquisitely between his fingers. Then his tongue traced the same path his fingers had taken until she could feel her nipple, congested now and aching with an agony too sweet for words, as it slipped into his mouth. He sucked it gently, and ran his tongue across it, so that it was fire and ice, velvet and steel, agony and ecstasy, all at the same time.

Candy made a strange, murmuring sound of passion deep in her throat. She closed her eyes again, waiting for the next move, longing desperately for it and yet afraid of it, too, for never had she gone this far, even in fantasy. She hoped she would not do something wrong, yet, deep inside, a primeval sense which was as basic and as deeply entrenched as humankind itself, guided her so that she was all things Rafe wanted her to be. She knew just when to position her body to his and when to open herself up to him.

White heat flooded through her when, at last, Rafe drove himself deep into her, and the heat, the sharp pain of initial entry and the lightning flash of passion all hit her at the same time. The pain receded almost instantly, but the heat and the passion remained. Instinctively she arched her back and raised her pelvis to meet him, pushing herself against him to share with him this thing which was

now so much a part of both of them. She gasped
with the pleasure of it and cried with the joy of it,
pushing aside all thought save this one headlong
quest for rapture. Her body was like a storm-
tossed sea as the first spasms of pleasure burst
over her. The pleasure was so intense as to be
beyond measure, and she cried with the joy of it,
and threw her arms around him and pulled him to
her so that she, Rafe, the sea and her passion
became one primeval force of nature unleashed in
splendid, furious energy.

Moments later, when the fires were no longer
blazing infernos but well-banked coals, they lay in
each other's arms, still naked and still drifting in
pleasure.

"I didn't want it to ever end," Candy said, her
voice full of wonder.

Rafe laughed.

"Why do you laugh?" Candy asked, raising
herself on one elbow. In such a position her breast
swung forward, pendulum-fashion, and the nipple
brushed across the hair on Rafe's naked chest. The
contact sent little currents of pleasure through both
of them.

"I laugh because I find you so delightful," Rafe
said. "And refreshing."

"I know a lady should never admit such a thing,"
Candy said.

Rafe reached up and took her nipple between his

finger and thumb. He massaged it gently, then pulled it to his lips and kissed it.

"You mean a lady should be dishonest?" Rafe asked.

"No, I just mean, well, it simply isn't proper; that's all," Candy said. She shivered. "Oh, Rafe, don't, please don't. You don't know what that's doing to me."

"I hope I know what it's doing to you," Rafe said. He stopped for a moment and looked at her. "And I hope you will always tell me," he said. "I want you to be honest with me, Candy. Why should we let our lives and our love be dictated to by what a bunch of old busybodies declare is proper. If they had ever been able to experience love as we just experienced it, they wouldn't be so stiff."

This time it was Candy's turn to laugh, and she did.

"What?" Rafe asked. "What is it?"

"Look who is calling whom stiff," she said, pointing to his reawkening condition. Then she giggled in the delightful pleasure of being able to make such a personal joke without succumbing to total embarrassment.

"I think we still have time to do something about it," Rafe suggested, pulling her to him. "Don't you?"

*   *   *

Candy shivered in the early morning darkness, and Rafe put his arm around her. The feel of his arm awakened the memory of their lovemaking just a few hours before, and she could still feel the heaviness of him in her and the warmth he had generated. The chill passed.

"No, not cold," she said. "I'm just excited. Oh, Rafe, do you think everything will go as it should?"

"Yes," Rafe said. "I don't expect any double-cross on this end of the deal; though I suspect Colonel Aldrich will throw a surprise at us later if we aren't careful."

"What do you mean?"

"Well, he will make a big thing of claiming that your father was taken from the two guards at gun point, and he will turn out the city to look for him."

"But how could he? He wouldn't want my father telling the truth, would he?"

"No," Rafe said. "He wouldn't want your father to talk, and I think he would take all precaution to see that he didn't."

"You mean, he might have my father shot?"

"Yes," Rafe said. "That's why I think we need to get away as quickly as possible."

"What do you have in mind?"

"As soon as we have your father, we will leave Washington and proceed to a secret cove in the

Chesapeake. Mr. McCorkle is going to meet us there with the *Delta Dancer*. While Colonel Aldrich is searching all the roads south, we will be safely at sea."

In the distance they could hear the hollow, clopping sounds of a horse's hooves on the cobblestone streets. There was also the sound of ironrimmed wheels rolling on cobblestone, and Rafe held his hand up.

"Listen."

"Oh, Rafe, do you think it's him?"

"Yes, the wheels sound like the wheels of an ambulance."

Rafe and Candy had been standing in the sheltered shadows of the doorway to a closed shop. They looked down the street and saw the ambulance approaching.

"Oh, it is him!" Candy said excitedly, and she started to run toward the ambulance, but Rafe restrained her.

"Wait," he warned. "Let's be sure there are no armed guards following it."

Candy waited, though impatiently, until finally Rafe was convinced that it was safe. Then the two of them stepped out of the shadows just as the ambulance approached.

"Hold it up there," Rafe called, and the driver and the guard called to the horse.

"You got somethin' to say, mister?" the driver asked.

Rafe remembered the passwords given him by Colonel Aldrich. No doubt it had been an example of Aldrich's brand of humor.

"Long live the Republic," Rafe said.

"I reckon you are the man all right," the driver said. "Ed, let the secesh go."

The guard leaned his rifle against the footrest of the ambulance, then hopped down and walked around to the back. Candy, impatient to see her father, followed him around. The guard pulled the pin in the latch and swung open the door.

"All right, doc, looks like your neck ain't gonna get stretched after all," the guard said. "Here's where you get out."

Dr. Pratt stepped hesitantly out of the back of the ambulance: then, when he saw Candy, he let out a little cry of emotion and went to her. They embraced for a long time.

"You men get on out of here," Rafe growled. "If a patrol came along, we'd all be in a pickle."

"Yeah," the driver said. "Get up here, Ed; he's right."

Ed climbed back up on the seat; the driver snapped the reins, and the ambulance moved away.

"Now we've got to go," Rafe said. "I don't trust Aldrich any further than I can throw him. He could come along any moment now."

"So, I have you to thank," Dr. Pratt said, shaking Rafe's hand. "I must confess, when Colonel Aldrich said he had arranged for my release, I didn't believe him. I came on the ambulance tonight, fully expecting to be taken out and shot."

"And you came anyway?" Candy asked.

Dr. Pratt patted Candy's hand. "Believe me, my dear, I would much rather be shot than hanged. I came willingly, no matter what the consequences were."

"Listen," Rafe said, holding his hand up.

They could hear the sound of horses and the jangle of soldiers' equipment as a patrol rode through the streets.

"Are you sure this is the place?" one of the soldiers asked.

"Yes. Colonel Aldrich said they would be around here somewhere," another answered. "Just keep your eyes open and your mouth shut. Remember, there is a five-hundred-dollar reward to the patrol that finds Pratt."

"Let's go," Rafe hissed, and he led his little party down an alley away from the patrol. He wasn't disturbed by them; he had expected them, and he was prepared for it.

Chapter Seven

"There she is," Rafe whispered. "See the fore-top? She's showing the signal of two green lamps and one red."

Rafe, Candy and Dr. Pratt were waiting in a small boat on the shore at Emerson Cove, looking out over the point toward Chesapeake Bay. The trees on the spit of land which guarded the cove prevented them from seeing anything but the top lights for a while; then, finally, the ship itself glided into view.

The lines, even when seen only in dark, unrelieved silhouette as tonight, were unmistakable. The silent ship which was sliding into the cove was the long, low, sleek hull of the *Delta Dancer*.

"Let's go," Rafe said, and he put his back to the oars to pull them out for the rendezvous.

"Welcome aboard, Cap'n Taylor," McCorkle greeted with a broad smile as Rafe, Candy and her father climbed the boarding ladder a few moments later.

"Did you have any trouble?" Rafe asked, shaking his first mate's hand.

"None, sir. The engine purred like a kitten all the way down here. Oh, and we had the barnacles scraped to get rid of the drag. The bottom of this ship is slick as a baby's bottom now."

Candy giggled at the analogy, and McCorkle, having forgotten her presence for a moment, coughed in embarrassment.

"I'm sorry, miss," he apologized.

"Don't worry about it," Rafe said. "Her father is a doctor. I'm sure Miss Pratt has seen more than one baby's bottom. What about the armor plate?"

"It's in place, Cap'n."

"Very well, Mac. Miss Pratt will have your quarters; you will share quarters with Mr. Carter. Dr. Pratt will share quarters with the ships' surgeon.

"Aye, aye, sir," McCorkle answered. "I thought as much. The lady's quarters are all ready for her."

"Very good. Pig Meat?"

"Aye, Cap'n," a huge man answered.

"Take Miss Pratt's bag and show her and her

father to their quarters. Mr. McCorkle, let's put about. I've no wish to be trapped in here."

"Aye, Cap'n, we're ready in all respects to get under way."

Candy followed the man named Pig Meat to her room. There, she examined it by the light of a dimly lit lantern which cast flickering shadows. There was a bed, though the bed itself took up more than half the room. In addition to the bed there was, built into the wall, a table, and above the table was a shelf with a handful of books. Small it may have been, but it was clean and dry, and as it had been several hours since Candy last slept, she got into the bed gratefully after Pig Meat left.

As she lay there, she could hear all the sounds of the ship. There was a rattle of chains and the creak of a windlass. A moment later she heard a voice from on deck.

"Cap'n, the anchor's aweigh."

"Aye," Rafe's voice replied. "Engine ahead one-third."

Candy could feel more than hear the engine, as it transferred its power not only to the ship's screw but through the very framing of the ship itself. The *Delta Dancer* got under way. The gentle rocking of the ship, the muffled sounds, and the fact that Candy was exhausted all combined to produce a soothing effect which Candy could no longer resist. Within a few moments she was sound asleep.

The bos'n's whistle awakened Candy the next morning, and she opened her eyes to see sunlight streaming in.

"All hands," she heard McCorkle's voice say. "All hands, turn out!"

There were more shouts, and she could hear footsteps running above her, so she went topside to see what was going on. She saw a very young man, not much older than a boy, actually, standing by the hatch. He was wearing the uniform of an officer, and she was surprised by that.

"You must be a very good seaman to be an officer at such a young age," she said.

The boy was startled by her voice, and he turned quickly toward her. He smiled and saluted.

"I'm not quite an officer yet, Miss Pratt," he said. "I'm a midshipman. Midshipman Carter. That means I'm an apprentice officer."

"I see." Candy looked around. "Oh, we are at sea."

"No, we are still in Chesapeake Bay," Carter said. "We're goin' to run through the Yankee blockade this afternoon, so as to let you 'n' your pa off down the coast. The cap'n figures Hampton Roads is too dangerous."

"Isn't it more dangerous to run the blockade?"

"Heck, no," Carter answered with a broad grin. "I reckon we've run the blockade 'bout as many times as any ship afloat. The Yankee blockade doesn't mean anything to Cap'n Taylor."

"Mr. Carter," McCorkle called. "Please take your place, sir."

"Aye, sir," Carter answered. He excused himself, then moved into his proper position when the ship's company was assembled.

Candy leaned against the shrouds and watched Rafe as he stood before his men. Now he was wearing the sea uniform of a Confederate naval officer, and authority rode with him as he addressed his men. Candy couldn't help but chuckle as she contrasted this stern commander with the tender lover she had come to know and love.

"Would you care to share your joke, daughter?" Dr. Pratt asked, coming topside at that moment.

"Oh, nothing, Father," Candy answered. "I was just watching Captain Taylor at work."

Rafe explained the presence of Candy and her father to the men, told them what they were going to do, then turned them over to Mr. McCorkle to set the watch. When McCorkle dismissed the men a moment later, they gave a rousing cheer for their captain.

"Your men seem fond of you, Captain Taylor," Dr. Pratt said.

"The feeling is mutual," Rafe replied. "You

know, most poor devils at sea are subject to the most brutal treatment. I don't know what it is about the profession I have entered, but it seems to attract an uncommon number of evil men, and of course, as the captain of a vessel at sea is an absolute monarch, the men have no recourse but to be the victim of his whims. As a result, when they encounter a captain who treats them fairly, they respond with loyalty and effort never seen by such brutal captains.''

"You would think every captain would attempt to get the most from his men by fair treatment," Candy said.

"Yes, you would, wouldn't you?"

"Cap'n, cannon fire ahead, sir!" the lookout shouted down, and everyone grew instantly quiet.

Candy strained to listen with the others; then she heard it, too. It was a low, distant rumble, like thunder rolling in faraway hills.

"What is it, Captain? Norfolk?" Dr. Pratt asked.

"It could be," Rafe said. "That or Fortress Monroe. Mr. McCorkle, crack on all sail; proceed at full speed. Let's find out what's going on."

"Aye, Cap'n," McCorkle said, relaying Rafe's orders.

"We'll be there in another half-hour," Rafe said. "Then we'll see for ourselves what is going on."

With a good following wind and the engine at

full speed, the *Delta Dancer* literally skimmed across the water for the next half-hour. A bow wake was raised which came halfway up the hull, and as Candy stood on deck, she felt an exhilaration at the swiftness of the vessel. Finally, they arrived at Hampton Roads, and as the sails were ruffed and the engine cut, they raised the Confederate flag, then signaled for a pilot to come at once. A small lighter put out from Norfolk, and a short time later a pilot climbed aboard.

"What was all the cannon fire we heard?" Rafe asked the pilot.

"You mean you ain't heard?" the pilot replied.

"No, we've been up the bay. We haven't heard anything."

"I'll tell you what's happened," the pilot said. "We've just taught the Yankees what-for—that's what happened."

"What do you mean?"

"Well, lookie over there, lad; what do you see?"

Rafe looked in the direction indicated by the pilot, and he saw some broken, tangled masts rising just out of the water.

"What ship was that?"

"That was the *Cumberland*," the pilot said. "And that'n over there, the *Congress*. They was both sunk yesterday. The *Minnesota* was run aground; I reckon we'll finish her off today."

"My God, you mean there was a battle right here in the Roads? But how could that be? There's so little maneuvering room no-ship-of-the-line would choose this place."

"It warn't no ship-o'-the-line," the pilot said. "It was the *Virginia*."

"The *Virginia?* You mean she's finally put in an appearance?" Rafe said. "Well, I'll be damned. I was beginning to think she was going to spend the rest of her days in dry dock."

"Not bloody likely," the pilot said proudly. "Not after yesterday. 'N' wait until you see what she does today. She's gonna clear out the rest of the Yankees. All the firin' you heard earlier was salutin'. She come out to take 'er bow, so to speak. Look," he said, pointing excitedly. "There she is again!"

Rafe looked toward the ship he had heard so much about but, until this moment, hadn't seen. He knew the history of the *Virginia*. It had originally been the *Merrimac*, a frigate of forty guns which has scuttled and sunk at the Norfolk navy yard at the commencement of the war. After the South took over the navy yard, they raised her and started converting her to a warship of a radical new design. Her hull was cut down to within three feet of her watermark, and a bomb-proof house was built on her gun deck. She was iron-plated and her bow and stern steel-clad with a projecting ram for piercing a vessel. She had no masts, depending entirely on steam for propulsion. She was equipped with four eleven-inch guns on each side and two one-hundred pounder Armstrong guns at the bow and stern.

There was excitement, not only on board the *Delta Dancer* but also on the other ships of the harbor and among the people ashore as the *Virginia* steamed out toward the Union blockade fleet. Rafe could hear the faint cheers from the Norfolk shore, and he saw hundreds of people lining the shore, waving flags and handkerchiefs at the little craft. From within Norfolk, whistles sounded their salutes.

The other ships of the harbor, Confederate and Federal alike, watched as the *Virginia* steamed out. The braces of the ships were manned by hundreds of sailors, who, for the moment, had forgotten all duties for the right to witness one of the greatest sea dramas in history.

Rafe saw that there was nothing protruding above the water but a flagstaff flying the Confederate flag and a short smokestack. The *Virginia* moved along slowly, venting steam, heading toward the grounded *Minnesota*.

Behind the *Virginia* were two other Confederate steamers, the *Yorktown* and the *Jamestown*. They were loaded with troops.

"There," the pilot said. "See them soldiers? They are our boys. The *Virginia* is goin' to destroy the Yankee camp over on Newport News, 'n' our boys'll take over. First, I reckon she's got to finish off the *Minnesota* though. That's where she's headed.''

Slowly but surely the *Virginia* headed toward the *Minnesota*; then, suddenly, another vessel appeared from behind the *Minnesota*.

"What's that thing?" the pilot asked. "It looks like some sort of oil drum. Is it a floating mine?"

Rafe reached for his glass and opened it to study the new craft which had appeared.

"No, my friend, that is no floating mine," he said. "That is Mr. Ericson's ironclad, the *Monitor*."

"What? You mean the Yankees got 'em an ironclad too?"

"That's right. We are about to be eyewitnesses to history. We are going to see the world's first battle between ironclads."

The pilot laughed. "What do they expect to do with that thing? Look how little it is? Where's the guns? Don't she have any guns?"

"She has two guns firing from the turret," Rafe said. "Mr. McCorkle, draw as close as we can," he ordered. "Perhaps we can benefit from this engagement. While the two ships are kept busy with each other, we can slip out."

"Will we not get to see the battle, Cap'n?"

"We'll watch it," Rafe said. "But all the while we are watching, we'll be edging toward open sea.

If we are lucky, all the Yankees will be so interested in what's going on that they won't notice until it's too late."

"Wait a minute," the pilot said. "I ain't takin' you into no blockade!"

"That won't be necessary," Rafe said. "I know these waters well enough. We can proceed without a pilot. You may disembark."

"Keep her away from the Rip Raps. That's the best channel, but most of the Yankee fleet is there," the pilot said. " 'N' don' pay no attention to the white buoys. They are to fool the Yankees. Ever' third red buoy will get you out of here."

"Thanks," Rafe said.

"Good luck," the pilot called as he went down the ladder to return to his own vessel.

"Mr. McCorkle," Rafe said. "Show the Union flag."

"The Union flag, sir?" McCorkle asked in surprise. "We're under our own guns, sir."

"I doubt any of our people will take the trouble to fire on one small sloop when they've a battle of ironclads to watch. The Union flag'll buy us a little time from the Yankee fleet."

"Aye, sir," McCorkle said. "You have a plan?"

"Yes. Put men in the braces as if watching the battle, but prepared to raise sail at a moment's notice," he said. "Use our best coal; show as little smoke as possible so that it appears as if our fires are banked. We'll creep along as slowly as possible, then, when we are in position, full sail and steam.''

"Aye, Cap'n,'' McCorkle said, and he began to transmit the necessary orders.

Rafe looked over at Candy.

"Are you frightened?'' he asked.

"A little,'' she admitted. She put her hand out to take his. "But I have confidence in you.''

The thunder of artillery fire rolled across the water, and they looked around toward the two ironclads. The guns had been fired by the Minnesota. She was aground, but her guns were still manned. The balls struck the *Virginia,* then glanced sharply upward from the sloping armored sides. The balls went straight up, one hundred or more feet, then fell back into the water with a splash. The *Virginia* had felt no effect from the broadside. Shortly after that, the *Monitor* fired its opening round, and, though the ball struck the *Virginia* near the water line, it, too, bounced off with no effect.

The *Virginia* then returned fire, racking the *Monitor* with a broadside from all four of its side guns and the stern gun. The balls fired by the *Virginia* had as little effect on the *Monitor* as those of the *Monitor* did on the *Virginia.*

Gunsmoke rose from the constant firing, and sometimes the two vessels were entirely obscured, but always, when the smoke rolled away, they would still be there, pouring shot into each other like two arm-weary boxers.

The *Minnesota* and another Union ship, the *Dragon*, also opened fire on the *Virginia*. The *Virginia* occasionally returned the fire of the two wooden vessels, and one of the shots penetrated the *Dragon* and caused her boiler to explode.

The battle raged on for another hour with the two ships moving around each other, trading shot and shell with no advantage being given either party. The *Virginia* was obviously the stronger, having the advantage of greater firepower, but the *Monitor* was the more maneuverable and was often able to evade the *Virginia's* broadsides.

All the while the battle was going on, the *Delta Dancer* was slowly easing its way toward the open sea. Finally, the *Virginia* began moving back toward Sewall's Point, and Rafe knew that the battle was about to end with no significant results.

"Mr. McCorkle!" he called.

"Aye, sir!"

"Crack on all sail. Engine, ahead full!"

"Aye, sir!" McCorkle answered with a broad grin, because the *Delta Dancer* had slipped by all the Union ships and was now well on its way toward the open sea.

"Cap'n, two Yankee ships have spotted us," the lookout called down. "They are making signals."

"What do they say?"

"Heave to for inspection," the lookout called.

Rafe laughed.

"Mr. Carter, show our true colors, sir."

"Aye, sir," the young midshipman said, striking the Stars and Stripes and running up the Stars and Bars to the cheers of the men on board.

The *Delta Dancer* had the advantage of having its steam well up and the sails set for maximum speed. They also had half a mile between them and the nearest Union ship. Add to that the fact that the *Delta Dancer* was one of the fastest vessels on the open sea, and there was absolutely no chance of them being caught. The two Union ships which started after them fired their bow chasers, but it was more in frustration than anything else. There was no real chance of them being hit, and, indeed, the balls fell so far away from the *Delta Dancer* that the splash of their impact could barely be seen.

The *Delta Dancer* was safely away.

Candy found a place on deck, out of the way, and she sat there for most of the day, just enjoying the voyage. She listened to the constant roar of the wind in the sails, the singing of the ropes, the creaking of the masts and the rushing of water by the hull. The engine was shut off to conserve coal, but so well-rigged was the ship that she still had enough speed to be exhilarating.

Lunch was served to the men on station. It was hard bread and a bit of cheese, and Candy ate with relish. She wished there was something she could do, some bit of work she could perform. She wandered around the ship for the rest of the afternoon, watching and learning, but always staying out of the way so as not to be a nuisance. She was excited at being at sea, and she wished she could convince Rafe and her father to let her stay on board, even when they reached Charleston.

That evening Candy stood at the rail looking back toward the west. They were well out of sight of land now, and she could see the sun, a great orange disk, just balanced on the horizon. Before the sun, and stretching all the way to the *Delta Dancer*, was a wide band of red, laid out like a carpet on the sea. The few clouds which dotted the western sky had purpled, and even the great white sails of the ship were rimmed with gold. Candy was sure she had never seen anything as beautiful as this sunset.

As she stood there, drinking in the beauty of the scene, she inhaled deeply and enjoyed the clean, fresh smell of the salt air. She heard a little sound behind her, then saw her father stagger toward the rail. He stood beside her for a moment, looking ashen.

"Father, what is it?" she asked, concerned by his appearance.

"I fear that I am suffering from seasickness," Dr. Pratt said. His face was bathed in perspiration, and he looked at his daughter with surprise on his face. "Don't you suffer it?"

"No," Candy said. "Not at all. I love it."

"But don't you feel it? Don't you feel the accursed rolling of this ship?"

"Yes," Candy said. "I do feel it, but I find it very exciting."

"Miss Pratt," Carter said, approaching them at that time.

"Aye," Candy answered, falling naturally into the sailors' way of speaking.

"The captain's compliments, ma'am, and he asks that you and your father join him in the great cabin for dinner this evening."

"Oh, yes, I think that would be wonderful. Don't you think so, Father?"

"Please," Dr. Pratt said in a pained voice. "Don't speak of eating to me now."

"But you don't mind if I go?" Candy asked.

"No, no, go ahead," Dr. Pratt said. "Just, for heaven's sake, don't mention it again." Dr. Pratt hurried down the railing while Candy and young Carter exchanged smiles.

*   *   *

Captain Raymond was at sea when the mail ship arrived from shore, bearing not only letters but newspapers as well. It was in the *Boston Evening Transcript* that Captain Raymond read the interesting account of the *Niagara* having witnessed the sinking of the *Delta Dancer*. He showed the article to Mr. Herrick.

"I don't understand," Herrick said, puzzled by the article. "Cap'n, you don't think we actually did get her, do you?"

"No," Raymond said. "Not for a minute."

"Then why would the captain of the *Niagara* claim to have watched her demise?"

"Why, indeed?" Raymond asked, moving his mouth into what may have been a smile. "You notice she was in Boston for repairs to her engine."

"You mean? Captain, you think the *Niagara* is the *Delta Dancer?*"

"I think that is a very distinct possibility," Raymond said. "So much so, that I think we should go to Boston and check out this vessel."

"Surely he wouldn't be foolish enough to bring the *Delta Dancer* into a northern port for repair, would he?"

"Perhaps a better word than foolish should be bold," Raymond said. "Boldness has often won the day, has it not? After all, who would suspect the *Delta Dancer* to be in Boston Harbor?"

"Yes," Herrick agreed. "Yes, you may be right."

It was a three-day run to Boston Harbor, and when the *Vanderbilt* docked, hundreds of people came down to look at her. She was already a famous ship, even before the claim that she'd sunk the *Delta Dancer*. She had been built as a very fast, very expensive yacht by one of the wealthiest men in the world. That alone was enough to arouse interest in her. Add to that the fact that she was now a warship, with a victory over one of the most famous ships of the Confederate Navy, and she would draw a crowd wherever she went.

There were half a dozen reporters who wanted an interview with Captain Raymond, but he put them off in order to be free to search for the *Niagara*. He didn't see her anywhere in the harbor, but he did hear that she'd had some work done at the B.T. Thompson Engine Works, so he went there to talk to the engineer who performed the work.

"Do I have drawings of the *Niagara*? Of course I do," Thompson answered. He shuffled through several loose papers on his drawing desk until he came up with what he was looking for. "Ah, she's a sweet, beautiful ship, I'll tell you that for sure. Here it is. Take a look at her."

One look was all it took.

"Ah-ha!" Raymond said, hitting his fist on the table. "It's her!"

"It's her? What's her?"

"This is the *Delta Dancer*," Raymond said, pointing to the engineering drawing of the *Niagara*.

"No, sir, this is the *Niagara*."

"Her captain may have passed the ship off to you as the *Niagara*, but she was the *Delta Dancer*. The captain, was he a big, handsome fellow, about twenty-eight or thirty?"

"That was him, all right. He told me his name was Steven Glover."

"His name was Rafe Taylor," Raymond said.

"That can't be," Thompson said. "Captain Raymond claims to have sunk the *Delta Dancer*."

"I'm Captain Raymond," Raymond said. He ran his hand across his bald head. "What was the nature of the repairs?"

"We replaced a slide valve," Thompson said. "And we put armor plate over the engine and boiler."

"When was the work concluded?"

"Yesterday," Thompson said. "The *Niagara*—that is, the *Delta Dancer*—sailed last night with the evening tide."

"I don't suppose you've any idea where?"

"No," Thompson said, shaking his head slowly. "I'm afraid not. Captain Raymond, I'm sorry, sir.

If I had known it was the *Delta Dancer*, you can be sure I would have never worked on her."

"Don't worry, Mr. Thompson," Captain Raymond said. "You aren't the first person Rafe Taylor has fooled. I have the dubious distinction of having been taken for a fool by him before he ever met you. But I'm keeping score, and, I promise you, the account will be settled."

Raymond studied the drawings for a while longer. "I'd like to keep these drawings, if I may."

"Yes, sir, of course you can."

"This is the area which is armored?" Raymond pointed to the shaded area on the drawings.

"Yes."

"How thick is the armor?"

"Four inches."

"Hmm, that would turn away all but conical shells with steel points. Tell me, Mr. Thompson, how quickly could you put the same shielding on the paddle boxes of the *Vanderbilt*?"

"I'll suspend work on everything else," Thompson said. "I can do it in three days."

"Make it two," Raymond said.

"Aye," Thompson replied. "Two days it is."

Captain Raymond looked at the drawing of the *Delta Dancer* again, then, under his breath, he chanted a little poem.

Two and two are four,
Five and four are nine,
I know all about your armor;
You know nothing of mine.

On board the *Delta Dancer*, now at sea, Candy prepared to take her dinner in Rafe's cabin. The captain's cabin was located just beneath the quarterdeck. It was as wide as the breadth of the ship, and as deep. It was perhaps four times as large as the small cabin Candy was using, and thus deserved the name of great cabin.

A table had been set up in the great cabin; it was covered with a fine, white linen and set with ship's crockery. A small ham, a hoop of cheese, a bottle of wine and a loaf of freshly baked bread comprised the fare, and as Candy had eaten only sparingly during the day, the food looked delicious to her.

"Your father isn't going to join us?" Rafe asked.

"I'm afraid not," Candy said. "He's feeling a little ill."

Rafe smiled. "Ah, I see. A little *mal-de-mer*, is it?"

"What?"

"Seasickness."

"Yes."

"Don't worry. He'll get his sea legs soon enough, and my guess is that when he does, he'll not be wanting to go ashore. You don't seem to be having any trouble.''

''No trouble at all,'' Candy said. ''And I don't want to go ashore.''

''What?'' Rafe asked, surprised by her statement. ''Surely you don't mean that.''

''But I do mean it,'' Candy said. ''Rafe, if I can talk my father into it, if I can gain his consent, would you let me stay on board the *Delta Dancer*?''

''No, of course not,'' Rafe said.

''But why not?''

''Because it is out of the question, that is why. It is simply out of the question.''

''That's no answer,'' Candy challenged.

Rafe poured a glass of wine for Candy and then one for himself.

''You'll be going ashore when we reach Charleston,'' he said.

''And when will that be?''

''Tomorrow night.''

Candy started to say something else, but she knew that any further conversation along those lines would be wasted now, so she let it pass. She fully intended to bring up the subject again later. Instead, she asked him about his first voyage.

Rafe began regaling her with stories of his first voyage, taken when he was still a midshipman at Annapolis. His description was animated and full of fun and laughter, with himself the butt of most of the fun, and Candy was so enjoying this time with him that she wished it could go on and on and on without end. She couldn't understand why he didn't share her feeling. Surely, if he cared as much for her as she did for him, he would be more than willing to allow her to stay aboard. She thought of what it would be like to stay on board with him. They had already become lovers; what more bliss could she ask for than to be with him? She thought of the prospect of making love with him every night, in this very cabin, and it suffused her with such a warm glow that she found it difficult to concentrate on what he was saying.

"The sea is getting heavy," he said.

"What?" She suddenly realized that he had completely changed the subject, yet she had missed it because of her secret fantasies.

Rafe got up from the table. He walked over to lean across his bed, which was fully twice the size of the one in her cabin, and looked through the stern windows.

"The sea has risen considerably. I'm afraid we are going to be in for a bit of a blow."

There was a knock on his cabin door at just about that precise moment. When Rafe opened it, Carter was standing there. He was soaking wet.

"Is it raining, Mr. Carter?" Rafe asked in surprise.

"No, sir; this is sea water, sir."

"The sea is that heavy?"

"Aye, sir," Carter replied. "I thought you might want to come on deck, sir."

"Mr. Carter, you should have called me earlier," Rafe said.

"Aye, sir, but you were having a meal with the lady. I had no wish to disturb you."

"A foundering ship would be disturbance, don't you agree, Mr. Carter?"

"Aye, sir," Carter admitted sheepishly.

"Never mind, lad, you'll learn. Let's get topside. We'll have to take in the sails."

"Aye, Cap'n. Mr. McCorkle has called for all hands," Carter said.

Candy went topside with Rafe and Carter. The *Delta Dancer* was plowing through very heavy seas, and just as Candy reached the deck, the bowsprit dipped and poked through a large swell, sending the breaking wave over its bow and throwing its spray the entire length of the deck.

"Reef the topsails," Rafe ordered, and the order was repeated by McCorkle. A handful of sailors scurried up the foremast, as it was the only sail that was square-rigged and thus required hands aloft to furl sail. "Make a proper furl, lads!" Rafe shouted into the wind.

The wind was blowing with gale force now, and the ship was crashing violently through the waves.

Candy steadied herself at the hatchway and watched as the men worked.

By now the wind was of near-hurricane velocity, and the waves were like mountains, battering against the hull of the ship with the impact of cannon balls. The *Delta Dancer* would be lifted by one swell, hang quivering over the waves, then slam back down into the sea, only to be caught up in another, even larger wave. The ship not only rolled to and fro, but was knocked from side to side by the impact of the heavy sea.

Finally, the sailors completed their work, and the ship was fitted with storm sails—special, smaller sails made of stronger canvas, and triangular-shaped—which were mounted close to the deck.

"I can't stand it!" a choked voice suddenly called. "Air! I must have air!"

Candy looked around in surprise to see her father push past her and head for the rail in a headlong rush. He grabbed the rail and hung his head over as if to throw up.

A huge wave broke over the ship, and the ship rolled into it so that its deck was awash. The rail, the capstain, Candy's father, and everything else on the port side went under water.

"Father!" Candy shouted in fear. "Father!"

The ship rolled back and the port side lifted out of the sea, dripping water from the rail and the braces.

Candy's father was gone.

Chapter Eight

The sea was as smooth as glass the next morning, when the entire ship's company was turned out for the burial ceremony of Dr. Pratt. Of course, they had no body to bury; Dr. Pratt had been washed overboard during the terrible storm of the night before, but the burial plank was in position at the starboard middeck, and it was covered with the Confederate flag, as if Candy's father's body lay under it.

The smoothness of the sea mocked Candy, for even the rolling which had caused her father's seasickness was absent now, and the ship might as well have been a house in a field, so steady was its ride.

171

Candy had gone to her cabin in shock after seeing her father washed overboard. Her grief was such that she was only vaguely aware of the storm which had so violently tossed the ship for the rest of the night. She cried at the irony of the situation. She had saved her father from the hangman's noose, only to see him killed at sea. And now, that which she had feared most, the loss of her father, had come to pass after all.

During the night Candy recalled a conversation she'd once had with her father. The conversation had occurred right after her mother died. She had stood with him beside her mother's grave, broken-hearted, hurt, confused and, inexplicably, a little angry. She was eight years old at the time.

"I don't want you to ever do that," she told her father that day, holding tightly to his hand.

"Do what, darlin'?" her father answered.

"Go away and leave me like Mama did. I didn't think Mama would ever leave me. I thought she loved me."

Candy's father had picked her up then, and held her close to him, barely managing to choke back a sob.

"Gracious, darlin', don't you know Mama didn't want to leave you?" he said. "She didn't want to leave any of us. She died."

"I don't want you to die."

"Sweetheart, we will all have to die. That's

Gods's plan for us. We are tested on earth, and then we die so we can be with Him in heaven.''

"I don't want you to be with Him. I want you to be with me," Candy had sobbed.

"But don't you see, darlin'? When we are all with Him, we will never be separated again."

"I don't care. I want you to stay with me forever."

"I will be with you forever, just as Mama is with you forever."

"But Mama isn't with me. She's gone. She's down there."

"No, Mama isn't there. What they buried was like a house where Mama lived, but she isn't there anymore."

"Then where is she?"

"Have you forgotten Mama already?"

"No."

"Then that's where she is. She is in your heart, and in mine, and she'll be there for as long as we live. You can feel her there, can't you?"

"Yes," Candy said, not exactly sure that the pain she was feeling was what her father meant, but certainly aware that she could feel something.

"That's the way it is when folks that you love die. I'm a doctor. I've seen lots of folks die, but I've always known that as long as there's someone left here that loves them, well, they're never truly gone. Darlin', when I die, that's the way it will be with me. I will come to live with Mama in your heart, and you'll have both of us until we meet again in God's heaven. That's the way things are.''

At exactly ten o'clock Mr. Carter sounded four bells, and the entire ship's company, except for Pig Meat, reported to the burial plank. Pig Meat stayed at the helm, but he, like the others, removed his hat. Candy and the ship's company stood silent for several seconds, staring at the flag-draped board as if it really did contain Dr. Pratt's body. It was quiet except for the wind whispering in the sails and the creaking of the ropes.

Rafe was carrying *The Book of Common Prayer* of the Episcopal Church. He had been introduced to the Episcopal prayer book by the first captain he had ever sailed with.

''I'm not Episcopalian,'' the captain told Rafe, ''but I'm not anything else either, and this book has all the prayers and sections clearly marked for every occasion, so it works out real fine. There is a God; nobody could sail across something as wide as the sea and not know in his heart that there is a God.''

Rafe looked over at Candy. Somewhere she had found the strength necessary to compose herself, and he admired her for that. He had never known anyone quite like her before. He would give anything if there was no war, if he had been able to meet Candy under normal conditions, if he could ask Candy to be his wife.

Rafe cleared his throat and began to read: "Unto Almighty God, we command the soul of our brother departed, and we commit his body to the deep; in sure and certain hope of the Resurrection unto eternal life, through our Lord Jesus Christ; at whose coming in glorious majesty to judge the world, the sea shall give up her dead; and the corruptible bodies of those who sleep in him shall be changed, and made like unto his glorious body; according to the mighty working whereby He is able to subdue all things unto himself, Amen."

"Amen," the others responded.

Rafe nodded at McCorkle, and McCorkle tipped the burial plank up, then let it slide into the sea from beneath the flag.

"Ship's company, dismissed," Rafe said quietly, and the men put on their hats and returned to their duties. Several of them looked toward Candy, showing by their glance their sympathy, and Candy felt warmed by it. She had no family remaining now, and had her father died ashore, she would have felt alone at his burial. Here she was not alone. Here she was . . . home.

Suddenly, and with a clarity so bright that it nearly stunned her, she knew what she wanted. She wanted to stay on board this ship, not only to be with Rafe, but because she had never felt more alive than she did when she was at sea. Even during the fiercest part of last night's storm she had felt grief for the loss of her father, but never fear or discomfort from the storm. She would go to Rafe and ask him to let her stay.

"No," Rafe answered resolutely. "Absolutely not!"

"Why not?"

"Why not? Because you are a woman, that's why not."

"Rafe, I promise, I won't be in the way. I'll find some way to make myself useful, I'll—"

"No," Rafe said again. "We'll be off the coast of South Carolina tonight; I'll have you ashore by tomorrow morning."

"With no regard as to what happens to me?" Candy asked.

"What do you mean?"

"I have no family, Rafe. I have nowhere to go."

"You are a resourceful young woman," Rafe said. "You will survive."

Candy blinked back tears. "Is that all I mean to you?" she asked.

"No," Rafe said. "Of course that's not all you mean to me. You mean. . . ." he paused, then sighed. "Candy, it's because you mean something to me that I don't want you to stay on this ship.

Don't you understand, girl? This is a ship of war. There are a dozen Yankee destroyers out there whose sole purpose in life is to find us and sink us.''

"They think you've already been sunk. I read it in *Harper's Weekly*.''

"They will learn soon enough that we haven't been sunk," Rafe said. "Or they may think we are yet another commerce raider. Either way, they will be coming after us, and that makes it very dangerous for anyone who is on board this ship.''

"You are on board.''

"I am the captain.''

"Rafe, don't you understand?'' Candy finally said. "If you won't say it, then I will. I love you, Rafe. I want to share my life with you. I want to share the risks with you. If anything happens to you, then I want it to happen to me as well.''

Rafe was somewhat taken aback by Candy's bold pronouncement, but he recovered quickly and he put his arms around her and drew her to him.

"Oh, darling,'' he said. "Don't you think I would give anything in the world if we could just be together forever? If there were no war and if this were a merchant ship, we could sail the seven seas as man and wife. I've seen captains with their wives at sea before, and it's not an uncommon thing. But, my God, Candy, we are at war! You can't ask me to let you stay aboard when we are at war!''

"Sails!" a shout drifted down from the lookout.

"Where away?"

"Hull down off the port bow," the lookout called back.

"Cap'n, look, there's smoke," One particularly sharp-eyed sailor called, and as Rafe looked, he could see a small wisp of smoke hanging above the horizon where the sails had been sighted. If the captain of the other ship was wasting his coal to sail under steam, that could only mean one thing. He was a warship, and he was coming after Rafe.

"Mr. McCorkle, light up the boilers," Rafe ordered.

"Aye, sir," McCorkle said. "Shall I alter course?"

Rafe knew that McCorkle was asking whether or not Rafe intended to fight. Rafe looked at Candy.

"What would you do if I weren't on board?" Candy asked.

"I'd fight 'er," Rafe answered easily.

"Then, do so," Candy answered. "You really have no choice anyway, and this would prove my point. Please, Rafe. Just act as if I weren't here. I want to show you that I could stay aboard your ship and not be a burden."

Rafe stroked his chin for a moment, then looked toward McCorkle.

"Maintain course," he said. "Gun crews to stations, but don't run out the guns until you receive my order."

"Aye, Cap'n," McCorkle answered with a wide grin.

"Gun crews!" he shouted. "Man your battle stations!"

"Hurrah!" the crew replied, and dozens of feet shuffled across the deck as the man bent to their duties.

Three men went aloft on the foremast to furl the sails. The other sails could be raised or lowered from the deck as necessary, but the foremast, being square-rigged, required men aloft; therefore, those sails were struck before battle. Another half-dozen men went aloft with rifles, ready to serve as sharpshooters when the ships closed to within rifle range of each other.

"Candy, before the battle starts, you are to go to my cabin," Rafe ordered.

"Rafe, I—"

"If you are going to stay aboard this ship, you must obey the captain!" Rafe said sharply. "Now, go to my cabin and assist the ship's surgeon, for that is where we set up the emergency hospital."

"All right, Rafe," Candy answered sheepishly. She had thought he was sending her below to get her out of the way. She was glad to see that he was at least going to utilize the nursing skills she had learned at her father's side.

Candy went below to Rafe's cabin. She saw that his door had been removed; its one end placed on the table where she had eaten dinner with Rafe last night, and the other end on a desk which protruded from the wall. She saw also that there were special pegs and holes to secure the door in this position, and realized that it was designed for just such a purpose. The door, then, became an operating table.

Beside the table the surgeon had removed the top tray of his sea chest, then placed the tray on the sea chest so that all his tools were readily accessible. Candy recognized the saws, blades, clamps and bone snips of his profession. There was also a mechanical tourniquet, a bullet probe and a generous supply of laudanum.

"Miss Pratt, are you to help me?" the ship's surgeon asked.

"Yes," Candy answered.

"Good, good. Go to the mess steward and get the slops bucket for me, will you?"

"The slops bucket?"

"Aye, lass, the slops bucket. We'll need something for the arms and legs."

"Oh," Candy said, feeling a bit weak in her stomach.

"Are you all right?" the surgeon asked, seeing the expression on her face.

"Yes, yes, I'm fine," Candy said. "I'll get it right away."

"Good girl."

Candy passed the powder magazine on her way to the galley, and she saw the powder cartridges being passed through a safety curtain of water-soaked blankets to barefooted men who then trans-ferred the cartridges to the gun crews on deck. Candy got the slops bucket for the surgeon, then went back on deck to wait for the battle to begin.

Candy saw that ropes and grappling hooks had been brought on deck and laid out for easy access. Everyone had removed their shoes, and those who had long hair had tied their hair back out of the way. The gun crews were all in position, and the men stood silently looking out toward the approach-ing vessel. Candy walked over to stand by the rail.

"Miss, I'm an old man, so what I'm about to say to you is like a friendly gran'pa talkin' to his gran'daughter, if you get my meanin'. I don't want you to take no offense," a sailor said. Candy didn't know his name, but she had seen him before and had noticed that he was even older than her father had been.

"What is it?" she asked.

"Well, miss, this bein' your first battle 'n' all, I think someone should advise you to—uh, well, there ain't no delicate way to put it, miss—" The old sailor sighed and ran his hand through his hair. "Miss, you'd best visit the head before the battle."

"The head? Oh," Candy felt her cheeks burning, but she suddenly realized the validitiy of the sailor's remarks, so she smiled at him and thanked him, then visited the place Rafe had set aside for her to use.

By the time Candy returned to the deck, the other ship had come very close, and now she could see the Stars and Stripes flying from the stern mast and smaller colorful flags flying in the upper rigging.

"Mr. Carter, what does she say?" Rafe asked.

Carter was in the shrouds, looking through his telescope at the other ship.

"She asks us to identify ourselves," Carter said.

"Very well, Mr. Carter. Show our identification. And run out the Stars and Bars."

There had been no flag showing until Rafe said this, and now, with a cheer, a couple of men ran the Stars and Bars up the flagpole at the stern. Carter showed flags identifying the ship as the *Delta Dancer*.

"Ha," McCorkle laughed. "That'll set their tongues wagging. They'll think us ghosts."

The other ship began maneuvering, and Rafe shouted orders to Pig Meat at the helm. The men laughed and cheered at the maneuvers, and then Candy realized what Rafe was doing. He was moving his ship in such a way as to not allow the

Union ship to bring its broadside to bear, while, at the same time, gaining the advantage of his own broadside to the other ship.

Suddenly, a cannon ball crashed through the rail on one side of the ship, passed across the deck without hitting anything and smashed through the rail on the other side. It splashed in the water a hundred yards beyond, having arrived and departed with only the whistling air and the smashing sound of timbers to announce its passing. The sound of the cannon report reached Candy's ears a second later.

"She fired her bow chaser!" McCorkle called.

"Return fire!" Rafe shouted, and all five guns on the *Delta Dancer's* gun deck boomed in reply. The ship rolled back from the volley, and smoke billowed out so thickly that, for a moment, nothing could be seen of the Union ship. Then, when the smoke cleared away, Candy saw that the first broadside had done tremendous damage to the other ship. Shattered spars and dangling rigging hung down over the deck, and a gaping hole appeared in the hull, just under the bowsprit.

"We raked her, Cap'n!" McCorkle shouted.

"Reload and fire again!"

"Aye, Cap'n!"

The Union ship answered fire, and Candy saw, to her amazement, that she could actually see the cannon ball as it came toward them. It was a terribly frightening experience, standing there watching this black speck of whistling death as it sped toward them. For a moment she had the idea that it was coming right for her, that it was going to hit her right in the chest, and she froze in fear and grabbed hold of the stanchion and held on as if, by bracing herself, she could resist it.

The cannon ball curved down toward the water; then she heard the crash of timber as it smashed through the hull.

"Mr. McCorkle, send a damage partly to find the impact of the ball," Rafe said. "If it hulled us at the waterline we must make rapid repairs to keep the water out."

"Aye, Cap'n."

"Cap'n!" Pig Meat shouted. "Cap'n, it hit our rudderpost, sir. We can't maneuver!" Pig Meat spun the wheel from side to side to demonstrate to Rafe.

"Damn!" Rafe swore. "Gents, we are well in for a fight now."

The Union ship, which was continually trying to gain position on the *Delta Dancer*, finally managed to do so, and once they were in position, they released their first broadside.

Eight balls crashed into the side of the *Delta Dancer*. One hit a gun and knocked it off its mounts. It fell on one of the gunners and crushed him dead, instantly. Another ball smashed into the deck and sent a shower of splinters. A large sharpened stake stabbed all the way through one sailor's leg, just below the knee, and he fell to the deck screaming in agony. The other balls crashed through the rigging, cutting rope and poking holes in sail.

Almost immediately after that volley, there was a second volley, this one from small cannon which had been loaded with grapeshot and taken into the shrouds of the enemy ship. A cloud of grapeshot hit the deck of the *Delta Dancer* like a sudden hailstorm of iron pellets, and still another sailor screamed in agony.

"Miss, the surgeon's askin' about you," one of the sailors said, and Candy, remembering then that she was to help the surgeon, went below, just as the first wounded man was brought in with the stake still protruding from his leg.

The surgeon didn't even look at the stake. Instead he dosed the wounded man with laudanum, then reached for the saw.

"The thing you got to remember," he said, as he began cuting through the leg, "is to leave enough skin to form a flap to cover the stump. Otherwise, it'll never heal, 'n' they'll die just as quick as if you didn't take the leg off in the first place."

Candy watched as the surgeon slowly, methodically cut through the leg. She suddenly felt an

overwhelming queasiness, then a giddy lighthead-
edness, then nothing.

"Are you all right?" the surgeon was asking,
leaning over her.

Candy opened her eyes. Outside she could hear
that the sound of battle was still going on.

"What happened?" she asked.

"You fainted when you saw me cut off the
leg," the surgeon said. "You don't have to feel
any shame from it. Lots of folks do the same."

"Yes, but my father was a doctor. I was trained
to be his nurse."

"What did you do for him?" the surgeon asked.
"Give a few immunizations? Administer tonic?"

"Yes," Candy said.

The surgeon laughed gently, and shook his head.

"It's not the same thing as seein' a man torn
apart by cannon balls," he said. "Go on, we'll
both do better if you are somewhere else."

"But I want to help," Candy said. "I need to
help."

Unspoken, though very real to her, was the fact
that she felt she had to prove herself. If she could
prove herself in this battle, perhaps Rafe would let
her stay. Anything else like her debacle in the
operating room would just convince Rafe that he
was right in wanting to put her ashore.

Candy stepped out into the bay area and saw a
powder monkey just about to go on deck with a

new charge. Just as he stuck his head out from the hatch, however, he was struck by a shot, and he tumbled back down the ladder. Candy bent down to tend to him, but saw that the shot had gone right through his forehead. He was dead before he even fell. She picked up his cartridge and took it up to one of the guns.

On deck she saw the ravages of the battle. Rope and sail and shattered spars lay in piles on the deck, itself pocked with holes and splinters. The Union ship was broadside with the *Delta Dancer* and they fired into each other like giants trading mortal blows. The Union ship had more broadside guns, and thus, with each exchange, it was gaining some advantage.

"Damn me, if we had twice the guns, we could make quick work of her!" McCorkle swore.

The *Delta Dancer* had presented her port side to the Union ship. On the starboard side, the guns were silent and cool, and the gun crews merely ducking the incoming shot and shell as they had nothing to do.

"Why not move the other guns across the deck and double the number of cannon?" Candy asked.

"Why, miss, we can't leave the starboard unprotected," McCorkle said.

"Why not?"

"Because you just don't do that."

"Candy's right," Rafe suddenly said. "What

the hell do we have to protect us from over there. Get those guns moved across deck. We'll have a little surprise for our friends.''

"Aye, Cap'n," McCorkle said. He started shouting orders, and even as the Union ship was pouring broadside after broadside into them, the men moved all the guns across the deck. It was a dangerous and difficult job, but they managed to do it with amazing speed. As soon as the guns were all in position, the entire broadside volleyed as one. There was a tremendous roar and the smoke, which was already thick, thickened to the point that it was aboslutely impossible to see for several moments. During those moments there was an unearthly quiet; then the quiet was shattered by a loud explosion from the other ship.

"Her boilers!" one of the *Delta Dancer* sailors called. "Her boilers went up." There was a loud cheer from the men, and then, when the smoke cleared away, they were able to confirm what the sailor said, for a white plume of steam was escaping from amidships. Her guns were silent, and Rafe saw the flag coming down, to be replaced with a white flag. A boat was being lowered from near the stern, and a handful of men climbed down into it. The little boat flew a white flag as the sailors started rowing toward the *Delta Dancer*.

"Looks like their cap'n's wantin' to call it quits," McCorkle said.

"Pipe him aboard with honors, Mr. McCorkle," Rafe ordered.

Everyone on board both ships stood silently by the railing as the little boat made its way across the water which separated the two combatants. When the boat scraped against the side of the *Delta Dancer*, the bo'sun sounded a pipe, and a moment later an officer appeared over the side. His arm was bandaged with a blood-soaked rag, and his face was black with spent powder, but, then, so were the faces of everyone on board the *Delta Dancer*, including Candy.

The officer turned to the stern and saluted the Confederate flag; then he came up to Rafe and saluted Rafe. Rafe returned the salute.

"Hello, Rafe," the officer said quietly. "I see Captain Raymond didn't sink you after all."

"The announcement of our demise was a bit premature. Hello, George; it's been a long time," Rafe answered.

"Not since I made you and your roommate walk three punishment tours at the Academy," George answered with a smile.

"I know," Rafe said. "Bill Herrick and I spent the entire weekend planning our revenge."

"Bill is first lieutenant to Captain Raymond on board the *Vanderbilt* now. Did you know that?"

"No, I didn't," Rafe said. "It's a hard thing, George, friends trying to kill each other like this."

The smile left the Union officer's face, and for a moment Candy thought he might break into tears. He composed himself, however.

"Yes," he said with a sigh. "Yes, it's a terribly sad thing." He looked around and saw the doubled cannon along the portside, and he smiled again and shook his head. "I wondered where you got the extra firepower from," he said. He sighed. "That's a good idea."

"Have you quit the battle, George?"

"Rafe, if it were me, I would fight you until one of us was at the bottom. But my captain has ordered me to tender our surrender."

"Who is your captain?"

"Cramsdale," George said. "Edward W. Cramsdale."

"I don't think I know him. Regular Navy?"

"Playboy, yachtsman," George scoffed. "He entered a yacht in the America's Cup trials, came in second out of a field of thirty, and decided he was a master of seamanship. The *Avenger* is his ship, donated to the Navy with the provision that he be the captain."

"Is he wounded?"

"No."

"George, what is the condition of your ship? Will it get you safely ashore?"

"I think so," George said. "We certainly can't

fight her anymore, though, if we run into anyone else like you."

"Lieutenant, there isn't anyone else like Cap'n Taylor," McCorkle said.

George smiled. "I knew that when we were in Annapolis."

"All right, George. Tell your captain I am paroling him on his honor. He can keep his ship."

"Thanks," George said. He saluted Rafe and turned to go back down the ladder to his boat. Just before he reached the railing, though, he turned back to Rafe.

"Rafe, we spoke to the *Vanderbilt* yesterday. They are right behind us. If I were you, I wouldn't hang around in these waters too long."

"I hadn't planned on it," Rafe said.

"You weren't planning on trying to put in at Charleston were you?"

"Maybe," Rafe admitted.

George shook his head.

"That's no good either," he said. "We have an entire fleet there now. Your best bet is to head for Nassau until you've recovered from this battle."

"Thanks, George," Rafe said.

"Rafe, I'll have to tell everyone that the *Delta Dancer* wasn't sunk. They'll be coming for you in full force."

"Yes," Rafe said. "I suppose they will."

George was silent for a moment longer, as if he

wanted to say something else. Finally, he just sighed and nodded as he started down the ladder.

"Good luck," he said.

The crew of the *Delta Dancer* gave another loud cheer as the little boat worked its way back to the *Avenger*.

"Mr. McCorkle," Rafe said.

"Aye, sir?"

"Set a course for Nassau." He looked at Candy. "Candy, it looks like you are going to be with us now, whether I like it on not," he said.

Candy smiled broadly, then moved over to him and put her arms around him. She kissed him fully on the mouth, in front of the crew, and the crew responded with a mighty cheer. When at last she stopped the kiss, she smiled to see that, beneath his powder-blackened face, shined cheeks of red. She had embarrassed him.

"You?" she teased. "The man who once so brazenly caught me in my bath embarrassed by a little kiss?"

"Don't worry," Rafe answered with a smile of his own. "The situation isn't terminal."

Chapter Nine

Candy stood at the open window of the Nassau hotel room and looked out over the sparkling blue-green waters of the harbor. A gentle breeze kissed her naked skin, and her nipples hardened and took on a glow, much as they had the night before, during her amorous moments with Rafe.

Behind Candy, also naked, Rafe lay sleeping. The sheets of the bed—indeed, the very room—held in erotic captivity the aroma of lovemaking.

Candy, Rafe, and the ship's crew had been in Nassau for three weeks. During that time the *Delta Dancer* had undergone repairs, and now it was fitted with a new rudderpost, new sail and shroud lines, and repaired decking and railing. Only the most discerning eye would ever notice the battle damage it had sustained. Now she was ready to sail again at the first target of opportunity.

At first the men had been happy to put in at Nassau. Their purses were all fat with prize money, and Nassau was teeming with bars which were only too happy to take their money and with fast women who would help them spend it. But many of the men had soon run out of money, and one by one, they came back to the ship as a refuge of last resort. Now those men, who were tied to the ship for economic reasons, were anxious to go to sea again and capture a few more prizes, so as to once again have some spending money.

So far Rafe had shown no impatience with their long sojourn, and Candy had enjoyed every minute of it. To Candy, it was as if she and Rafe had found some private paradise in which to while away the remainder of the war. The thunder of shot and shell and the screams of men in agony seemed but a distant memory now, and it was not a memory she was all that anxious to arouse.

There was a quiet knock on the door behind her; Candy padded back over to the bed and slid in under the sheet to cover her nudity. She did it without hurry or concern, because she knew who it would be. It would be John, the hotel bellboy, with their breakfast. He brought them breakfast in bed every morning.

Rafe stirred as she slipped into bed with him. She felt a small tingle of supressed excitement as the naked skin of her long, smooth legs lay pressed against the skin of his hard, hairy legs.

"What?" he mumbled. "What is it?"

"I think it is John," Candy said.

Rafe sat up in bed and rubbed his eyes. The sheet fell down, exposing his broad shoulders and muscular chest, and, at the same time, her breasts.

"Good," he said. "I'm starving."

"How can you wake up hungry?" Candy asked.

"You know what they say," Rafe defended. "One should eat the breakfast of a king, the lunch of a prince and the dinner of a pauper. Come in, John!"

Candy realized that her breasts were exposed, so she managed to clutch the sheet to her bare breasts just before the door opened. An old, white-haired black man pushed in a wheeled cart laden with silver-covered serving dishes. The first morning John had come in, Candy had not expected him and she hadn't covered herself up. Though she was nude in front of him, John had acted as if there was nothing out of the ordinary, and he'd set up the breakfast table with as much ease and dignity as if Candy and Rafe had been fully dressed and down in the dining room. Now, though Candy did make a point to cover her nudity, she was no longer embarrassed when John came into the room.

"What have we for breakfast this morning, John?" Rafe asked, looking at the tray eagerly.

"Sausage and scrambled eggs, sir, and fresh fruit. Also coffee and a nice coconut pastry."

The first time Candy heard John talk she had been amazed. He was black, but he didn't have the slurring dialect of the blacks she had always known and been exposed to. In fact, John's language was decidedly more cultured than Rafe's, or her own, as well as the majority of all the whites she knew, including those in high government positions.

"Sounds good," Rafe said.

"Shall I serve, sir? Or would you prefer that I leave them in the warming trays, so that you may serve yourself at your leisure?"

"You serve, John," Rafe said. "I'm starving to death right now. Nothing is going to keep me from that breakfast."

Under the sheet, and thus away from John's eyes, Candy slowly, but deliberately put her hand on Rafe's hip. She could feel the heat of his skin in her fingers and, or so she thought, a small tingling of excitement, generated in him by her touch. She moved her hand across the smooth skin of his hip, over to the growth of hair on his lower abdomen, and finally into the thick tangle of hair which crowned his now-inert manhood. She felt him draw a quick, sharp breath.

Candy smiled and continued her teasing. Her

hand moved on until her fingers grasped, and then gently squeezed. She felt it twitching and growing in her hand.

"Are you really so hungry, Rafe?" Candy asked in a low, husky voice.

"Uh," Rafe said. "John?"

John looked around at Rafe and Candy. Candy's unseen fingers continued to squeeze and caress with the skill she had acquired over the last several weeks. She smiled at John. The expression in John's face didn't change, but his eyes twinkled in amusement and Candy knew that he knew what was going on.

"Yes, Captain?"

"On second thought, just leave everything in the warming trays. Maybe I'm not quite ready to eat just yet."

"Yes, sir, I think the captain has made a wise decision," John said. His eyes continued to twinkle knowingly as, with an impassive expression, he replaced the warming covers. He turned and gave a slight bow toward the bed, then left the room.

"I thought you were ready to eat breakfast," Candy teased. "Please don't let me detain you. Would you like me to serve you?" She started to get out of bed, but Rafe reached for her and pulled her back into the bed.

"Come here, you," He said roughly. He captured her mouth with his in a deep, probing kiss.

When it started, it had been a game, a teasing ploy with Candy well in control. Now, as the kiss deepened, Candy felt herself losing control, falling into the abyss created by the white heat of the erupting fires in her body. The joke, the time, the place, even the circumstances of her being here in Nassau, were all washed away, and the only reality left was the contact of their lips.

Rafe's hand went to her bare breast, and his fingers gently massaged her nipple. She floated in the bliss of langurous sexual excitement, and her body trembled with the fire of her blood as he planted kisses on her and searched and probed her body with his hands and fingers.

Candy went from a floating sexual pleasure to an all-consuming need, and her hands and fingers, which had been gently persuasive, now became demanding.

"Rafe, don't torture me so," she gasped. "Don't make me wait any longer. I want you now!"

Rafe moved over her, then into her, and the exquisite pleasures, the silken sensations she had experienced with Rafe on each previous time, returned; only each time they seemed greater than before.

Candy had clearly been the instigator of this sexual encounter, and now she was definitely more than just a passive partner. She was, in fact, the aggressor. She could scarcely contain the pleasure which was building up inside her, and she wanted to share with Rafe all that she was feeling. She thrust against him, and wrapped her arms and legs around him, and pulled him to her, taking all he could give, yet demanding still more.

She felt herself speeding to the edge of all sensation, and she hung balanced there for several precarious moments, suspended as if in a ship just behind the crest of a breaking wave. As she was playing the dominant role, she was able to escape from her own body, and she became aware of Rafe's own pleasure. It was as if she felt what he felt, and their sensations conjoined in a headlong rush to the ultimate ecstasy which, with an explosion of rapture, burst over them.

Even though her goal had been attained, Candy didn't drop away from the peak of rapture in one full swoop. Instead, she floated down, pausing to experience new pinnacles of pleasure, exploring them one by one until, finally, there was nothing left but the contented warmth of what had been a blazing fire. Then, and only then, did Rafe disengage himself and roll over on his back to lie there breathing heavily with the contentment of total satiation.

Candy lay there in bed beside the man who had become her lover. He was not her husband; he was her lover—and as she thought of it, she wondered how she had reached this point of wantonness.

Most of Candy's life had been spent without a mother, but her father had certainly instilled a sense of propriety in her. She had been raised a lady, and she knew to blush when she heard a swear word or any remark which might be construed as off-color. She had certainly been mortified on that occasion Rafe had caught her nude in the bathroom. And yet, as she lay there beside her lover, both of them heavy with the sweat and smell of sex, she remembered that, even then, an unbidden feeling of pleasure had suffused her body.

Perhaps it was the war. Perhaps it was the realization that, at any moment, she could die. That certainly made life more precious, and it made folly of the inhibitions and taboos which would limit a person's right to enjoy life.

And sinful or not, right or wrong, Candy was certainly enjoying life.

By noon the sun above the harbor had grown brilliant in its intensity. The sky was a bright blue, and the roofs of the town of Nassau glowed in shimmering silver from the reflection of the bright light, sending back a wavering image, as if the town were being studied through an imperfect lens.

A United States warship slipped into the harbor, moving under steam power alone, with all its sails furled. It was a side-wheeler, and the paddlewheels churned the water into white froth beneath the gray, ironclad wheel covers as the ship moved across the bay.

On the deck of the *Vanderbilt*, Captain Raymond stood just aft of the wheel and looked out over the forest of masts which stabbed into the brilliant sky. Finally, he saw what he was looking for, and he let out a long, slow sigh.

"Well, my friend," he said under his breath, "I have finally caught up with you."

"Cap'n, I see the *Delta Dancer*," the lookout called from the foretop.

"Yes, thank you," Raymond said. "I see her. Helm."

"Aye, sir," the man at the wheel answered.

Captain Raymond leaned against the compass binnacle and surveyed the harbor. "Come around so that we have her to our lee."

"Aye, sir," the helmsman answered.

"Cap'n, her cap'n ain't aboard," the lookout called. "The pennant isn't flying."

Raymond looked toward the *Delta Dancer*, and as his lookout had noticed, the captain's pennant wasn't flying. Rafe Taylor was ashore.

"Very well," Raymond said. "When we drop anchor, I'll go ashore to look him up."

Mr. Herrick was on deck then, and he leaned against the railing as he looked ashore.

"Captain, even if you find him, this is a neutral port," Herrick said. "You can do nothing."

"I can get him to come out of port and meet me," Raymond said.

"I don't think you can."

"Oh? You are his close, personal friend, Mr. Herrick. Are you telling me that he is a coward?"

"No, of course not, and I think you know that as well."

"Then he will come out of port and meet me on the high sea."

"Why would he do that, sir? His primary mission is as a commerce raider. It would be a violation of his mission orders for him to meet you, unless it was an accidental encounter at sea."

"Because I have something he wants. Or, rather, I have something that Miss Pratt wants, an that is just as well."

"You really think Miss Pratt can exercise that much influence over him?"

"Yes," Raymond said.

"We have no proof that Miss Pratt is still with him."

"Where else would she be?" Raymond asked.

"I don't know."

"She is here," Raymond said. He rubbed his bald head. "She is here and so is our good friend Mr. Taylor."

"What do you have in mind?"

"I'm going to let our prisoner go, in return for Mr. Taylor's promise to meet us on the high sea."

"Captain, you can't let the prisoner go. We have to return him to Washington. Remember, he is under the sentence of death."

"As far as I'm concerned, so is Rafe Taylor," Raymond said. "And I'm much more anxious to see that his sentence is carried out. How is our prisoner, by the way?"

"He is in excellent shape," Herrick said. "It is truly amazing when one realizes what he has been through. It really would be a shame to see him hanged after all this."

"Yes, twenty-four hours in the open water, clinging to a piece of driftwood—it is a miracle that Dr. Pratt is still alive. It's a miracle that Divine Providence designed it just for me, to ensure that I would have the opportunity to fulfill my mission. Now, Mr. Herrick, I want you to go ashore and look up Mr. Taylor. Extend him my compliments, and inform him that we have Miss Pratt's father safely on board. Tell him, also, that we will let Dr. Pratt go, if he will meet with me, privately, and make the arrangements for a fair fight."

"Aye, sir," Herrick said.

"Oh, Rafe, don't you wish we could go on like this forever?" Candy asked. They were walking through an open-air market, and Candy was holding a small coconut and a straw doll. It had been so cleverly fashioned by the smiling black woman who sold the doll to her that Candy had fallen in love with it at once and teased Rafe into buying it for her. He did so, only after laughing at her and accusing her of being just like a little girl.

The smile left Rafe's face.

"Yes," he said, quietly. "I do wish it could, Candy, but it can't. Already the crew is beginning to grow anxious to get back onto the trade routes. It is only when we take commerce ships as prizes that anyone gets paid."

"I know," Candy said. "And I've been wondering why we haven't set out again. After all, the ship is fully repaired, isn't it?"

"I haven't gone out again, because I don't want to leave you."

"Leave me? Why must you leave me? I'll go with you."

"No," Rafe said.

"Rafe, what are you saying? Of course I'll go with you."

"Candy, you were on board when we fought the *Avenger*. You heard the screams of the men who were wounded. You saw the ones who were killed. Don't you know that could happen to you as well?"

"Or to you."

"Yes, but I'm prepared for it."

"Who is to say that I'm not?" Candy said.

"Rafe, I love you, and I am ready to face any hardship, any danger, just to be with you. I had hoped that you loved me as much."

Rafe put his arms around her. "You know I love you as much," he said. "I love you so much that if anything happened to you, I wouldn't want to live. Don't you see? I just couldn't take it."

"You must let me go with you, Rafe. You simply must," Candy begged.

As they stood there in each other's arms, Rafe suddenly grew aware of someone staring at them. He looked up, then gasped in surprise.

Candy heard his gasp and felt him stiffen, and she pulled away from his in curiosity.

"Rafe, what is it?" she asked. She saw that Rafe was looking intently at someone, and she followed his gaze. She saw a man about the same age as Rafe, a little shorter and darker, perhaps, but remarkably similar in bearing. He, too, was wearing a naval uniform, but his uniform had the brass buttons and accounterments of the U.S. Navy.

"Hello, Rafe," the man said quietly.

"Bill," Rafe replied. "I heard you were with Captain Raymond on the *Vanderbilt*."

"Yes," Herrick said.

"Is the *Vanderbilt* in port?"

"Aye, we arrived this morning," Herrick said. Herrick looked at Candy and touched his hat in a salute. "You must be Miss Pratt," he said.

"Yes," Candy said, surprised that he would know her name. "How did you know that?"

"I was told you were with Rafe," Herrick said. He cleared his throat. "I reckon I've got some pretty good news for you, Miss Pratt."

"Oh? What?"

"Your father is alive and well."

"What?" Candy asked in a small voice. Once, when she was a young girl, she had fallen from a tree and had the breath knocked out of her. It had been a terrifying experience, lying there for a long moment, unable to breathe, not knowing whether she would ever breathe again. She felt like that now, and her knees grew weak. She might have fallen, had Rafe not been supporting her with his strong arms. "What did you say?"

"I said your father is alive," Herrick said again.

"See here, Bill, that's a cruel jest to make," Rafe said angrily.

"It isn't a jest, Rafe, believe me," Mr. Herrick said. "Dr. Pratt was washed over in a storm, was he not?"

"Yes," Candy said.

"A nearby ship must have foundered, or at least been damaged to the point that some of it was cast adrift. Dr. Pratt found a piece of flotsam and managed to cling to it. We picked him up twenty-four hours later."

"Oh! Where is he?" Candy cried. "Please, take me to him! I want to see him!"

"He's on board the *Vanderbilt*," Herrick said. "In our brig."

"In your brig?"

"Yes, ma'am," Herrick said. He cleared his throat. "Uh, ma'am, you must know that your father is an escaped prisoner—and a condemned man, at that."

"Bill, are you telling me that Raymond intends to take Dr. Pratt back to Washington?"

"I'm afraid so," Herrick said. "Unless . . ." He let the word hang.

"Unless what?"

"Captain Raymond has authorized me to tell you that, if you will agree to meet privately with him and work out the details for an open sea battle, he will let Dr. Pratt go."

"What? That's all I have to do? Of course I'll meet with him," Rafe said. "When? Where?"

"I wouldn't be so eager," Herrick said. "Rafe, the *Vanderbilt*'ll get the best of the *Delta Dancer*. We'll sink you sure."

"Maybe you will, and maybe you won't," Rafe said. "I'm willing to take that chance if it means freedom for Dr. Pratt. The question I have for you is, will Raymond actually let Dr. Pratt go?"

"If it means getting you, yes," Herrick said. "I'm not sure I know why, but Captain Raymond

has an obsession about you. He is willing to let
Dr. Pratt go and risk court-martial, dismissal from
the Navy and a lifetime of disgrace, just to get
you.''

"I suppose I should be flattered," Rafe said.
"Now, when and where does Raymond want to
meet?"

"Do you know Bell Rock, at the south end of
the island?"

"Yes."

"He wants you there tonight, at seven."

"Tell him he must first set Dr. Pratt free."

"I think he'll let him go tonight, when you
meet."

"No," Rafe said. "I must have some assurance
that he won't try and use Dr. Pratt as bait. When
Dr. Pratt walks into my hotel room, a free man,
then I'll go down to Bell Rock and meet with
Raymond."

"I don't know if Raymond will go along with
that," Herrick said.

"That's my offer," Rafe said. "If he is as
obsessed with getting me as you think he is, he'll
go along."

"All right," Herrick agreed. "I'll tell him. What
is your hotel?"

"The Victoria," Rafe said. "Room 312."

Herrick turned to leave; then he looked back at

Rafe. "You're looking good, Rafe. I'm glad to see you haven't been wounded."

"Yes," Rafe said, shaking his hand. "I've been lucky, so far."

"So have I," Herrick said. "I hope our luck holds out . . . for both of us."

Chapter Ten

Candy paced back and forth nervously as she and Rafe awaited her father's release. They had returned to the hotel room shortly after the meeting with Mr. Herrick, and there, in accordance with Herrick's instructions, waited for Dr. Pratt.

The waiting proved to be very difficult for Candy, and she went to the window many times to look out over the bay, almost as if expecting to see him come ashore in one of the many boats which were plying the harbor. Rafe lay on the bed behind her, reading newspapers and magazines from the States.

"Hah, listen to this," he chuckled, reading from "Humors of the Day." "Why is a solitary cry like Captain Rafe Taylor's ship?"

"I don't know," Candy replied. "Why?"

"Because it is a private-tear," Rafe said, laughing.

"Oh," Candy said. She brushed her hair back nervously and looked through the window one more time.

Rafe looked up and saw how nervous she was, and realized that she had scarcely heard the joke. He put the paper down.

"Darlin', why are you so worried?" he asked.

"It's just that I had almost gotten used to thinking Father dead," she said. "Now I am given new hope, and if it proves to be false, I shall have to go through a period of mourning again."

Rafe walked over to her and put his arms around her, pulling her to him.

"If Bill Herrick says your father is alive, he is alive."

"Do you trust him that much? He's a Yankee, isn't he?"

"I trust him," Rafe said. "North or South, he is still a man of honor."

There was a light knock on the hotel door, and Candy took a quick breath.

She looked at Rafe with hope barely daring to express itself in her eyes.

"Who is it?" Rafe called out.

"Cap'n Taylor?" a voice called from the other side of the door.

"Yes."

"Cap'n Taylor, I'm Boggs, sir, bos'n from the *Vanderbilt*," the voice answered. "I have someone here for you."

Rafe started for the door, but Candy wouldn't be denied. She let out a little cry of joy and rushed across the room to jerk the door open. She saw her father standing between two men.

"Father!" she shouted, and she threw herself into his arms with such energy that the two men who had been holding him by the arms were startled into letting him go. They started to reach for him again, but the bos'n, by a glance, told them to let him be.

"Oh, my darlin' daughter," Dr. Pratt said, embracing Candy with all his might. "I feared I would never see you again."

For a long, silent moment, the two embraced, exchanging in that time all the love and joy which each had thought gone forever. The bos'n and the two men who brought him, and Rafe, stood by silently, allowing father and daughter this moment alone. Finally, the bos'n spoke.

"Cap'n Taylor, sir, Cap'n Raymond's compliments, and he says to tell you that he has kept his word. Now he'll be wantin' you to keep you yours, sir. Will you meet with him to make the plans?"

"Tell your captain I'll be there this evening," Rafe said.

"Very good, sir," the bos'n said with a little salute. He nodded toward his two companions and they started back down the hallway. Rafe closed the door so that the three of them were alone in the room.

"Doctor, it is indeed good to see you again," Rafe said, shaking Dr. Pratt's hand.

"The feeling is mutual, I assure you," Dr. Pratt said. He looked around the hotel room. "It is not only good to be alive, but it is equally good to be free." He rubbed his wrists, and only then did Candy noticed there were marks on them from manacles.

"What is that?" she asked.

"They kept me chained to a bulwark in the 'tweendecks," Dr. Pratt said.

"Oh, how cruel of them!" Candy said angrily.

"I suppose it was the only way they could keep me in restraint," Dr. Pratt said. "Their brig was too small and was used only for recalcitrants from their own crew." Dr. Pratt laughed—a short, humorless laugh. "I don't know if they were doing that to protect their crew from me or me from their crew."

"Tell me, Doctor," Rafe said. "How did you escape?"

"We thought you were . . . were dead," Candy said.

"Yes, I even wasted a perfectly nice burial-at-sea ceremony on you," Rafe teased.

"Well, as you know, I was terribly seasick," Dr. Pratt said. "And when the storm came up, I began to feel closed in. So closed in that I thought I couldn't breathe. I know how foolish it was, but I couldn't contain myself. I rushed to the deck and hung onto the railing. It was about that time that the ship took a monstrous roll, and the next thing I knew, I was in the water."

"I know," Candy put in. "I saw you! Oh, I was never so shocked in my life! One minute you were there, and the next you were gone."

"Yes," Dr. Pratt said, smiling. "Well, you should have seen it from my end. I tried to call out, but every time I opened my mouth, it filled with salt water. Besides, it wouldn't have mattered; you would not have been able to hear me above the roar of the sea. And could you have heard me, you wouldn't have seen me, for the truth is, I could scarcely see the ship, so high were the waves. I tell you now, I made my peace with God, because I knew I was a goner."

"And then what happened?" Candy asked. They had crossed the room and were now sitting on a sofa, with Candy holding on to her father's arm as possessively as if she had no intention of ever letting him go again.

"I was bumped by a large floating piece of

wood, a hatch-cover of some sort. Evidently it had washed overboard from another ship. It made a sizable raft, and fortunately, I had the strength to climb on. I rode out the rest of the storm, and indeed the calm of the following day, on top of that tiny raft.'' Dr. Pratt laughed. ''It's funny. There, on board a large ship like the *Delta Dancer*, I was so seasick as to foolishly risk my life. But on the tiny raft, whose tossing and throwing about was many times more severe than the action of the *Delta Dancer*, I felt no sense of seasickness at all. I am a doctor, and yet I've no explanation for that.''

''Perhaps I can explain it,'' Rafe said.

''How?''

''Many times I have seen sailors who were seasick, just before we engaged in a battle. During the battle their malady disappeared often, only to return when the battle was quit. I believe the mind makes one seasick, and when the mind has other more important things to worry about, seasickness won't occur. When you were on the raft, your mind was not worried about seasickness, it was worried about survival, hence your relief from the malady.''

Dr. Pratt smiled. ''Perhaps you are right,'' he said. ''Maybe someday I can write a medical paper to that effect.'' Dr. Pratt looked around the hotel room. "This is a nice room," he said. "Whose is it?"

"Mine," Rafe and Candy said together. Candy blushed mightily as her father stared at her in surprise, but Rafe spoke up quickly.

"That is to say, I have taken the room for Candy," he said. "I thought it more fitting accomodations for her, than for her to remain on board the *Delta Dancer* with the rest of us."

"Yes, yes, well, that is quite nice of you," Dr. Pratt said. Candy, unable to look her father in the face for a moment, stood up and walked over to the window. When she looked out over the bay and saw all the ships, including the *Delta Dancer*, she remembered the price they were paying for her father's release, and she returned around.

"Rafe, don't go out and meet him," she said.

"What?"

"Captain Raymond. Don't take his challenge. Stay here, in port. He'll have to leave soon. The Navy won't let him stand off Nassau for the entire war, will they?"

"They might," Rafe said. "But whether they do or not doesn't matter. The point is, I gave my word to Captain Raymond, and I intend to keep it."

"But your heard Mr. Herrick. He said that the *Delta Dancer* wasn't the equal of the *Vanderbilt* in battle."

Rafe smiled. "He's first officer of the *Vanderbilt*, he has to think that way. But the truth is, the *Vanderbilt* is quite vulnerable. All we have to do is put a ball in the paddlewheels and the *Vanderbilt* will be totally unable to maneuver."

"That will be easier said than done," Dr. Pratt said. "The *Vanderbilt* has iron plating over the paddlewheels, from the top to the waterline. The plating is the same thickness as is on the *Monitor*, and you saw how the *Monitor* turned away cannon balls."

"The paddlewheels are armor-plated?"

"Yes," Dr. Pratt said. "And the engine and boilers as well."

"Hmm that does make it interesting, doesn't it? But, of course, we may have a few surprises of our own. He doesn't know that I have plated the engine and boilers of the *Delta Dancer*."

"Oh, but he does, my friend," Dr. Pratt said. "He not only knows; he has detailed drawings from the people who did it."

"What?"

"I overheard some of the men talking. This Captain Raymond is a pretty smart man. He read in the paper of the ship *Niagara* landing in Boston. Somehow he new the *Niagara* was you, and he went to Boston to try and catch you there. He just missed you, but he found out that you had repairs made, and he got engineering drawings of the armor plate you added to your ship. I tell you, Captain Taylor, he is a very smart man.''

"I've never had any delusions about that," Rafe said.

"Why does he hate you so?"

"I don't know that he hates me, exactly," Rafe said. "I think it is simply that I am his enemy and he is dedicated to doing his duty—that is, to destroy the enemy."

"No," Dr. Pratt said. "It is more than that. It is much more than that. I overheard his discussion with Mr. Herrick. Mr. Herrick cautioned him that releasing me to get to you might result in his dishonorable dismissal from the service, but Captain Raymond allowed as it was worth it for the opportunity to get you."

"Rafe, such determination frightens me," Candy said.

Rafe smiled.

"Don't worry. Oftentimes such determination makes a man careless. I think Captain Raymond will have his task cut out for him if he tries to take the *Delta Dancer*."

"Are you going to meet with him?"

"Yes, of course," Rafe said. When he saw that Candy was truly worried, he put his arms around her and pulled her to him. "Listen, I'd rather go into battle this way, knowing what to expect, than be surprised by an unexpected appearance. It's best this way, believe me. I'll fight the *Vanderbilt*, defeat her, then be back before you know it."

"I don't suppose there is any chance you will let me go?"

"No chance whatever," Rafe said, and he kissed Candy on the forehead. For the moment, they seemed oblivious of Candy's father, and he, discreetly seemed to find something interesting to examine out on the bay.

"And now, my dear, I must get to the meeting with my old friend, Captain Raymond," Rafe said.

The *Vanderbilt* lay lee of the *Delta Dancer*, isolated not only from it but from many of the other ships in the harbor as well. It stood above its own reflection in the still waters, with the Stars and Stripes hanging limply from the sternpost and the Captain's pennant hanging just as limply from the mainmast tack.

Charles Raymond leaned on his palms on the sill of his cabin windows and looked toward the *Delta Dancer*. He was glad it had survived its battle with the *Avenger*. If that fool yachtsman had bested the *Delta Dancer*, it would have been humiliating for Raymond.

Raymond turned away from his cabin window and looked at his reflection in his cabin mirror. He had the somewhat pugnacious appearance of a bulldog, and could have as well earned that sobriquet as Old Cannon Ball.

Charles Raymond should be a captain now. Or at least a full commander. He was, instead, an acting lieutenant commander, with the permanent rank of lieutenant. His permanent rank was no higher than that which had been held by Rafe Taylor, when Rafe Taylor was still in the Union navy. Raymond had gone to sea at the age of eight, as cabin boy for David Porter. There was no sea on earth he had not sailed, no ship, sail or steam, he could not command. And yet he had come up from the ranks, apprenticing as a midshipman at sea, while Rafe and others like him received a gentleman's education at the Naval Academy in Annapolis. And the crowning blow was when he saw the promotion list and realized that Rafe Taylor was being promoted to lieutenant commander with a permanent rank. That meant that Taylor, who had been his first lieutenant, would outrank him.

Livid with rage and green with envy, Raymond had gone to his old friend, Farragut, to ask why.

"Old warhorses like you and me, Charley, are being pushed aside," Farragut said. "We've got to make room for the new Navy. But, as it's for the good of the Navy, I'm willing to do so, and so should you be. After all, isn't the Navy what counts?"

"But this fellow has worked for me," Raymond

had protested. ''He came to me, still wet behind the ears. Everything he is, he learned from me.''

''Then you should be proud that he has been selected for early promotion, Charley,'' Farragut said. ''After all, that speaks well of you, for one of your command to be advanced so rapidly.''

''While I cool my heels as a lieutenant?''

''Yes, if need be,'' Farragut concluded, finally growing a little impatient with Raymond's complaining.

Of course, Rafe Taylor was never promoted to lieutenant commander because he resigned his commission to present himself for service to the Confederacy before the promotion list was activated. In fact, he never even knew he had been selected and thus was unaware of why Charles Raymond had conducted such a personal vendetta against him.

For Raymond, of course, the fact that Rafe had resigned from the Navy just before his promotion, simply bore out his own contention that the Department of Navy didn't know what they were doing. Not only were they attempting to promote someone who was junior to him in time and grade, but they were also willing to promote someone who had shown by his resignation to be a disloyal officer.

After Rafe left the Navy, Farragut wrote a letter to Raymond, apologizing for having had a hand in selecting one of Raymond's junior lieutenants over him. Farragut assured Raymond that his name had been inserted into the promotion list in place of Rafe Taylor's, and with the coming of war, he should attain a permanent rank to match his temporary position soon. Raymond didn't bother to thank Farragut. After all, he figured it was only his due. Besides, why should he be satisfied with being a mere lieutenant commander now? He felt that the war had provided him with an excellent opportunity to go even further. Commander, captain, perhaps even the lofty rank of commodore, if all his plans worked out.

Of course, Mr. Herrick was concerned that he may have left himself open for court-martial by releasing Dr. Pratt. What Mr. Herrick didn't know was, Raymond had no intention of allowing Dr. Pratt to remain free. As soon as he had taken care of Rafe Taylor, he would deal with Dr. Pratt.

There was a quiet knock on the cabin door, and Raymond interrupted his musing.

"Yes?"

"Cap'n, it's me, Boggs, sir."

Raymond opened the door. "Did everything go all right?" he asked.

"Aye, sir. Cap'n Taylor will meet you like you asked."

"Good. What about McCorkle?"

"Uh, well, sir, that's what I wanted to talk to you about."

"You mean you couldn't find him?"

"Yes, sir, we found him all right."

"Well, then, what is the problem? I told you to find him and take him prisoner. Did you do that?"

"No, sir. That is, not exactly," Boggs hedged.

"What do you mean not exactly? You either have him prisoner or you don't. I told you, I wanted him out of the way."

"He's out of the way all right," Boggs said. He looked toward the floor. "He's dead."

"Dead?"

"Aye, sir."

"How did that happen?"

"Well, sir, we found 'im in a bar jus' like we figured we would. But he had a pistol stuck down in his belt 'n he put up a fight. We didn't have no choice, Cap'n. It was him or us. We had to kill him."

Raymond rubbed his bald head for a moment; then he sighed.

"Well, I reckon if you had to kill him, you had to kill him," he said. "It's over and done, 'n' there's little we can do about it. Now, have you got everything else set up?"

"Aye, sir," he said. "I've got four armed men in the rocks, just waitin' for your signal."

"And Mr. Herrick doesn't suspect a thing?"

"No, sir," Boggs said.

"Very well, Bos'n, let's get on with it. Let's go meet Mr. Taylor."

"Aye, sir."

At approximately six thirty, Rafe, Candy and her father climbed the boarding ladder to the deck of the *Delta Dancer*. They were greeted by Midshipman Carter, who saluted Rafe, smiled self-consciously at Candy, then gawked in barely restrained shock at Dr. Pratt.

"That's right," Candy said, smiling broadly. "This is my father."

"But . . . how can it be?" Carter asked. "He was lost overboard."

"And rescued," Candy said.

"He'll have time to tell you about it," Rafe interrupted. "I want Miss Pratt and her father to remain aboard until after my meeting. I trust Bill Herrick, but I don't trust Captain Raymond."

"What meeting?" Carter asked.

"Captain Raymond rescued my father," Candy explained. "And now he has set my father free, in exchange for the chance to meet the *Delta Dancer* in a battle at sea."

"Ha!" Carter said, clapping his hands together. "Captain Raymond has just signed his own death warrant!"

"I said I didn't trust Captain Raymond," Rafe

said. "I didn't say he was a stupid man. If he didn't think he could beat us, he wouldn't challenge us. How many men are back aboard?"

"About eighty percent of the ship's company is aboard now, Cap'n," Carter reported.

"Good. Send parties ashore to find the rest of the men. Go into every bar and brothel on the island if you have to. Where is Mr. McCorkle?"

"He's still ashore, sir."

"Find him as well," Rafe said. "Make ready in all respects to get under way."

"When will that be, sir?" Carter asked.

"I don't know," Rafe answered. "I'm to meet with Captain Raymond now, and we'll work out a time and a place." Rafe started toward the ladder to return to the small boat; then he stopped and looked back at Carter. "Oh, by the way, there is a British warship in harbor, I believe. The *Wasp?*"

"Aye, sir," Carter said. "I met one of her midshipmen."

"Find out if they have any conical shells with steel points we can use for our parrot gun. I think they are equipped with a parrot gun of the same caliber."

"And if they do?"

"Try and buy a few rounds from them if you can. The *Vanderbilt* has iron plating over her sidewheels. Solid shot would be useless, even if we scored a direct hit there."

"Aye, Cap'n, I'll try," Carter said.

Rafe waved good-bye to Candy and her father, then climbed down the ladder and got into the boat. He looked back at the *Delta Dancer* as a hired man pulled at the oars of the water taxi. Seen from this angle, the *Delta Dancer* was clearly the most beautiful ship, perhaps the most beautiful creation, ever fashioned by the hands of man. It would be a shame to lose her in battle, and yet he couldn't very well refuse to fight her. After all, that was the purpose of her existence.

Rafe shook his head. There must be something inherently wrong with mankind if the most beautiful of all their creations was designed just for war.

Though it wasn't cold in these latitudes, it was still early enough in the spring that it was nearly dark by seven o'clock in the evening. When Rafe walked down to Bell Rock, a dark band of deep purple had already claimed the eastern horizon, and the shades of night were rapidly closing over everything else.

There was a wide spit of open sand between the line of palm trees in scrub brush and the edge of the water where a cluster of rocks were gathered around the one large rock known as Bell Rock. Sitting all alone in front of Bell Rock was Charles Raymond.

Rafe remembered the first time he had ever seen Captain Charles Raymond. He had looked nothing

at all like the picture of a commander Rafe had
constructed in his mind. Charles Raymond lacked
the polish of the officers Rafe had known at the
Academy. Rafe remembered wondering how such
an oaf ever rose to the rank of officer, let alone
managed to be placed in command of a ship.

Appearances were deceiving, however. Raymond
was an expert seaman, and he commanded with
the authority of one who expected his every order
to be carried out. He was, Rafe thought, a bit too
brutish for his tastes, too quick to administer
punishment. Rafe recalled being sickened at the
sight of grown men stripped to the waist and tied
to the tee for a lashing. It was a punishment
Captain Raymond was not loath to administer.
Despite all that, Rafe was willing to admit that his
service with Charles Raymond had been a valuable
experience. He had learned much, and he regretted
that they now found themselves on opposite sides
in a war.

Raymond stood as Rafe approached.

"Ah, Mr. Taylor," Raymond said. "Forgive
me. As you once pointed out, I lack the social
graces, and so I may have addressed you incorrectly.
Should it more properly be Captain Taylor? What
is your rank in that garbage scow navy, anyway?"

"I am the master of my own ship," Rafe answered easily. "That's all that matters."

"Yes, indeed," Raymond said. "You are the

master of your ship, and I am the master of mine. And, as you say, that is all that matters.''

"Captain Raymond, if you don't mind, sir, I would like to get on with the arrangements,'' Rafe said. "I have much to do to get ready for another battle so soon after the last one. I'm sure you can understand.''

"Oh, yes,'' Raymond answered. "I understand.''

"Then you will be so kind as to tell me when and where you wish us to meet?''

Raymond held his arm out, then, with the palm of his hand facing up, made a lifting motion. Four men suddenly stood up from the rocks, and all four were pointing pistols at Rafe.

"I figure this place is as good as any,'' Raymond said with a little chuckle.

Rafe looked around in surprise. "What the hell is this?'' he demanded. "What's going on? Who are these men?''

"These men are loyal, able-bodied seamen,'' Raymond said. "And you, Mr. Taylor, are my prisoner.''

"What? You can't do that,'' Rafe sputtered. "We are in a neutral port! I'm not subject to seizure.''

"You are a pirate, Mr. Taylor, and as such you are subject to seizure anywhere I find you.''

"What are you going to do with me?'' Rafe asked.

"Why, I'm going to take you back to the States in chains and disgrace," Raymond said. "Along with the nameplate of your ship, because when your ship finally does decide to come out, we'll be waitin' for her. Without you in command, she should be little more than target practice for my cannoneers."

"You forget Mr. McCorkle," Rafe said. "The ship will perform quite ably under his command."

"Oh, yes, Mr. McCorkle, your ex-first lieutenant."

"My ex-first lieutenant, you say?" Rafe asked, surprised by the statement. "What are you talking about?"

"I'm afraid your Mr. McCorkle met with an accident," Raymond said.

"What sort of accident?"

"When we tried to convince him that he should come aboard the *Vanderbilt* as our guest, he pulled a secreted gun and began shooting. We had no choice but to shoot back. He's dead, I'm afraid."

"Mac's dead?" Rafe asked in a tight voice.

"Quite dead," Raymond replied. "But this is war, after all, Mr. Taylor, and people do get killed in wars. Don't forget, you Southerners brought it all on."

"But this is a neutral port!" Rafe said again.

"So you said. I'm afraid I don't recognize neutrality," Raymond said. "Not when dealing with a pirate. Now, you will come aboard the *Vanderbilt* with me, and when the *Delta Dancer* does come out, you will have the distinction of seeing your own ship defeated in battle, from the decks of the opposing ship. How many are afforded that opportunity?''

"You're a madman," Rafe charged.

"If you mean mad in the sense that I have an unswerving desire to do my duty, then I plead guilty as charged," Raymond said. "But, if you will but stop to see the logic of my reason, you will be forced to admit, albeit reluctantly, that my plan is brilliant. Deprived of her two top officers, the *Delta Dancer* should be easy enough to defeat. I will have rid the sea of a scourge, and duty will have been served."

"You know what they say, Captain Raymond," Rafe said. "The plans of mice and men oftimes go awry."

Raymond smiled. "Yes, but I am pleased to report that, thus far, everything is going as planned. And I shall have an added bonus for you. Even now my men are at the Victoria Hotel. Miss Pratt and her father are being taken to the *Vanderbilt* where they, like you, will have the privilege of witnessing the final battle of the *Delta Dancer*, before you are all returned to Washington. Perhaps you and Dr. Pratt will share the same gallows."

For the first time, Rafe smiled.

"You smile," Raymond said, confused by Rafe's reaction. "Why do you smile?"

"Because," Rafe said, "it's too late. I have already anticipated your treachery, and Miss Pratt and her father have been moved to a safe place."

"I would have thought you knew by now," Raymond suggested.

"Knew? Knew what?"

"There is no such place as a safe place."

Chapter Eleven

Candy stood at the rail with Carter and her father, looking down toward the water as the longboat touched against the hull.

"Pig Meat? Did you find the captain or Mr. McCorkle?" Carter asked. Candy heard a note of anxiety in the young midshipman's voice.

"It ain't good, sir," Pig Meat said, climbing the boarding ladder. The two sailors who went ashore with him climbed up behind him, and they all stood in the splash of green light which the position lantern threw on the deck. It was now nearly midnight, and no one had heard from Rafe since he'd left for his meeting with Captain Raymond of the *Vanderbilt*.

"What?" Carter asked. "What is it?"

"Well, sir," Pig Meat said. "Mr. McCorkle, he's dead."

"What?" Carter gasped. "Are you certain?"

"If I ever seed a dead man, I'm certain," Pig Meat said. "They got 'im lyin' out on a table in the back of the constable's office."

"Well, what is it? What happened?"

"He was shot dead," Pig Meat said. "Some say it was in an argument, others say it was Yankee sailors offen the *Vanderbilt*."

"And Captain Taylor?"

Pig Meat shook his head. "Now, they ain't no one seen hide nor hair o' the cap'n since he went ashore," Pig Meat said. "It's like as if he's plumb disappeared. You want my thinkin'?"

"Yes, go ahead," Carter said.

"My thinkin' is this. The *Vanderbilt* cap'n knew he couldn't whup us iffen Cap'n Taylor was aboard, so they kilt him."

"No!" Candy said in an explosive breath. "No, that isn't true! Rafe isn't dead. I know he isn't."

"Maybe not, miss," Pig Meat said easily. "I was jes' givin' you my thinkin', that's all."

"But why?" Candy asked. "Why would Captain Raymond lure Rafe out to kill him?"

"So he would have a better chance in a fight agin us," Pig Meat said. "Then, jes' to make the chances better, they up 'n' kilt Mr. McCorkle, too.''

"No," Candy said. "No, I won't believe Rafe is dead. You didn't see his body, did you?"

"No, ma'am, I truly did not."

"But you did see McCorkle's body. If they left Mr. McCorkle's body for you to see, don't you think they would have left Captain Taylor's body as well?"

"Maybe so," Pig Meat said. "At any rate, Captain Taylor ain't nowhere on the island, and Mr. McCorkle is dead."

"What do we do now?" Carter asked.

"Well, sir, you bein' the only officer left on the *Delta Dancer*, Mr. Carter, I reckon you're gonna have to take command," Pig Meat said.

"I can't take command," Carter said. "I'm only seventeen years old," Carter said.

"That may be, but you are cap'n of this ship now," Pig Meat said. "You gotta tell us, Mr. Carter. What are we gonna do?"

Before Carter could answer, the sailor on watch called his attention to a light blinking from the deck of the *Vanderbilt*.

"Mr. Carter, signals from the *Vanderbilt*."

"What do they say?"

"They are in Morse code, sir; I can't read them."

"I can read them," Carter said. He looked at the signal for a moment, then turned away with a frightened expression on his face. "Oh," he said. "Oh, my."

"Mr. Carter, what is it?" Candy asked.

"They have demanded that we surrender the ship to them," he said. "If we don't, they are going to wait just out of the harbor and sink us the moment we leave."

"What are you going to do, Mr. Carter?" Pig Meat asked.

"I don't know," Carter said quietly. "I . . . I wish the captain was here. I don't know what to do."

"Well, I know," Candy suddenly said with a resolution which startled everyone. They looked at her. "We are going to fight."

"How can we fight without the captain?" Carter asked.

"You still have the same cannon, the same gunner's mates, the same powder monkeys as before, don't you?" Candy asked.

"Yes," Carter agreed.

"Then it seems to me that we have no choice. If we surrender this ship, you, Mr. Carter, will probably hang for piracy. Everyone else on the crew will be given long prison sentences. My father will be returned to have his sentence carried out, and I'll be put in prison as well. Is that a happy future for any of us?"

"The lady has a point, sir," Pig Meat said.

Carter walked out of the splash of green light and stood looking over toward the *Vanderbilt* for a long moment. Finally, he turned to face the others; he leaned against the rail and folded both arms across his chest. Candy had seen Rafe assume this same posture many times, and she wondered if Carter knew that he was imitating his commander. She felt good about seeing him in such a pose, for she believed it meant he had come to a decision.

"Pig Meat, light the signal lantern," he said. "I'm going to tell them that we will fight."

Pig Meat smiled broadly. "Right you are, sir!" he said.

Ding, ding. Ding, ding.

The ringing of four bells echoed through the otherwise quiet ship. It was two o'clock in the morning, and Candy was sure that everyone on this ship, with the exception of the deck watch who had just rung the bells, was sound asleep. She wished she could join them.

Candy fluffed up her pillow and turned over to try and find a more comfortable position. She closed her eyes, but it was to no avail.

It had been two hours since the conference on deck concluded. Two hours since Carter had made the decision to give battle to the *Vanderbilt*. No, more properly, that should be two hours since she had goaded Carter into making that decision.

Why had she done that? By her action she might well be condemning them all to death, for it wasn't inconceivable that the *Vanderbilt* could sink the *Delta Dancer* with all hands. Especially as Rafe wasn't in command.

Where is Rafe? Is he dead?

No. Candy didn't know where Rafe was now, but she was quite sure he wasn't dead. If he were dead, she felt she would know it.

Candy heard the measured pace of footsteps on the deck above her, and finally, she sat up. A bar of soft moonlight streamed in through the air scupper, projecting a perfect circle on the wall. That tiny bit of silver light made her feel confined in the small cabin. She was sleeping in a nightgown, so she wrapped a blanket around her shoulders, got up and opened the door.

She stepped out into the bay and heard the heavy breathing and snoring of a dozen men. They were lying on coils of rope, curled into corners and wedged between bulkheads. It had surprised her the first time she discovered men sleeping there, but she soon learned that there were no quarters, as such, for the seamen. They were expected to sleep wherever they could find a place.

Candy picked her way through the sleeping bodies until, finally, she reached the ladderway which led topside. She climbed up to the deck and walked across to stand at the railing. The moon danced a ghostly image across the bay, and a dozen ships rocked in gentle sleep.

The *Vanderbilt* was gone!

Candy let out a little gasp as soon as she noticed it.

"She hauled anchor about an hour ago," a voice said.

Candy turned around to see Carter standing behind her.

"She's out there," he said. "Just waiting on us."

"Let her wait," Candy said. "We are the measure of her."

"No," Carter said, shaking his head.

"You don't think *Delta Dancer* is as good a ship as the *Vanderbilt?*"

"I think *Delta Dancer* is a wonderful ship," Carter said.

"You have no confidence in the men?"

"This ship's company is the finest crew I've ever encountered," Carter said, and so sincere was his declaration that Candy stifled the grin which would have said that she knew this was the only crew he had ever encountered.

"Well, then, what is it?" she asked.

"It's me," Carter said, and his voice nearly broke. "Miss Pratt, I can't command these men; I'm not even a man myself."

Candy measured the anguish of the young

midshipman; then, in a sudden flash of clarity born amidst the precariousness of their situation, she knew what she must do. She must make him a man.

There was a faint welling of protest from the woman whose propriety had not all been subverted by her uninhibited love affair with Rafe Taylor. But that little spark of protest was quickly beaten down by the strong feeling that what she was going to do was right and proper under the circumstances. And though she didn't want to admit it to herself, even now, there was a secret spark of excitement over the prospect.

"Of course you are a man," Candy said in a low, throaty voice. "Do you think years make the man? A person becomes a man by his experiences and by his feelings. You have been aboard the *Delta Dancer* for nearly a year now. That should count for something."

Candy shivered. She did it partly because the night air had grown cool and partly because she wanted to make Carter think she was cold. And part of it, she knew, was in anticipated pleasure, for though she tried to tell herself that she was doing this for the good of the ship, she knew also that it did not hold the prospect of being an unpleasant duty.

"Are you . . . are you cold, Miss Pratt?" Carter asked.

"Yes, a little," Candy said. She moved to him and put her head on his shoulder. Instinctively, Carter put his arms around her. That was exactly what Candy had in mind, and she used his expression to maximum advantage. She leaned into him, pressing her body against his. She was wearing only a thin nightgown, and she knew that he would be able to feel the fullness of her breasts, the hardness of her nipples, and the warmth of her flesh through the thin material.

"You . . . you don't feel cold," Carter said, and the words were strained.

Candy increased the pressure, and now her flat stomach and thighs were glued to his body. She felt a bulge in the front of his pants, and she smiled as she realized she had been successful.

Abrubtly, Carter drew away.

"I . . . I'm sorry, Miss Pratt," he said. "Please forgive me. I had no right to take advantage of you like that."

"I forgive you," Candy said. She shivered again. "But I am still cold. Perhaps you would take me to the captain's cabin and give me a bit of rum? That would warm me, I'm sure."

"I . . . I can't go to the captain's cabin, miss," Carter said.

"Of course you can," Candy said. "After all, you are the captain, aren't you? And my name is

Candy. Now, are you known by any name other than Carter?''

"Jesse," Carter answered.

"Let's go to the captain's cabin, Jesse, shall we?" Candy invited.

Candy led the way, moving quietly so as not to awaken anyone, but resolutely so Carter wouldn't lose his courage.

"I think you will find some rum there, in the top left drawer of the desk," she said, pointing to the desk when they entered the cabin.

"You've been in here before, then?" Carter asked.

"A few times," Candy answered with a smile.

Candy sat on the bed and let the blanket she was carrying drop. The nightgown was open at the neck, and the creamy tops of her breasts were clearly visible. Carter looked at them, then looked away pointedly, but not before Candy was able to see the raw hunger in his face. The bulge in his trousers had returned, too, and despite Carter's attempt to stand in such a way as to disguise it, it was clearly visible.

"Oh, uh, here is the rum," Carter said. He poured some into a glass and handed it to Candy.

Candy tossed it down quickly. Normally, she didn't care much for drink, but she felt that, under the present circumstances, a drink would be beneficial.

Carter was still standing over her, and Candy put the glass down, then looked up at him and smiled, holding him in a long, penetrating gaze. Carter tried at first to look away, but he found that he couldn't. Then, as if having lost control over his own actions, he leaned down and put his lips to hers in a kiss.

He was very young and inexperienced, but the state of sexual arousal to which Candy had pushed him made up for his inexperience. She felt his mouth firm against hers, and she allowed her tongue to dart out and flick across his lips. The effect was instantaneous, and he gasped and pulled away in shock.

"I . . . I'm sorry," he said again.

"Don't apologize, Jesse," Candy said. "You are a man, and you are experiencing the feelings of a man. It is natural. Just as it is natural for me, a woman, to respond to you."

"You . . . you are responding to me?" Carter asked in a choked voice.

"I can't keep my hands off you," Candy said, and she put her arms around his neck and pulled him down to her. She put her mouth to his neck and nibbled on it gently, then moved back up to his lips. She kissed him again, and this time, when her tongue darted across his lips, he opened them, making way for her tongue to stab inside him and plumb the depths of his mouth.

Carter practically lost all control then, and he began fumbling with her nightgown, trying to pull it up, while at the same time pulling at the buttons and ties of his own clothes.

"Let me," Candy said. "I'll take care of it for both of us."

Gently, Candy pushed Carter down on the bed, then, in one easy motion, she pulled the nightgown up and over her head. She was on her knees beside him, and she was totally nude. Her body shined in a soft gold from the subdued light of the gimbals lamp, and she displayed it before Carter unashamedly, proudly.

Carter had never seen a naked woman before, and he stared at her hungrily. Candy looked down into his big brown eyes, open wide now in eager innocence. She could practically see her own reflection in those eyes. Carter took in the smooth, uninterrupted flow of her skin from the upthrusting breasts and tightly drawn nipples, all the way down to the soft, glowing triangle of hair to which his eyes inevitably traveled.

Candy smiled at him, then leaned over to begin loosening his clothes. She found that she was enjoying the role of seducer immensely. Here was a young virgin, a boy who would soon become a man, and all because of her. It was a sense of power she had never before experienced. She didn't feel the same degree of sexual excitation she felt with Rafe. With Rafe, there was a willingness to share, to be both the aggressor and the dominated. With Carter, she was the aggressor only, and she was reluctant to relinquish that position.

Slowly, Candy removed Carter's clothing. First came his shirt, then his shoes, and finally his trousers. Her fingers brushed against his skin, and she felt the heat of his body flare up beneath her touch. She could feel the fierce beating of his heart and she could understand the excitement he was feeling. She had felt the same thing her first time with Rafe—fear, wonder, pleasure and desire, and now, vicariously, she was feeling it all again.

"I . . . I have a confession to make," Carter said in a choked voice. "I, uh," he cleared his throat. "I've never done this before."

"You will enjoy it," Candy said. "I promise you, you will enjoy it."

Candy kissed him on each of his bare shoulders, then in the hollow of his neck. She leaned down so that the nipples of her breasts rubbed against his burning skin, and she felt the heat transfer from his skin, first through her nipples, and then it spread through her entire body. Until now she had been experiencing a degree of pleasure, but it had been a detached pleasure, as if she were watching someone else. Not until this moment did her own internal heat flare up, lighting her body as if it were a furnace whose fires had just been stoked.

She had been telling herself that she was seducing Mr. Carter to strengthen his will, to lead him into manhood. The hot dampness of her womb belied that now. She was seducing him because she wanted him.

Candy lay down beside him then; she raised the arm nearest him and put it behind her head. The action made her breast flatten out into a gently rounded mound, though the tight rosebud of a nipple still protruded from the graceful curve of her body. The nipple, thus accented, seemed to inflame the young midshipman's ardor all the more, and he bent down to it and took it between his lips with a sweet, sucking sound.

Candy looked down at him, at his dark, boyishly unruly hair resting on her breast, while his lips and tongue worked a magic which had to come by instinct and desire since he'd had no previous experience. She put her hands on his head and ran her fingers through his hair, while his own hand moved, tentatively at first, then with increasing eagerness, down her naked body. It hesitated just at the edge of that part of her which now throbbed for want of attention, and she moved her body so that his hand plunged into an area totally new to him. The heat and tactile sensations emboldened him to further experiment, until Candy felt him moving instinctively into position over her. She helped him where such help was needed;

then, with a little gasp of pleasure, she felt him thrust into her.

Candy no longer held any illusions about what she was doing or why. She surrendered herself to her desires and Jesse Carter's youthful eagerness. She felt his weight on her and she thrust herself up against him, sharing with him the limits of her experience and passion.

It was all new for the young midshipman, but, in a sense, it was new for Candy as well. She had come to think of herself as one experienced in this sort of thing, but that experience was limited to one man in the person of Rafe Taylor. Now she was discovering that her passions and desires could be awakened independent of love.

It started then, a tiny but familiar tingling which began deep in her womb, then pinwheeling out and spinning faster and faster and faster until every part of her body was caught up in a whirlpool of pleasure. She felt as if her body had been wound like the mainspring of a clock, tighter and tighter, until, finally, a burst of rapturous pleasure washed over her, and her body achieved the release and satisfaction it had long yearned for. She felt as if her skin were pricked by a million tiny pins, and she shivered in total delight.

Shortly after she had experienced her own sweet pleasure, she remembered that she had begun this experiment to introduce young Carter to manhood.

She concentrated on just that, and a moment later she was rewarded by hearing his involuntary cry of joy, and feeling a racking through his body as he was struck by a shattering climax. Unexpectedly, she was carried along with him, and a second, then a third orgasm swept over her, bringing her to a peak of fulfillment greater even than the first time.

Finally, they were convulsed by one last shudder of ecstasy, and they collapsed onto the bed, lying in each other's arms for a long, long moment, before either of them spoke.

Inexplicably, Carter giggled.

Candy, surprised by his laugh, raised herself up on one elbow and looked down at him.

"Why did you laugh?" she asked.

"You know, I've heard the men talk and talk and talk about it," he said. "Sometimes, it seems like that's all they talk about. And I've wondered, *why?* What was there about it which could so affect a person as to dominate all conversation? And now I know."

"Now you know what, silly?" Candy asked, smiling.

"Why, I know what it's all about," he said. "I'm a man. At last, I'm a man. And it's wonderful!"

Candy laughed gaily, and throughout the ship sailors stirred in their sleep, with their dreams

enriched by the sudden and unexpected appearance
of a beautiful, laughing maiden.

The sky was bright blue, but the Gulf Stream
was running heavy, and there were deep troughs
between the waves. The *Delta Dancer* was pitch-
ing and rolling, yet Candy, who stood just beneath
the mizzenmast, clutching the shroud, felt not in
the least queasy. Even her father had acquired his
sea legs, and he was standing close by.

Near the helm, with binoculars to his eyes and
his legs spread and braced against the sea swell,
Midshipman and now acting Captain Jesse Carter,
looked out across the tossing Atlantic. He had
been gone from the bed when Candy awakened
this morning. They had not spoken of the night
before at all today, though once she did catch
Carter looking at her, only to see him then look
away with an embarrassed smile.

There was, however, one other sign of what had
transpired during the previous night. Carter seemed
possessed of a new confidence and a more manly
bearing which the crew noticed. They put it off as
merely an example of a young boy growing instantly into a man's job. Candy felt that her own
contribution had been significant.

The object of Carter's attention was a piece of
sail which jutted just above the horizon off the
starboard rail. The lookout reported that the distant

ship was making sail, and there was little doubt in anyone's mind as to who it was. It was the *Vanderbilt,* waiting for them, just as Captain Raymond had promised.

"Cap'n, the ship is ready in all respects to do battle, sir," the bos'n reported. "Though with this roll it's going to be hell to get our guns to bear."

"The *Vanderbilt's* in the same sea," Carter answered. "We'll just have to do the best we can."

"Aye, aye, sir," the bos'n replied, saluting and returning to go down the gun deck and talk with each gun captain.

"Dr. Pratt, you'll assist me in surgery, sir?" the ship's surgeon asked, poking his head up through the hatchway.

"Yes, of course," Dr. Pratt said, jarred out of his complacency. "I'll be right there." He looked over at his daughter. "Where will you be during the battle?" he asked.

"I'll be where I can do the most good," she answered easily.

Dr. Pratt raised his hand. "Not that it will do any good to tell you," he said, "but do try and be careful."

"Don't worry about me, Father," Candy said. "I'll be all right, I promise."

Candy watched her father disappear down the

hatch; then she walked over to stand by Midshipman Carter.

"How long do you think it will be?" she asked.

Carter looked at her. Last night she had been the one with the experience. It had been her skill and knowledge and courage which had led them. Today it was a different story. She was coming to him for solace, and it made him feel good.

"Less than an hour, I'd say," Carter replied. "Are you frightened?"

"Yes," Candy answered. "Are you?"

"No," Carter replied hastily. Then he smiled and looked down at the deck. "That's a lie," he said. "I am frightened. But I know I won't be so scared as to do anything foolish."

"That's what real bravery is," Candy said. "Doing the best you can do, even if you are frightened by it."

"Miss Pratt," Carter started, and Candy put her hand on his arm.

"Don't you think we know each other well enough for you to call me Candy?" she asked.

"Candy," Carter said. He put his hand on top of hers. "I want to thank you for last night."

Candy smiled. "It was a pleasure," she said.

"Yes, it was," Carter agreed, and she thought she saw a tiny blush appear. "But that's not what I mean. I became a man last night. If something happens to me today, if I am killed in battle . . . ."

"No," Candy said, putting her fingers to his lips. "No, you mustn't even think that. You're young. You're much too young to be thinking of death."

Carter smiled, and suddenly their roles were reversed. She felt the young innocent.

"No, I'm old," Carter said. "I'm very old. Everyone is old when they are killed in battle. You can't get any older than dead."

"But, please, don't talk like that," Candy said.

"It is a possibility which must be faced," Carter said. "I only wanted to tell you that I can face it better today than ever before. At least, if something happened to me now, I won't have to die never having known the pleasure of a woman. And for that, Candy, I thank you more than words can say."

Candy wanted to answer him, but she couldn't. Suddenly and inexplicably, her eyes had filled with tears and her throat grew choked. She turned away from him and watched the approaching sails.

Chapter Twelve

Rafe Taylor sat on the floor in the 'tween decks, forward of the port wheel box. There was a steel cuff around his ankle and a length of chain, about six feet long, running from the cuff to the forward bulkhead.

There was not enough room to stand upright in the 'tween decks, and the gun crews who were readying their guns had to move around in a semi-crouch.

When he first came aboard, Rafe Taylor had been the object of much attention and teasing. He didn't realize how much fame his name had generated in the North until some of the sailors came back later and, quietly, asked him for his autograph.

None of the officers had spoken to him, including Bill Herrick. Rafe regretted that, though he imagined that Bill Herrick was quite ashamed of his unwitting role in the deception which had led to Rafe's capture.

From up on deck, Rafe could hear the long drum roll. There were shouted orders and the scuff of feet as people ran across the deck. Powder boys began passing leather pouches of powder about, and shoes were removed as the gun crews started preparing for the impending battle. Bare feet could grip the deck more securely if the deck became soaked with blood. The breeching ropes were checked and the tampons were removed from the muzzles of the cannon.

The captain of the gun which was nearest Rafe was an old Irishman with many years at sea. Rafe knew him fairly well, for the Irishman had served under Rafe when Rafe was a gunnery officer on the *Congress*.

"Mike," Rafe asked. "What is it? Why are the guns being readied?"

" 'Tis your ship, sir," Mike replied. "Sure'n the *Delty Dancy* has poked her beautiful nose outta the hole. I 'spect we're gonna be in for a wee bit of a fight."

"You're sure it's the *Delta Dancer*?"

"As sure as we know where her armor lies," Mike said. "You see, Mr. Taylor, we have drawin's o' the *Delty Dancy* plastered all about. Each gun crew has the drawin' right over the gun port, like this.''

Mike pointed to a piece of paper tacked to the side, just above the gun port, and even from this distance, Rafe could tell that it was an excellent likeness of his ship.

"That's her, all right," Rafe said. He tried to lean forward to see through the gun port.

"She's not in position to see now, sir, but she's maneuverin' about," Mike said. "When she comes up, I'll tell you so you can have a look-see."

"Thanks, Mike."

" 'Tis no bother," Mike said. "The truth is, I allus liked you, Mr. Taylor. You were the whitest gunnery officer I ever knew. You really cared 'bout your men. 'Tis a shame you've gone to the other side.''

"It's a shame there *is* another side," Rafe answered.

"Sure'n that's the truth now."

"Hey, Mike," one of the other gun captains called. "How'll we charge our pieces?"

"I'd say sixty-four pound solid ball with a ten pound propellant charge," Mike answered.

Rafe leaned his head back against the bulkhead and closed his eyes. Mike's prescription was exactly right. There had been a few times when his ship had been struck with what would have been a fatal blow, except for mistakes made by the gunners. A projectile which was too light and a propellant charge which was too heavy concentrated whatever destructive energy the ball had when it hit its target so that it localized all its force on the point of impact. Such missiles usually passed right through without doing much more damage. A good hit from the ordnance mix Mike had suggested, however, would have a terrible effect. A heavy low-velocity ball would spread its energy out on impact, stoving in sides and crushing spars and frames.

"Rafe?"

Rafe opened his eyes and saw Bill Herrick standing over him.

"Rafe, it's the *Delta Dancer,*" Bill said. "She's showing fight; she's already backed her sails and is coming around to offer her broadside."

"It looks as if Raymond is going to get his fight, after all," Rafe said.

"Who's in command?" Bill asked. "With you here and Mr. McCorkle gone . . ."

"Mr. McCorkle murdered, you mean," Rafe interrupted.

"Rafe, I regret that," Bill said. "I regret it more than you can know. But, I swear to you, I didn't have anything to do with it."

"You are the first officer," Rafe said. "You must share in everything your captain does."

"And so I must," Bill admitted. He sighed. "But what is done is done. Now, tell me, who is in command of the *Delta Dancer?* Who is your third in command?"

"Bill, you know I can't tell you that."

"Then tell me this. Do you think there is any chance your ship will surrender if we give them the opportunity? I ask this because, without you in command, they have no chance. There are going to be many lives lost. I seek only to prevent that."

"It's too late for that, Bill," Rafe said. "Lives are going to be lost."

"Mr. Herrick to the deck," someone called, and the call was repeated by someone even closer so that Herrick, with a sigh, had to leave Rafe at his point of confinement and return to the deck.

"Mr. Taylor, you can see your ship now, sir, if you look through the gun port," Mike said, and Rafe, thanking him, moved up to take a look.

The *Delta Dancer* was beautiful—lean and trimmed for battle, rolling in the heavy swells at about a thousand yards distant.

Rafe saw a puff of white smoke erupt from the *Delta Dancer*. About one second later he heard the flat thump of the explosion.

"There's a ball, goin' over our head by a mile," Mike said, and everyone on the forward gun deck laughed nervously. "No," Rafe said under his breath. "You must time the swells. Fire at the wrong time and the swell will lift the gun too high.''

"Let that be a lesson to you, mates,'' Mike yelled to the other gun crews on the forward deck. "You can't fire when you're on the upswell.''

"Where the hell did that shot go?'' Candy heard one of the men on the *Delta Dancer* ask.

"It went high!'' Carter yelled to the gun crew which had fired the first round. "It went way over their heads. We've got to fire at just the right time.''

The entire port side of the *Vanderbilt* poured out smoke then, followed a second later by a loud, flat-sounding thump. Candy heard the balls whistle just overhead; then she saw them raise geysers of water behind the *Delta Dancer*. The *Vanderbilt* had also fallen victim to the swells, though their calculations had been closer than those of the *Delta Dancer* gunners.

"They got closer than we did,'' Candy said.

"Yes,'' Carter replied. "They'll be on target with the next volley.'' Carter picked up a speaking trumpet and yelled to the gunners on the starboard side.

"Men, remember Captain Taylor, and remember Mr. McCorkle. Fight as if they were by your side!''

The men cheered.

"Mind the swell now, men!" Pig Meat called. "Gunners at the ready!"

The ship caught an upswell and the guns rose high. Pig Meat measured the swell; then, as the ship started coming back down, he shouted: "Fire!"

Candy watched as every gun on the starboard side fired. There was a deafening roar and a tremendous billowing of smoke. The guns all kicked back against the breeching ropes, and the ropes strained against the recoil until Candy feared they would break. Water splashed up near the *Vanderbilt*. There were no hits, but this volley was much closer than the first shot had been.

Immediately after the guns fired, one man on each crew rammed a wet sponge down the barrels. Candy knew that was to make certain there were no burning sparks remaining inside, waiting to set off the next charge of powder prematurely.

The *Vanderbilt* was maneuvering under the power of its side paddles. By reversing one and going forward on the other, she was able to come about almost at once, and now she presented her starboard side. The distance between them had closed considerably, and when her starboard batteries discharged, the sound was almost instantaneous.

With the guns so close, it wasn't possible to follow the path of the cannon balls while they were in flight. But it wasn't hard to see where they hit. They missed the *Delta Dancer*, but they were so close that they threw water up on the deck, and Candy was drenched by the spray.

The *Delta Dancer* loosed another salvo, and this time they hit the *Vanderbilt* with two of the balls, though the strikes were against the iron plating which covered the side-mounted paddlewheels. Both of the balls bounced high into the air with no apparent damage to the ship.

The next volley from the *Vanderbilt* dealt a telling blow. Balls crashed through the side of the ship, and Candy could hear the crunch of heavy timbers being carried away below deck. The distance between the two ships grew shorter.

"Sharpshooters aloft!" Carter shouted, and half a dozen riflemen went aloft, ready to fire at targets of opportunity on board the *Vanderbilt*.

A sudden cheer told Candy that the last volley loosed toward the *Vanderbilt* had struck home. She saw a gaping hole appear just behind the wheel box, and the cannon which had been firing from that position tumbled out and into the sea.

The cheer soon turned to groans, however, as another *Vanderbilt* volley struck home, this time killing and wounding all the men in one of the gun crews.

The ships continued to maneuver and fire for the better part of an hour. Time after time the volleys found their targets, so that the deck of the *Delta Dancer* became a mess with fallen masts and yards and cordage. Then a new danger presented itself as the *Vanderbilt* began firing canister shot. Clouds of flying metal tore into the side of the *Delta Dancer*, poking holes in the decking, cutting through the lines, and leaving in its path half a dozen dead and dying men.

"Candy, they're using grape!" Carter shouted. Though there was a slight difference between grape and canister, the two names were often used interchangably. "Get below decks, you. . . ." That was as far as Carter got because his warning was cut off by another volley of grape, this time aimed for the helm. Carter and the man at the helm were both cut down.

"Jesse!" Candy shouted, running over to him. She dropped down beside him and heard his breathing, rough and ragged. There was blood on his chest and it bubbled as he spoke.

"I was doing all right, wasn't I?" he asked. "You'll tell the captain I was doing all right?"

"You were doing magnificently," Candy said. She looked up and saw Pig Meat dragging a body away from the nearest gun. "Pig Meat, it's Mr. Carter. Get him below quickly, please."

Pig Meat came over and picked Carter up gently, then looked into his face. He looked at Candy.

"I'm sorry, Miss Pratt," he said quietly. "The boy's gone."

"The helm! She's falling away!" someone

shouted, and Candy saw that the wheel was spinning hard as the ship was turning away from the *Vanderbilt*. This way, none of the *Delta Dancer's* guns would come to bear, while her stern was offered for a raking hull shot.

The *Vanderbilt* took immediate advantage of the situation and a volley smashed through the poop of the ship. Again there was the terrible sound of crushed timbers, followed by terrible screams of agony.

"The cap'n's cabin has been stove in!" someone shouted. "The ship's surgeon, Dr. Pratt, all the wounded, they've been kilt!"

"Father?" Candy shouted. She started for the hatch, but one of the sailors grabbed her.

"You don't want to go down there, miss. It ain't a very pretty sight."

How cruel, Candy thought. Her father was rescued from the gallows, then lost at sea and found again, only to be killed while attending to others.

"Miss Pratt, take the helm!" Pig Meat called. "The bos'n's been kilt!"

"What do I do?" Candy asked, stepping up to the wheel.

"Just keep us broadside of the other ship," Pig Meat said.

"Pig Meat, the conical shells!" Candy shouted. "Fire the conical shells at the paddlewheels."

"Aye, lass, that's a good idea," Pig Meat said,

and a moment later the rifled gun which fired conical shells was put in position. The first round penetrated the iron plating over the paddlewheel, then exploded. Pieces of the wheel flew everywhere, and the *Vanderbilt* began burning amidship.

The men on the *Delta Dancer* cheered, and at Pig Meat's instruction, they loaded a second shell and fired it. This one penetrated the *Vanderbilt's* hull just in front of the paddlewheel, and everyone waited with bated breath for it to go off, for they believed it to be near the powder magazine. An explosion in the powder magazine, they knew, would be the end of the *Vanderbilt*.

When the paddlewheel was hit, fragments of wreckage flew in all directions like shrapnel. A dozen men fell with mortal wounds, and had Rafe been in a kneeling position as he had been just a moment before, he would have been killed as well. As it was, the jagged piece of metal which poked through the bulkhead just above him sprayed him with splinters which, while causing no serious injury, did bloody his face.

"Mr. Taylor, sir, are you badly hurt?" Mike yelled at him.

"No," Rafe answered.

"What was that? I didn't think they had a ball that could crash through the iron plating."

"It was a conical shell with a steel point," Rafe said. "I brought twenty of them aboard."

"I hope they aren't all lucky hits," Mike said.

At that instant another shell crashed into them, this one coming right through the gun port of Mike's gun. The gun was dismounted, and the shell, after having done that damage, plunked into the center frame. The steel point of the shell dug about fourteen inches into the wooden beam, while the end of the shell stuck out. The fuse was still burning. It was about two feet away from Rafe.

"Mike, this shell is going to explode!" Rafe yelled.

There was no answer.

"Mike!" Rafe yelled again. All this time he had been unable to take his eyes off the smoldering, sputtering fuse of the shell. Death was just twenty-four inches away, and he was resigned to watch it happen. When Mike didn't answer, he looked around and saw that Mike had been killed by the dismounted gun. Two of his crew had been killed with him, and the others were so dazed as to be insensible.

Rafe looked back at the shell. This was it. He was going to die now. He thought of Candy and of the brave men on the *Delta Dancer*. It was ironic, he thought, that he should be killed by his own men. And yet, even though it meant his death, he was proud of the way the ship had fought.

The shell popped about as loudly as a pistol report, but there was no explosion. The powder charge was defective.

"Rafe! Rafe, are you still alive?"

Rafe recognized Bill's voice, but he couldn't see him. There was a great gaping hole in the side of the ship, through which sunlight poured, but, though the darkness of the 'tween decks had been dispelled, it was still impossible to see because of the smoke. Sunbeams stabbed through the smoke to create an opaque wall of brilliance.

"I'm over here," Rafe said.

Bill worked his way through the smoke until he reached Rafe. He knelt beside him and began unlocking the ankle cuff.

"There's a boat tied onto the rudderpost," Bill said. "If you go out through the side, do you think you can make it to the boat?"

"Yes," Rafe said. He rubbed his ankle gingerly. "What's happening? Why are you letting me go?"

"The captain's been wounded," Bill said.

"Badly?"

"He may lose a leg, but he'll live. The surgeon's operating on him now. I'm going to break off the fight."

"Is your ship hurt that badly?"

Bill pointed to the paddlewheel. "We can't maneuver," he said. "Without the ability to maneuver, we can't fight. I just hope there's enough cordage to hold the sail we need to get out of here.''

"When he finds out that you let me go, there's going to be hell to pay, you know."

"I'm not going to tell him I let you go," Bill said. "I'm just going to let him wonder what happened to you."

"Bill, you know we'll meet again, don't you?" Rafe said. "He's not going to let it go at this."

"I know," Bill said. "Now go. And good luck!"

Rafe stepped over the dismounted gun and up to the jagged hole in the side of the ship. He took a deep breath, then dived out to the side. There was a breathtaking drop; then he hit the water. He stayed underwater as he swam toward the stern of the *Vanderbilt*. He saw the smashed paddlewheel, hanging down from its well in pieces, and as he passed it by, he felt a heavy concussion very close by. He was startled by the concussion and looked around to see a cannon ball passing by, its momentum checked by the water. Even though the water had checked its momentum, he realized that it could have easily broken his back had it hit him squarely.

Rafe finally surfaced astern of the *Vanderbilt*, and he drew a deep breath, glad to be into the air once again. He saw the boat there, just as Bill had told him it would be, and he pulled himself over the side, then cut the boat loose and let it drift

away. At about the same time, he saw sail going
up on the *Vanderbilt*, and her one remaining paddle began beating fiercely against the water. The
rudder was hard a'port to compensate for the loss
of the port wheel, and the *Vanderbilt* started pulling away.

Rafe looked back toward the *Delta Dancer*, and
then realized why Bill had set him free. The *Delta
Dancer* was leeward of the *Vanderbilt*, but, with
power, it had the proper angle to cut off any
retreat the *Vanderbilt* might try and make. However,
with Rafe cast adrift, the *Delta Dancer* would
have to change its heading, then back down to
pick him up. All that would take several minutes,
and by the time Rafe was safely aboard, the
Vanderbilt would be gone.

Rafe sat in the bobbing boat and watched his
ship as she came toward him. He knew he had
been seen, and recognized, by the resolute way
she advanced toward him. On the one hand, he
was happy he was being rescued. On the other, he
regretted the fact that the *Vanderbilt* was getting
away, and reluctantly, he had to give Bill Herrick
his due. It was a good plan.

It took nearly twenty minutes for the *Delta
Dancer* to make its approach. Rafe watched as it
drew near. The fighting sails were riddled with
cannon ball and canister, and he could see loose
cordage hanging from the arms. There were holes

in the hull, and he noticed that the spanker gaff had been shot away. He realized, also, that the holes in the hull meant there was a very good chance of even greater damage which couldn't be seen.

Despite the damage and despite the heavy swells of the rolling sea, the *Delta Dancer* came straight on. At last he saw the sails spilling air, and he heard the change in the engine as the ship backed down, then crept up alongside. A ladder was dropped to him and he climbed it to the deck.

"Darling!" Candy greeted him as he stepped over the railing. She put her arms around him and they stood together in a long embrace. "You're home," she said.

Rafe returned her embrace, then looked around at the ship. Only one cannon was dismounted, but there were holes and broken timbers everywhere. He saw a dozen men in bloody bandages.

"Oh, you're hurt!" Candy said, putting her hand to Rafe's bloody face.

"Not badly," Rafe said, taking her hand in his.

"When did it happen?"

"When you hit the paddlewheel," Rafe said. "That was a good shot."

"Pig Meat aimed the cannon," Candy said.

Rafe looked over and saw Pig Meat at the helm.

"Good job, Pig Meat. That turned the tide of battle. Where's Mr. Carter, and Andy?"

"Dead, the both of them," Candy said. "Along with the ship's surgeon and my father." Though she had been brave up until now, her voice cracked with her last statement, and Rafe put his arms around her again. He pulled her to him and patted her hair softly.

"How many men did we lose?" he asked.

"Seventeen killed, twenty-two wounded," Candy said.

"What about below decks? What kind of damage down there?"

"Your cabin was totally demolished," Candy said. "In fact, that was when we lost most of our men, because there were half a dozen wounded in there, besides my father and the surgeon."

"What about structural damage, Pig Meat? Any damage to the keel that can't be repaired?"

"The ship was shot up pretty good, Cap'n," Pig Meat said. He smiled. "But she warn't broken."

"And you were here during all of that?" he asked Candy.

"She was a lot more than just here, Cap'n," Pig Meat said. "She took the helm after the helmsman was kilt."

"You had the helm during the battle?" Rafe asked in wonder.

"Yes," Candy said.

Rafe chuckled. "I can't seem to get rid of you, can I?"

"I'm not that easy to get rid of," Candy admitted. "So you might as well quit trying."

"Maybe I will, at that," Rafe said. "Pig Meat?"

"Aye, sir?"

"Let Candy have the helm, and you summon all hands."

"Aye, sir," Pig Meat said, and he relinquished the wheel to Candy, who took it with complete confidence. Pig Meat left to gather all hands while Rafe stood quietly, hands on his hips, surveying the damage to the ship. He wasn't sure how badly hurt she was below deck, but the damage he could see up here was mostly superficial.

A few minutes later, all hands were gathered aft, and Rafe stepped up onto the hatch cover to look out over them. There were about fifty left, nearly half of whom were wounded.

"Are there any more?" Rafe asked.

"This is all, Cap'n."

"Any wounded besides these men?"

"No, sir, all the wounded are walking wounded."

"Thanks," Rafe said. He cleared his throat and looked out over the assembled company. "Men, as you know, I was on board the *Vanderbilt* during our recent battle. I saw, firsthand, what kind of punishment the *Delta Dancer* can dish out, and let me tell you, gentlemen, it is something to behold."

"Was you scared, Cap'n?" someone asked.

"Scared? Men, I tightened up so tight I won't

be able to visit the head for a week," Rafe said, and everyone laughed.

"It wasn't all tea and cakes on this end," one of the sailors cracked, and there was more laughter.

"I can tell by looking," Rafe said. He cleared his throat. "But I can tell something else, too. The *Vanderbilt* got the worst end of the fight. She's badly hurt."

"We could tell that," one of the men shouted. "We figured that's why she showed us her tail."

"She figures to pick up an escort from the Federal fleet, then put in to Baltimore for repairs," Rafe went on. "Her captain's wounded, and at least two of her guns are destroyed, and she's beating along on one paddle. The only thing in her favor is that we are so shot up we'll have to go back to Nassau." Rafe paused for a moment, then smiled. 'At least that's what Captain Raymond thinks we'll do."

"You mean we ain't puttin' in to Nassau?" someone asked.

"Not a bit of it," Rafe answered. "Gentlemen, we are going to hunt the *Vanderbilt* down—and we are going to sink her."

The ships company broke out into a big cheer.

"I have to be honest with you, though," Rafe said when the cheer died. He held up his hands. "If she manages to rendezvous with any ship from the Federal fleet, we are going to be in for it. In our current condition we can just barely hold our own with the *Vanderbilt*. An undamaged ship would have the advantage of us. Two undamaged ships could destroy us.''

"Not with you in command, Cap'n!" Pig Meat said, and his retort was met with a cheer from the rest of the crew.

"There's one more thing," Rafe said. "As you know, Mr. McCorkle and Mr. Carter are both dead. That means we are going to have to appoint a new first officer. I'm going to let you men do that. Have you any suggestions?"

"Aye, sir, I've a suggestion, and a good one, too," Pig Meat said. He looked around at the rest of the crew as if daring them to challenge him.

"All right, Pig Meat. Who do you suggest?"

"Cap'n, I suggest you make Miss Candice Pratt the first officer."

"What?" Rafe replied in surprise.

"Yes, sir," someone else said. "Miss Pratt should be our first officer."

"Gentlemen, I appreciate your suggestion," Rafe said. "And I'm sure Miss Pratt is very flattered, but. . . ."

"There ain't no buts about it, Cap'n," Pig Meat said. "She's the one who come up with the idea of doublin' our guns, remember?"

"Yes," Rafe said.

"And she's the one who give Mr. Carter the

gumption to come out fightin' this mornin'," Pig
Meat went on.

Candy blushed at that statement, though no one
noticed, or if they did, no one knew the cause of
her blush. She was certain none of the crew knew
just how she had given Mr. Carter the gumption to
come out fighting.

"And you should have seen her in the battle,
sir," another sailor put in. "She was that cool that
she just stood there while shot and shell was all
aroun'. I tell you, I was 'bout ready to cut 'n' run
oncet myself, till I looked over 'n' seen how brave
she was takin' it all."

"You mean you men don't mind having a woman
as the first officer? You'll take her orders without
question?" Rafe asked.

"Aye, 'n' with pleasure beside," Pig Meat
answered.

Rafe looked at Candy. There might be an advantage to having her as his first officer, after all. Just
as the sailor had said, there would be something
inspiring about having a woman facing the same
dangers. Few of the men would be willing to show
fear in front of her, and with a crew greatly re-
duced by battle, he would need the full measure of
valor from everyone on board. It just might be that
Candy could ensure that for him. He smiled.

"All right," he said. "Miss Pratt, by the powers invested in me by the Department of Navy of the Confederate States Government, I hereby appoint you an acting Lieutenant, and assign you as First Officer of the *C.S.S. Delta Dancer*.''

Chapter Thirteen

Captain Raymond sat on a stool on the *Vanderbilt's* deck. The stump of his right leg was bandaged and resting on a pillow which was on another stool. The sea which had run so heavily in the Gulf Stream during the battle of a few days earlier had now receded, and the *Vanderbilt* was rolling easily in the gentle swell.

The deck of the *Vanderbilt* was alive with working parties as holes were patched, cannons were remounted, cordage was spliced and re-strung, and canvas sails were sewn together again. The port paddlewheel cover was stripped away and half a dozen men were working to repair it as well.

"Cap'n Raymond, signals from the *Tuscarora*, sir."

"What do they say?" Raymond asked.

"They want to know what assistance we require."

"Extend my compliments to the captain of the *Tuscarora* and ask if he would be so kind as to allow me the use of a couple of his carpenters and mechanics."

"Aye, sir," the signalman answered.

"And ask Mr. Herrick to report to me," Raymond directed.

"Aye, sir," the signalman answered again.

Raymond reached down and rubbed the end of his stump gingerly. He wished he had a peg leg attached so he could get around, but the thought of that stump end supporting any weight now was excruciating. It was funny, but he could swear the pain he felt was in his foot. Not the stump, but the amputated foot which, by now, was food for the sharks. He'd heard other amputees talk of such pains, but he had not been able to understand. Now he was experiencing the pains himself, though he still couldn't understand.

Raymond rubbed his stump for a moment longer, then looked out over the railing across the gently rolling, bright blue sea. Out there, just over the horizon somewhere, was the *Delta Dancer*. They had fought to a draw the last time, but he had been felled by one of the earliest volleys. When the *Vanderbilt* showed her stern, he was below decks, unconscious. Mr. Herrick had been in command of the vessel.

When Raymond came to and discovered that the battle was over and with no definite result, he was angry. He would have fought until one of them was in Davy Jones' locker. Then, when he discovered that Rafe Taylor had gotten away cleanly, had actually been seen transferring from the rowboat to the *Delta Dancer*, he was more than just angry; he was furious. Not only had the *Delta Dancer* escaped, but its captain as well.

The last few days had mellowed his attitude somewhat, however. With him out of action, a victory during his incapacitation would have been credited to Mr. Herrick. Captain Raymond wanted the *Delta Dancer* and Rafe Taylor all for himself. It was better this way, after all. This gave him another chance at the elusive ghost of the sea.

Mr. Herrick approached Captain Raymond, and stopped a few feet away. Mr. Herrick was without his tunic, and there was grease on his arms, hands and trousers.

"You sent for me, Captain?"

Raymond looked at him, squinting in the afternoon sun.

"Tell me again how badly hurt the *Delta Dancer* was."

"She suffered a lot of damage in her upper braces," Mr. Herrick said. "And we hulled her pretty good with a couple of broadsides. Also, our sharpshooters in the braces reported that the canister had a devastating effect on her crew.''

"You think he's putting back into Nassau for repairs?"

"I doubt it, Captain," Mr. Herrick answered. "I'm sure Rafe figures we'll have at least one ship in a blocking position to cut him off. No, I think it more likely that he's heading for Grenada."

"Ha," Captain Raymond said. "Probably limping along at one or two knots, secure in the knowledge that we are putting into Baltimore."

"That's my belief, sir," Mr. Herrick said.

"Which means he won't be expecting us when we suddenly pounce on him."

"No, sir."

"How go our repairs?" Captain Raymond asked.

"We are actually quite lucky, sir," Mr. Herrick said. "The bearing and wheel shaft are undamaged. The damage seems to be limited to the paddles themselves."

"Can you repair it?"

"Aye, sir, we can repair the wheel so that she will gain purchase for us," Mr. Herrick said. "But without taking the wheel off and giving it a proper balance, we're likely to have vibrations when she's in use."

"How bad will the vibrations be? Will the ship hold together long enough to get us to Grenada?"

"Aye, sir. But over a period of time the vibrations are sure to warp the shaft and flatten the bearings."

Captain Raymond waved his hand impatiently.

"I'm not concerned with what might happen over a period of time," he said. "All I want is to make certain that these paddles answer to power now. I'm not going to let Taylor get away. We're going to patch things up; then we're going back after him."

"Aye, sir," Mr. Herrick said.

"You don't sound too happy about that."

"It is good that we will have the opportunity to meet the *Delta Dancer* again," Mr. Herrick said.

"But? Go on, finish it," Captain Raymond demanded.

"But what, sir?"

"You said it is good to have the opportunity to meet the *Delta Dancer* again, only there was an unspoken *but* at the end of your statement. What is bothering you?"

"A couple of things, sir," Mr. Herrick said.

"Let me hear them."

"Well, sir, for one thing, even without Rafe Taylor, the *Delta Dancer* fought us to a standstill. When a ship fights as well as she did without her commander, and without her first officer as well, it can only speak of an exceptionally well-trained ship's company."

"Have you found the ship's company of the *Vanderbilt* wanting?" Captain Raymond asked.

"No, sir, not really," Mr. Herrick said. "I think we have a fine crew. The fact that I can speak so highly of the crew of the *Delta Dancer* is because their action impressed me, even considering the excellence of our crew. And now Rafe is back with them. That can only make them the more dangerous."

"Yes, but Mr. Taylor has a damaged ship," Captain Raymond said.

"So do we, sir."

"The *Tuscarora* is sending over a few extra carpenters and mechanics. With the assistance of the Federal fleet, I'm positive we have made more progress in our repairs than Mr. Taylor could have, working alone. Don't you agree, Mr. Herrick?"

"Aye, sir," Mr. Herrick said again.

"Then we've nothing to worry about, do we?" Captain Raymond said. "You just see to it that the repair work is swiftly carried out."

"Aye, sir."

"Oh, and send our best gunner's mate to me. I imagine that would be Mike Flynn on number-one gun, wouldn't it?"

"Aye, sir, it would have been," Mr. Herrick said. "Unfortunately, Mike Flynn was killed in the fight."

"Oh? Well, I'm sorry to hear that. We'd served

together for quite a few years. Very well, send the next best gunner's mate we have."

"That would be Pippen, sir," Mr. Herrick said. "I've got him supervising the remounting of the guns, but I'll send him to you."

"No," Captain Raymond said. "No, that's all right. That was what I wanted to talk to him about anyway, so if he is already usefully employed, why should I detain him? Carry on with what you were doing, Mr. Herrick."

"Aye, sir," Mr. Herrick said, obviously glad to be leaving.

So he doesn't care much for me, Captain Raymond thought, as he watched Mr. Herrick leave. *He probably doesn't care for me because he knows I am going to kill his friend. I wouldn't be surprised if he didn't let Taylor go. I'll bet it wasn't an escape at all.*

Less than twenty miles away, riding the same calm swells as the *Vanderbilt*, the *Delta Dancer* was also a beehive of activity. Though the *Delta Dancer* had no fleet to help it with its repairs, it was doing quite nicely on its own. The windows which had arched across the stern of the raider were all gone, shot away by cannon fire during the battle with the *Vanderbilt*. There was other damage to the captain's cabin: The bed and desk had been smashed by cannon balls and the walls sprayed with canister. The bed and desk had been repaired and the canister holes patched. Of course, there was no glass to replace the windows, so the windows were simply boarded up. It made the captain's cabin considerably darker, but it kept out the wind and the sea spray and would do the same for rain; so it rendered the cabin adequate for its purposes.

Though several cannon balls passed through the sides and the upper deck of the *Delta Dancer*, there had been no severe structural damage. That meant that several jerry-rigged patches, some liberally applied caulking and a few splices sufficed to make the ship sound enough for the heaviest of seas.

The men had worked magic on the *Delta Dancer*, and now Rafe was ready to take her back into battle.

Rafe knew that Captain Raymond would figure on his returning to Nassau or some other port for repair. That would give Rafe the opportunity to surprise Raymond at sea. He would find him tomorrow, and tomorrow they would do battle.

Because they were going to do battle tomorrow, Rafe wanted to do something for the men tonight. He decided they would roast their one remaining pig for supper, and eat, not at their stations, but out upon the deck in a sit-down dinner.

The *Delta Dancer* had left Nassau with three live pigs and two goats. Both goats and two of the pigs had disappeared during the battle. A cannon ball had destroyed the pens, releasing the animals. The theory was that the two goats and two of the pigs preferred the unknown sea to the hell of being on board a frigate during a pitched battle. The pig which stayed on board was found shaking and afraid under a canvas in the forecastle.

Rafe realized that this pig may take the path of its brothers, should it be subjected to another battle. Therefore, better to eat it now than to lose it the next day.

Eb had been cooking it for the last three hours, spitted whole and turning slowly over open coals so that the rich, succulent aroma permeated the ship and reached the nostrils of everyone on board, whether he be at the helm, on the highest yard, or way down in the orlop deck.

Candy had offered to help Eb with the cooking, but Eb had insisted that, as the first officer, it wouldn't be seemly for her to bear a hand with such a chore. Therefore, Candy wandered around the ship watching the men work. At first she thought she would just be in the way, but soon she discovered that she could be of some benefit by coordinating the efforts and moving someone from a job which didn't require as many hands over to another job which could use him. Before long she was proud of the efficiency she was introducing to the repair work, and she moved about the boat with a confident step. Toward evening, as the meat neared readiness and the aroma filled every nook and cranny of the ship, she found that she was looking forward to the meal as eagerly as the men.

Then, later that evening, just as the sun was sinking into the western horizon, she saw some of the sailors rigging a sail canvas screen near the forecastle. A short while later, she saw two men manning the bilge pump and a third spraying the hose out behind the screen. There was a lot of laughing and shouting going on, so she wandered forward to find out what they were about. Pig Meat stopped her.

"Beg 'pardon, ma'am," Pig Meat said, holding up his hand. "But the men are all takin' a bath for the supper. Best you don't go up there."

"My," Candy said. "This must be quite an occasion if they are taking a bath."

"Yes'm, I reckon it is," Pig Meat said. Candy turned away with a wistful expression on her face. Suddenly, she envied them. Of course, it wouldn't be practical for her to stand there naked while two men pumped and the third directed a hose at her, but she would dearly love to take a bath.

Pig Meat noticed the expression on her face and felt sorry for her.

"I ain't supposed to tell you, ma'am," he said.

"But Eb 'n' the Cap'n have rigged up a tub for you in the cap'n's quarters. With hot water."

"Oh!" Candy squealed. "Really? Now?"

Pig Meat laughed and Candy, forgetting for the moment that she was the first officer and thus committed to show some restraint, turned and ran across the deck, then down the ladderway and aft to the door of the captain's cabin. She saw Eb pouring a large pot of boiling water into a big, round tub. Steam was coming up from the water which was already in the tub.

"Pig Meat said there was a tub in here," she said.

"Here it is," Rafe said, smiling.

"Well, where has it been? Why have I never seen it before?"

"It's the bottom half of the spare boiler," Rafe explained. "The top half got holed by a ball during the battle, and we were about to drop it overboard as useless, when we thought of making a bathtub from the bottom half. I thought you might enjoy a bath."

"Oh, Rafe, you've no idea!" Candy said, and so excited was she by the prospect that she started to unbutton her shirt even as Eb was pouring in the last of the water.

"Uh, don't you think you had better wait just a moment longer?" Rafe asked, laughing and indicating Eb's presence.

"Oh, yes, I suppose so," Candy said, and she stopped and looked pointedly at Eb. "Isn't it full enough now?"

"Yes, ma'am," Eb said. "I think so. Anyway, I'd best be gettin' back to the supper."

"How about you?" Candy asked Rafe after Eb left. "Don't you have some place to go?"

"I thought I would stay and help you bathe," Rafe suggested.

"No, thank you," Candy said. "I'm quite capable of handling this by myself."

Candy pushed a protesting Rafe out of the room, then eagerly hurried out of her clothes and stepped down into the tub. She found a bar of soap and she wet it, then passed it across her body. The sensation of soap bubbles sliding across her skin was so luxurious as to be almost erotic. Never had she enjoyed a bath more than she was enjoying this one. She leaned her head back against the edge of the tub and closed her eyes to allow her body to soak. Not until the water turned from warm to tepid did she open her eyes again and continue her bath. She lifted one leg and held it out over the edge of the tub and examined it critically. It was smooth and unmarked, and showed no sign of the strenuous and somewhat unusual life she had been living of late. To the naked eye there had been no change in her appearance. But, inside, much had happened.

Candy thought of the twists and turns her life had taken over the past month. She had lost her virginity to one man and taken the virginity of another. She had fought in two battles, one of which cost her her father, and this was the eve of another fight. She was on a ship in the middle of the ocean, the only woman among many men, serving as an officer over them. And she was with the man she loved.

The question, of course, was where would she be tomorrow night? Would she survive the battle? Would Rafe survive the battle? And if they survived, would they survive it in one piece? It was a question men had asked themselves on the eve of battles since time began. But, Candy wondered, how many women had asked it of themselves?

Finally, Candy stepped out of the tub. Her skin was pink and glowing, and she reached for a towel with her arm extended, her breast fleshed full and the nipple upturned, when the door to the cabin opened and Rafe stepped into the room.

At first Candy was startled, but when she saw it was Rafe, she smiled at him.

"It seems to me we've been in this position before," she said. "Do you always come in just as a lady is getting out of the bath?"

"Only if that lady is you," Rafe said. He put his arms around her and drew her clean, soft body against him. "This is what I wanted to do the first time, you know."

Candy giggled. "Would you think me awfully bold if I confessed that I had thoughts of you doing this very thing?"

"Why didn't I?" Rafe asked. "Think of all the time we wasted."

"Think of the time we are wasting now," Candy said. "Why are we standing here talking, when we could be. . . ."

Rafe interrupted her with a kiss. Though they had kissed before, had made love before, this kiss seemed possessed of a particular urgency, as if the unspoken affirmation of the fear that this might be their last night together.

The kiss set Candy's head spinning. She could feel his tongue brushing across her lips and she opened her mouth to it, showing by such an action that she was surrendering herself to him completely. For the moment she was so overwhelmed by the sensations thus evoked that she forgot where she was and what was going on. Just a few feet away, on the other side of the thin walls of the cabin, she could hear the scurrying feet of the sailors who were preparing for their supper party. She knew that a prolonged absence of both of them would be suspicious to the men, but she didn't care. In fact, at this moment, she wouldn't have cared if they had been on deck in full view of everyone, for no one else existed. There were only the two of them, alone on the vast ocean.

Familiar hands burned paths across her body, to a breast, then across her stomach until it reached between her legs at the center of all her feeling.

Somewhere in the back of Candy's mind, she recalled her experience with young Mr. Carter. She had been the aggressor then, and it had been mildly stimulating by reason of its taboo. But the stimulation she had felt then was but a soft spring breeze compared to the hurricane winds of passion which were sweeping over her now. In Rafe's skilled hands and powerful masculinity she felt like a helpless victim. The very thought of that, however, left her weak, and her body was trembling with desire.

Rafe picked her up and carried her over to the large bed. He laid her gently upon it, and she floated in a languorous haze brought on by extreme sexual arousal as, quickly, Rafe removed his clothes. She felt a sweet aching in her loins as she anticipated what was to come.

Rafe came to her then, and her skin tingled with a thousand teasing little flames. As Rafe had his way with her, new waves of pleasure came up, building second by second like the constantly changing patterns of a storm-tossed sea. When their bodies were finally connected, a rapture shot through her like a bolt of flame, generating enough heat to ignite a signal rocket and send it arcing through the night sky.

Rafe thrust into her, pushing onward and inward, carrying her from ecstasy to rapture and back to ecstasy again, jolting her with such sharp sensations that they were beyond pleasure, almost painful, but delightfully so. Then, suddenly, she felt her body leap forward in a final, shattering, white-hot explosion, and she felt as if she were falling away from some great, heretofore unreached and un-dreamed-of height.

They lay there for a long moment, draining their pleasure into each other.

Suddenly, there was a knock on the cabin door.

"Cap'n? Cap'n, are you in there?"

"What is it, Pig Meat?" Rafe asked. Rafe made no effort to disengage himself from Candy, and she felt a keen awareness of lying here under him, feeling him still in her, while he spoke with some-one just outside the door. There was a sense of excitement to it which, suddenly caused her to have a new, smaller, though still intensely satisfy-ing orgasm, and she shivered in delight beneath him and opened her mouth on his neck to drown out her involuntary moans of pleasure.

"Cap'n, the cook says the supper's ready, 'n' the men are growin' a bit anxious."

"We'll be right there," Rafe promised.

Rafe got up then, and smiled down at Candy.

He touched her still congested nipple with his fingers, and she could feel one last small charge of sensation coursing through her body. She could smell her own musk, and she wished they really were alone so she could work on him to reawaken his desires. But they weren't alone, and tomorrow it might be all over, and what they had shared here tonight would become only a whisper in time.

The sun was completely set by the time Candy appeared on deck, but there was still the twilight and half a dozen lanterns to light the deck. The sailors were all standing, waiting for her, and she saw that they had put on their cleanest and best uniforms for this occasion.

"I don't know if a first officer is supposed to notice such things," Candy said as she joined them, "but I have never seen a more handsome group of men."

The men all beamed under her praise as if they were children being complimented by their favorite teacher. Finally Pig Meat stood up. He had a package in his hand, and he cleared his throat importantly.

"Uh, Miss Pratt," he said. "I would like to give you. . . ."

"It ain't jes' you, Pig Meat!" someone called. "It's from all of us!"

"Yes!" one of the other men put in. "Don't you go takin' all the credit for it."

Pig Meat cleared his throat and started again.

"We would like to give you this," he said, holding the package toward her.

"Why, I thank you, Pig Meat," Candy said, accepting the gift. She opened the brown paper then gasped. She was silent for a long moment. The package contained a Confederate battle flag. There were holes in the flag, and there was blood on the banner. Her eyes suddenly welled with water and a tear began sliding down her cheek.

"She don't like it," someone said.

"She's just moved by it, you dumb bastard," someone else said. "Don't you know anything about women?"

"It's the battle flag, ma'am," Pig Meat said. "It's the one was flyin' when you was commandin' us."

"Yes, I know what it is," Candy said. "I . . . I don't know how to thank you. It's the most wonderful, most moving gift I have ever had."

Suddenly and impulsively, Candy put her arms around Pig Meat and hugged him affectionately.

"Hey, wait a minute!" someone shouted. "I told you that it's a gift from all of us, not just Pig Meat."

"Well, then, I shall have to give each and every one of you a hug, won't I?" Candy said, and with a whoop of delight the men all stood up and got in line, then passed by one at a time for Candy's thank-you embrace.

After the hugs were all dispensed, except to Rafe who stood back watching and smiling, the ship's company sat down to enjoy Eb's meal. It was fully as magnificent as the aroma had promised that it would be. Afterward, when everything was eaten and everyone lay around with their stomachs full and in good spirits, as relaxed and unconcerned as if they weren't expecting a battle the next day, one of the sailors pulled out a flute.

"Give us a tune here, Earl," someone shouted.

"Yeah, give us a tune we can dance the hornpipe to," another said.

Earl, with a happy smile, began playing a lively tune, and a couple of men got up and began to dance the hornpipe.

During the dancing, while the other men were clapping and keeping time to the music, Rafe came over and sat beside Candy. He reached out and took her hand in his, then raised it to his lips.

Candy had been smiling at the antics of the sailors, and she looked over into Rafe's eyes at the moment he kissed her hand. The smile left her lips then, as she saw through his eyes, all the way to his soul. He was a man in deep, deep agony at that moment.

"Rafe? Rafe, are you all right?" she asked.

Rafe looked at her for a moment, then smiled.

"Yes," he said. "I'm all right."

"What is it? You looked so . . . so strange, there for a moment."

"I was just thinking," he said.

"What about?"

Rafe sighed. "I was thinking how wonderful this could all be if the *Delta Dancer* was a cargo ship. Maybe a trader which doubled the Horn and made for China for the tea trade. I could take you as my wife, and we could raise our family right here on board."

Candy put her other hand on top of his.

"I know," she said softly.

"Would you?" Rafe asked.

"Would I what?"

"Would you marry me under such conditions?"

Candy laughed. "Rafe, my darling, don't you realize by now that I would marry you under any conditions? I love you."

"And I love you," Rafe said. "Almost enough to. . . ."

"To what?"

"Nothing."

"What were you going to say?"

"I can't put it in words," Rafe said. "For if I do, I will show myself to be a coward and a man totally without honor."

"But if you—"

"No," Rafe said, putting his fingers on her

lips. "Please, if you do love me, speak of this no more."

"All right," Candy answered. "If you wish."

Silently, Rafe patted Candy's hand; then he got up and walked away.

Candy would have liked to follow him, but she knew that he wanted a few moments alone. Besides, she felt that she owed it to the others to spend some time with them, and she laughed with them and clapped her hands to keep time to the music, and watched as the sailors vied for the right to show their dancing prowess to her.

Rafe stood at the taffrail and looked out over the night sea. He had always liked the sea at night. It was his favorite time . . . a time when he could be alone with his thoughts.

The night air was clear and sharp, and the sea stretched to the horizon in gently rolling magenta, textured by the foam which rose like a candle flame when a wave spilled over. In the water just below the ship, hundreds of brilliant green streaks, phosphorescent fish, glowed like the gas lamps of a city.

During such moments Rafe was able to reason things out more clearly than at any other time. Two nights ago when Candy tearfully confessed that she had made love with Midshipman Carter, he had come here to be alone with his thoughts. Here, under the clarity of the stars and the brilliance of the moon, he realized why Candy had done it, and he understood. In fact, he even felt a sense of joy for the boy who had been his friend and who, because of Candy, had managed to taste some of the sweet fruits of life before he died.

It was here, too, that he came to realize that he loved Candy with all his heart and with all his soul, and he wanted to share the rest of his life, however long that might be, with her. And now, tonight, he was trying to face the question of what he should do. A professor at Annapolis once told Rafe that it wasn't hard to do the right thing. What was hard was in knowing what the right thing was. That was the question which plagued him now.

Chapter Fourteen

The morning sun, its disk blood-red but not yet painful to the eyes, brightened the east and made the horizon indistinct. The pear-gray blue of the sea and sky seemed to blend so that the *Delta Dancer* wasn't a ship at sea, but a ship suspended in timeless space.

The water was as smooth as glass. In fact, it was so still that it looked solid, and as Rafe stood at the railing, he had the illogical illusion that he could simply step off the ship and walk across the surface of the water.

Rafe had slept unsoundly the night before. Candy had slept with him, sharing his bed in sleep for the first time ever. When Rafe got out of bed before the sun this morning, Candy's long tawny hair was fanned out on the pillow, and the bed covering was pushed down so that one breast was visible in its sweet, white, rosy-tipped innocence.

Rafe left her sleeping and climbed to the deck to watch the sun rise. He had watched the sun set the night before, had contemplated the moon, then watched the last morning star wink out before the sun rose again. And in all that time he had been thinking.

Rafe recalled the young soldier he had met in the Philadelphia railroad station. He had lost one leg and yet was still game and able to offer a friendly word to a stranger. There was nothing unusual about that; the young man was an American, and thus eager to share his friendship and enthusiasm with his fellow countryman.

But Rafe wasn't a fellow countryman. Rafe was an enemy. An enemy of the flag he had taken an oath to protect.

Rafe thought of Mike Flynn on board the *Vanderbilt*. Mike told Rafe he was the best gunnery officer he had ever worked for, and he credited Rafe with teaching him a lot. The truth was, Rafe knew the book about gunnery, but it was for Mike Flynn and others like Mike Flynn to convert the classroom theory of Annapolis into practical experience at sea.

And now Mike was dead.

Rafe thought of Mr. McCorkle, and the bos'n, and Mr. Carter, and of Dr. Pratt. They were as dead as Mike now, and all because of a war which was pitting countryman against countryman, friend against friend, and sometimes, even brother against brother.

It wasn't right. It wasn't right that politicians who were safe in Richmond and Washington should create policies which would get men like Mike Flynn and Jesse Carter killed. The young man in the Philadelphia railroad station should not have lost his leg. The thousands of young men who had died on the battlefields, and whose death postures were so vividly described by the writer for the *Boston Evening Transcript,* should have been allowed to live their lives, to help build the country. Instead, the cream of this generation was devoting all its energy, skill, courage and cunning to destroying the country.

Rafe was at sea, using the skills he had learned in the Naval Academy, not to protect the United States against some foreign aggressor, but to do battle against the United States. He had met a woman whom he loved, but he couldn't plan upon building a life with her because he was caught up in a war—a war not of his own making or even of his support. It wasn't right, and Rafe had been thinking about it all night. His thoughts had finally

produced a course of action, though, and now he
knew what he wanted to do.

Rafe heard someone behind him and he turned
to see Eb bringing him a cup of coffee.

"Thanks, Eb," he said.

"Will the cap'n be wantin' breakfast?" Eb asked.

"No," Rafe said.

"Very good, sir," Eb answered. He turned and
started to leave.

"Eb?"

"Aye, sir?"

"Eb, how long have we served together?"

"Le's see, sir," Eb said. "I was mess mate on
board the ole *Mohawk* when you come aboard a
new ensign. I make that six or seven years."

"And when I left the Navy to fight for the
South, you came with me," Rafe said.

"Aye, 'n' so did Mr. McCorkle, 'n' Andy 'n' Pig
Meat, 'n' a dozen or so others I could name," Eb
said.

"Why?"

"Why, sir?"

"Yes, why?" Rafe repeated. "You're not all
Southern-born. Some of you aren't even Amer-
ican-born."

"We come to be with you, Cap'n," Eb said
easily, as if that explained it.

"Eb, you know I'm trying to cut the *Vanderbilt*
off before it makes port?"

"Aye, sir."

"And if we do, there'll be another battle."

"Aye, there's no escapin' that," Eb said.

"Some will be killed."

"That's for certain, Cap'n," Eb said.

Rafe took another swallow of his coffee.

"And yet the men are ready to follow me into battle without question?"

"Aye, sir."

Rafe paused for a long moment before he asked the next question.

"Would the men follow me out of battle?"

Eb looked surprise. "Beggin' the cap'n's pardon, sir, I don't know what you mean."

"Suppose I decided not to chase down the *Vanderbilt*," he said. "Suppose I told you I was going to let it return to port unmolested. What would you think?"

"I'd think the cap'n had his ideas," Eb said.

"Suppose I told you that I didn't want to fight anymore," Rafe said. "Suppose I told you I wanted to take the ship back to Charleston and turn it over to the Confederate Navy and resign my commission."

"The men would be for followin' you, then, if they could," Eb said. "The thing you maybe forget, Cap'n, is you're an officer. An officer can quit the war by jes' resignin' his commission. Let a ordinary sailor do that 'n' it ain't resignin'; it's desertion.

We'd either have to stay in the Navy with a new officer or be shot.''

"Yes," Rafe said. 'That's why I've come up with another idea.''

"Another idea, sir?''

"Eb, I'm going to put our ship into commercial service. I'm going to quit the war, but we're all going to quit it together.''

Eb smiled broadly. "Is the cap'n serious?''

"I'm very serious," Rafe said.

"But, Cap'n, won't that make us pirates?''

"Hell, Eb, we're pirates now," Rafe replied with a smile. "Don't you realize that if any of us are ever captured by a Union ship, we would all be hanged?''

"Aye, that thought has crossed my mind," Eb admitted.

"So what does it matter if we become pirates to the South as well? Besides, if the North wins, then we will be heroes.''

"Cap'n, I've got an idea. Suppose you turn the *Delta Dancer* over to the Yankees. Maybe they'd pardon all of us 'n' you could keep the ship.''

"No," Rafe said. "I don't want to fight for the South anymore, but I won't fight against the South. We have papers of registry which authorize us, as the *Niagara*, to carry on Atlantic commerce. That's just what I intend to do.''

"No more fightin'?''

"Not unless we are jumped by pirates," Rafe teased. "And I mean real pirates. Now, tell me, Eb. What do you think of that?"

Eb smiled broadly. "Cap'n, who wouldn't like that idea?"

"Then you believe the men would go along with it? It's a treasonous act, disloyal to the Confederacy."

"Cap'n, the men of this ship don't know treason; they only know mutiny. Their loyalty isn't to the Confederacy; it's to their ship, and to you. If you lead them, they will go wherever you take them."

Rafe smiled. "All right, I'll tell them this morning," he said.

"Cap'n! Sails and smoke!" the lookout called down.

"Where away?"

"Five points off the starboard bow!"

Rafe climbed the braces and opened his spyglass to look toward the ship the lookout had spotted. The fore and aft masts, the swept-back smokestack, the side mounted paddlewheels, all combined to unmistakenly identify the ship as the *Vanderbilt*. Rafe stepped down onto the deck. How could that be? By rights, the *Vanderbilt* should be halfway to Baltimore, limping along under sail only. She wasn't halfway to Baltimore; she was right here, and she looked as if she were making full steam.

"It be the *Vanderbilt*, Cap'n," Pig Meat yelled

down from the upper braces, confirming Rafe's silent identification. "She's comin' dead on, sir. She shows no sign of damage!"

News of the sighted *Vanderbilt* spread quickly through the crew, and within a moment or two the entire ship's company was on deck, including Candy.

"We've spotted the *Vanderbilt?*" she asked.

"Yes," Rafe said. Rafe walked over to Eb, who was standing a little away from the others.

"Old friend, I guess we'll have to delay my plan for a while," he said. "Under the circumstances, it would probably be best if no one else knew about it."

"Aye, Cap'n," Eb answered.

Candy walked up to them, and Eb drifted away.

"Rafe, why is the *Vanderbilt* coming toward us? I thought we would have to overtake it." Candy said.

"I thought so, too," Rafe said, rubbing his chin with his hand and looking toward the distant ship. "But it looks as if Captain Raymond has decided to play my game."

"You mean repair his ship at sea instead of going to port, and coming after us?"

"Aye, he thought he'd catch us limping back to a neutral port. I'm sure the sight of our ship has caused some surprise on the decks of the *Vanderbilt*," Rafe said.

"Then there is to be fighting?" Candy asked.

"Yes. Did you think otherwise?"

"I . . . I don't know," Candy said. "I know it was an unreasonable hope, but I thought, well, that is, I hoped," Candy let it her sentence die.

"You thought maybe I would just turn away and not fight?" Rafe asked quietly.

"Yes," Candy said.

"I must confess, I had given that very thing some thought," Rafe said. "But the truth is, Candy girl, Raymond has his sights set for me and he's not going to let go until the issue is settled. If we tried to run away now, he would come after us, and he would stay on us until he caught us. I learned a long time ago, if you are forced into a fight, you can fight better if you're facing the enemy. I won't show tail now. It's too late for anything except fighting."

"He frightens me," Candy said. "I've never met him, yet anyone with such bulldog determination is frightening."

"Aye, he can be that," Rafe said. "All the more reason it's better to get this settled now."

Rafe raised his glass and looked toward the *Vanderbilt*. Both paddles were beating at the water and her bow was raising a wake. She was rapidly cutting the distance between them.

"Beat to quarters," Rafe ordered, and Candy, who had been in two battles, was now an experienced veteran and she knew what to do. She summoned the drummer to sound the long roll.

As the drum roll sounded and the men hurried to their battle stations, Rafe saw that the *Vanderbilt's* guns were already run out. He noticed that the hole in the port bow had been repaired and new cannon were in place. The *Vanderbilt* backed down her sails and turned to present a broadside. Rafe knew that Raymond was anxious to get in the first blow.

"Cap'n, shall I come about?" the helmsman called.

"No," Rafe said. "Continue as you go."

Rafe was heading straight for the *Vanderbilt*. "We are going to end this today, lads. We're going to sink the *Vanderbilt* and have no more trouble with Captain Raymond."

A flash of light and a great cloud of smoke billowed from the side of the *Vanderbilt*. Cannon balls arced toward the *Delta Dancer*, one cutting some cordage aloft, but the others splashing into the sea around them. As the *Delta Dancer* was coming head on, she didn't offer that much of a target for the *Vanderbilt* gunners. A series of dull thumps reached Rafe's ears, the delayed sounds of the cannons being fired.

The *Vanderbilt* backed one paddle and seemed to spin in the water before them, presenting the other side for a second broadside.

The *Delta Dancer* had not altered course during the whole time, and the gunners on the *Vanderbilt* were surprised to see the ship so close upon them. Again, bow on, the *Delta Dancer* did not present an easy target and the second broadside was as ineffective as the first.

"Candy, how are the guns?"

"They are laid in and ready," Candy replied, having checked with all the gun captains.

"Helmsman!"

"Aye, sir?"

"Come hard a'starboard. Candy, when we are in line, fire."

Candy hung onto the mizzenmast shroud as the ship heeled over so sharply that, for a moment, Candy was afraid they were going to roll all the way over. As soon as the ship was broadside, she shouted out to the port gun crews.

"Fire!"

The guns fired with a thundering roar and the ship rolled with the recoil. She emerged from the cloud of gunsmoke, and looking across the distance, incredibly short due to Rafe's maneuver, she saw the damage their first broadside had done. Two of the *Vanderbilt's* guns were now unmanned.

"Helm hard a'port!" Rafe shouted, and the *Delta Dancer* descried a large letter "S", winding up by presenting its starboard side to the *Vanderbilt*. The *Vanderbilt* was in the midst of turning when Candy ordered the second broadside. By now the space had been cut down to one hundred yards and it was virtually impossible for any of their shells to miss the mark. This time they were close enough to hear the screams of the sailors of the *Vanderbilt* as they were caught in the barrage.

"Helm, when we come about again, we'll be right alongside," Rafe said. "Port batteries, load with canister. Pig Meat!"

"Aye, sir!"

"Grappling hooks at the ready! When we are alongside, lash us together."

"Aye, sir!" Pig Meat yelled, and he and half a dozen others went into the braces.

The helmsman had the wheel turned hard a'starboard to repeat the "S" maneuver, and when they came out of the turn, they were right alongside the *Vanderbilt*.

"Fire!" Rafe shouted, even before Candy could give the order, and the canister shot raked the decks of the *Vanderbilt*. This time the volley went unanswered.

"Reload with ball!" Rafe shouted. "Pig Meat, secure us together! Marksmen, keep them away from their guns!"

There were some marksmen aloft in the braces of the *Vanderbilt* as well, but they were unable to prevent the gun crews of the *Delta Dancer* from reloading with solid shot. Rafe's marksmen, on the other hand, had the advantage of following up on the carnage caused by the volley of grapeshot, and they picked off every *Vanderbilt* sailor who approached one of the guns. As a result, the *Delta Dancer* guns were reloaded with solid shot and a broadside was released from pointblank range right into the side of the *Vanderbilt*. The sides of the *Vanderbilt* stoved in under the pressure, and the boiler burst, sending a jet of steam a hundred feet straight up into the air.

One of the solid shots cut the mizzen, and the sharpshooters who were high in the mizzen braces fell, screaming, to the deck or the sea.

The smoke rolled away from the last volley, and Rafe looked over at the deck of the *Vanderbilt*. It was indescribable. The deck ran red with blood, and the bodies were almost indistinguishable from the rest of the wreckage lying about. The *Vanderbilt* was, obviously, a mortally wounded ship.

The roaring of the cannon ceased, and the shrill hiss of steam grew quiet. The only sound now was the crackling of half a dozen fires and the quiet moans of the wounded men on board the *Vanderbilt*. Incredibly, not one person on the *Delta Dancer* had sustained a wound.

The ships drifted along together, grinding and bumping into each other. Water was pouring into the bowels of the *Vanderbilt* and she was beginning to settle.

Rafe saw Bill Herrick standing amidship. Herrick was holding his shoulder as blood spilled between his fingers. Herrick was looking around in shock, as if unable to believe the total disaster that had overtaken them in this brief, but bloody fight.

Rafe raised his speaking trumpet.

"Bill, I can't send another broadside into your ship; it would be murder," he called. "Do you surrender?"

"No!" another voice answered, and Rafe saw Captain Raymond trying to pull himself up from beneath a pile of wreckage. Raymond's face was bloody and one arm hung uselessly at his side. Despite his wounds, he managed to sit up.

"I do not surrender, sir!" he called. "I do not surrender!"

"Cap'n, shall we give them another broadside?" one of the gunners called.

Rafe looked at the *Vanderbilt*. She was settling by the starboard, which was the side adjacent to the *Delta Dancer*. Already, none of her guns could be brought to bear, even if there were men to man them.

"No," Rafe answered. "The *Vanderbilt* is finished."

"I have not surrendered my ship, sir!" Captain Raymond called out loudly. "My flag is still flying!"

Rafe called to Captain Raymond.

"Captain Raymond, sir! Request permission to take your men aboard."

By now more than two dozen men had made it to the deck of the *Vanderbilt*, and they stood huddled together, waiting for their captain's word on their fate. They looked stoically at Rafe, and he knew that, to the man, they would stay on board the sinking ship if Captain Raymond ordered it of them.

"Permission granted," Raymond answered.

"Pig Meat, get a party to help with the wounded," Rafe called.

"Aye, Cap'n," Pig Meat answered, dropping down from the braces to respond to the order.

Candy came over to stand beside Rafe. She had been in two previous battles, but she had never been in one as furious as this one had been. She was beyond shock, beyond ability to be sickened or saddened by what she saw. She could only stand by Rafe and feel thankful that the both of them were still alive.

"Bill," Rafe called. "You'd better hurry aboard. There's not much time left."

"Thanks," Mr. Herrick replied. "But I'll stay with my captain." He moved over to stand by Captain Raymond, and he moved a piece of timber away to make Raymond more comfortable.

"Captain Taylor, sir," Raymond said. It was the first time he had ever called Rafe captain.

"Aye, sir?"

"You'll tell them? You'll tell them my flag was still flying?"

"Aye, sir," Rafe answered. He saluted Captain Raymond and Mr. Herrick. Raymond was unable to answer the salute with his right hand, so he saluted with his left. Mr. Herrick's wound was in his left shoulder, so he was able to answer the salute.

"Pig Meat, cut the lines. Helmsman, pull away," Rafe said, after the last of the survivors were transferred to the *Delta Dancer*.

The lines had already grown taut as the *Vanderbilt* was settling fast. They were cut away; then the *Delta Dancer* steamed ahead, then turned in a great circle to come back and witness the last moments of the *Vanderbilt*, now a little over one hundred yards away.

The boiler fires were extinguished and there was another burst of steam. Next, some of the internal bulkhead collapsed under the water pressure, and the creaking and groaning made it sound as if the ship were alive, sounding its own death knell. The last of the cannon were unshipped, and they slid across the deck with a loud clatter, then splashed noisily into the sea. Finally, the *Vanderbilt* keeled completely over, and Rafe's last view of Captain

Raymond and Bill Herrick was as they were sliding into the sea. The ship rolled belly-up, rode that
way for a few moments, then slipped under the
sea. Thirty seconds after she went under, a giant
air bubble burst to the surface, then dissipated.
The *Vanderbilt* was no more.

There was no cheering.

Rafe went below deck and into his cabin without saying a word. He lay on his bunk and put his
hands behind his head. Unbidden, bits and pieces
of memory came back to him.

"Hi, I'm William T. Herrick, from Ohio.
We are going to be roommates while we are
in the Academy. What kind of name is Rafe?"

"It's a family name. I'm from Virginia.
Virginians are big about keeping family names
going."

"Midshipmen Taylor and Herrick are singled out for their joint project on the coeffi-
cients of drag and hull design."

"You've got to take my watch, Rafe. I've
met the most beautiful woman in the world, and
if I'm not there, Wingate will beat my time."

"Mr. Taylor? I'm Captain Raymond. I am

master of this vessel, and as far as you are concerned, sir, I am only slightly lower in authority than God!''

''Mr. Taylor, it grieves me to think of you throwing away a brilliant naval career to join up with the secesh. Such action is treasonable, sir.''

''Rafe, I guess this is good-bye. We've been together since our first year at Annapolis. I wish we could both wake up in the morning and find out this is just some bad dream. My God, to think that we, that you and I might someday actually have to fight each other.''

Rafe was stirred from his memories by a knock on the door. He pinched the bridge of his nose and, when he did so, discovered tears. He had been crying.

''Rafe? Rafe, it's me,'' Candy called.

Rafe sat up.

''Come in, Candy,'' he called.

Candy opened the door. It was dark inside because the windows were still boarded over and the only light was that which seeped in through the air scuppers.

''Are you all right?'' she asked.

''Yeah,'' Rafe said. ''Yeah, I'm all right.''

Candy sat down beside him and took his hand. She may have noticed the tears in his eyes, but she said nothing about it.

"According to some of the men we took on board, there's a large Federal fleet near. If they heard the sounds of the guns, they'll be here soon. We have to get away."

"I know," Rafe said.

"Where are we going?"

"We are going to Bermuda."

"Bermuda? Why?"

"Because Bermuda is a neutral port and I can release these men to the American counsulate there."

"You mean you aren't going to try and take them back as prisoners?"

"No," Rafe said. He put his arm around Candy. "Candy, would you lose respect for me if I did something which some might consider dishonorable? Would you think me a coward? Would you quit loving me?"

"No," Candy said softly. She put her fingers on his cheek. "I could never quit loving you, nor could I ever lose respect for you or think you a coward."

"But you don't know what I have in mind to do."

"I don't care what you do," Candy said. "I will love you for it, simply because you are you."

Rafe brushed his hair back and took a deep breath.

"This victory today," he said. "It was a hollow victory for me. Those men I killed were once my shipmates . . . my friends."

"I know," Candy said softly.

"But it isn't just these men," Rafe went on. "It's everyone in this war. It's insane. Why are we killing each other?"

"I don't know the answer to that question," Candy said. "I don't think anyone does."

"Perhaps not," Rafe agreed. "But I know the solution. The solution is simply not to kill anymore."

"How are you going to avoid that?" Candy asked.

"How am I going to avoid it? By quitting the war. I had already made up my mind before the *Vanderbilt* showed up. If I could have avoided the fight with Raymond, I would have done so. But I couldn't. I can avoid killing any more Americans. Candy, I'm taking this ship, and this crew, out of the war. We are going to South America to find cargo. We are going to be the commercial ship you and I spoke of."

"You mean you are stealing this ship?"

"No," Rafe said. "I'm not stealing it. I bought it. I paid for it with the blood of my comrades. It is my ship—she belongs to me and to the men who sail on her.''

"You left something out," Candy said.

"What?"

"The men who sail on her . . . and the woman."

Rafe looked at Candy and a big smile lit up his face.

"Candy, you mean it? You will go with me?"

"Try and stop me, Rafe Taylor," Candy said, pulling his lips to her for a kiss.

IN THE TRADITION OF *THE YOUNG LIONS* AND *FROM HERE TO ETERNITY* . . .

THE QUICK AND THE DEAD
A Novel of Viet Nam
by Robert Vaughan

Major Jake Culpepper, the product of four generations of career Army men, was unprepared for what he found upon arriving in Saigon as a military advisor in 1963, and he asked, early on, "How do we know who the bad guys are?" His story is a sweeping novel of the war with no victors, only victims. It is also the story of Mot, anguished secret agent of the Viet Cong; of Kristin, fervent Freedom Rider, intensely in love with Culpepper, who stands for all she opposes; of Culpepper's two sons—Andy, who refused a commission and fought as a "grunt," and Mike, who went to Canada and defied the draft; of Larry Cantrell, a black man with a brilliant future who risked everything in a war he hated; of Melinda, high-priced plaything of generals who at last found her true, impossible love. . . . Here is a panoramic novel that chronicles more completely and vividly than ever before the years of the nightmare war which could never be won.

Robert Vaughan, author of the acclaimed mini-series, *THE WAR-TORN*, and most recently *A DISTANT BUGLE* (a startling new novel of Custer's Last Stand, as lived by a secret survivor), is a much-decorated Viet Nam veteran with a fast-growing reputation as one of the outstanding war novelists of our time.

DON'T MISS
THE QUICK AND THE DEAD
—A DELL/BRYAN'S PAPERBACK ON SALE NOW—